Caffeine

SCREAM, YOU DIE

The first DS Scarlett Macey Novel

Michael Fowler

Fiction aimed at the heart
and the head...

Published by Caffeine Nights Publishing 2015

Published in Great Britain by
Caffeine Nights Publishing
4 Eton Close
Walderslade
Chatham
Kent
ME5 9AT

www.caffeine-nights.com
www.caffeinenightsbooks.com

British Library Cataloguing in Publication Data.
A CIP catalogue record for this book is available from the British Library

ISBN: 978-1-910720-04-2

Cover design by
Mark (Wills) Williams

Everything else by
Default, Luck and Accident

 Michael Fowler was born and brought up in the Dearne Valley area of Yorkshire where he still lives with his wife and two sons.

At the age of 16 he left school with the ambition of going to art college, but his parents' financial circumstances meant he had to find work and so joined the police.

He has never regretted that decision, serving as a police officer for thirty-two years, both in uniform and in plain clothes, working in CID, and undercover in Vice Squad and Drug Squad, retiring as an Inspector in charge of a busy CID in 2006.

Since leaving the police he has written and painted professionally. As an artist he has numerous artistic accolades to his name, and currently, his work can be found in the galleries of Spencer Coleman Fine Arts at Lincoln and Stamford. As a writer he is the author of the DS Hunter Kerr series and the DS Scarlett Macey series. He has also written a true crime novel.

He is a member of the Crime Writers Association and International Thriller Writers.

Find out more at www.mjfowler.co.uk
or follow him on Twitter @MichaelFowler1.
and on facebook

This is for the real Scarlett Macey

Also by Michael Fowler

DS Hunter Kerr series

Heart of the Demon
Cold Death
Secrets of the Dead
Coming, Ready or Not

Black & Blue
(e-book novella)

Acknowledgments

I am passionate about writing, but like my previous career it requires the support of a team to provide the end result, and to that end I owe thanks to my initial proofreader Sam Swanney, my editor Emma Grundy Haigh, Mark (Wills) Williams for the cover design and Darren Laws, CEO of Caffeine Nights. Without them this would never appear on bookshelves.

Once more I want to thank my good friend Stuart Sosnowski, crime scene investigation supervisor. I continually drag him along to the crime scenes I conjure up for my stories and he always provides me with the evidence for my characters to work with.

I owe a debt of gratitude to Detective Superintendent Lisa Ray, who gave me an insight into her working practices and decision making when a murder enquiry was ongoing.

Many thanks also to my friend Giles, who helped me with much of the scene-setting in and around Richmond upon Thames.

Finally, I also want to thank ex-colleague Nick Kinsella QPM, currently working with the United Nations Office on Drugs and Crime, who passed on both his knowledge and information into the cruel and degrading issue of human trafficking in certain parts of the world, and in particular how difficult it is to tackle. And, although this is a piece of fiction, I hope my story highlights the tragedy of what is happening to some of the world's most vulnerable.

One

It was almost midnight on Halloween and Scarlett Macey was chasing demons. Tonight though, it wasn't her usual inner demons she was contending with, but the two masked thugs who twenty seconds ago had steamed into her, bowling her over, and nicked her shoulder bag.

Now she was haring after them, arms and legs pumping in unison, like a sprinter exploding out of the starting blocks. Even in her heavy motorcycle boots, and them getting a good fifty-yard start, she could see that she was beginning to gain ground.

Grabbing a lungful of air she bellowed, "Stop, police!"

Her cry got a reaction. The one wearing the *Scream* mask looked back over his shoulder, losing some of his pace. But it was only momentary. Kicking up his heels he shouldered his accomplice, shot him a sideways glance and split left across the road. The one to the right took a few more runs and ducked into a side street, disappearing from view.

For a second the action threw Scarlett, but only briefly. She still had the guy in the *Scream* mask in her sights – and he was the one running away with her bag. She clawed in more air and drew on her training: as a junior champion at the fifteen hundred metres and a competitive runner at university she knew she had a chance as long he didn't start scrambling over walls and gardens, though with shop fronts as far as the eye could see there was no chance of that. She upped her pace and zeroed in on her prey.

Seconds later Scarlett caught him glancing over his shoulder again. She was getting closer. She would have loved to see his face behind that mask. On any other occasion she might have broken into a triumphant smile, but her mouth was sucking in and blowing out air almost simultaneously, as she squeezed that little bit more from her ever-tightening chest. It had been a long time since she had sprinted like this and it was telling.

Conscious of her ragged breathing she caught herself and sucked in extra air. The adrenaline was kicking in. She could hear the blood beating inside her ears and her footfalls echoing back. The pace was good – measured, fast.

Another ten seconds you little shit! When she caught up with him she was going to make damn sure he would regret this.

Then from nowhere a speeding human shape appeared at the corner of her eye. Although the vision was fleeting her brain registered this was her thief's accomplice who had dodged away at the beginning of the chase. She had no time to react and he smashed into her with the force of a wrecking ball, scuttling her feet from beneath her. She hit the ground hard, hip first, followed quickly by her upper arm and then shoulder. All the air broke out from her lungs and fireworks exploded behind her eyes.

Gasping for air, the flashes and sparks dancing before her soon subsided and a cloudy night sky entered her vision. She became conscious of running footsteps fading out of earshot. From her prostrate position she gazed along the street. Her two attackers were together again, the one in the *Scream* mask jogging backwards and staring back at her, waving her shoulder bag in the air as if it was a trophy. She could hear them both laughing.

The mask's grimace bore into her and she tried to push herself up but a sharp pain tore from her hip joint, making her wince.

For a second she lay there fighting to catch her breath, her clothing wet through from the puddle she'd fallen into.

Clenching her teeth, she cursed, "Bastards!"

Rolling onto her hands and knees she eased herself up and in a fit of temper and frustration kicked up a spray of water from the wet tarmac.

Two

An intermittent trill pounded Scarlett's ears, forcing open her eyes. For a second the noise confused her. It wasn't a sound she was familiar with. Then last night's episode tumbled inside her head and she remembered that she'd had to set her morning wake-up alarm on her work's BlackBerry. Her own phone had been in her shoulder bag.

She rolled over and groaned as a sharp pain registered in her left shoulder. Another vision of last night flashed inside her head. Closing her eyes for a second she speedily relived it, then flashing them open, propped herself up on one arm and snatched up her BlackBerry. She tapped off the alarm and flopped back onto the pillow. Pain wracked the left-hand side of her body.

Taking a deep breath she hoisted herself up, threw aside her duvet and slung her legs over the edge of the bed.

Still got to go to work.

Groggy and sore, for a couple of seconds she sat there, her eyes roaming around the bedroom, waiting for the pain to subside, simultaneously summoning up enough strength to make the dozen or so steps to the bathroom.

The room was in gloom and she could tell from the dull coruscating light coming through her curtains and the sound of traffic sloshing through puddles outside that she faced a lousy day ahead.

Placing her hands on her thighs, easing herself up, she spied last night's clothing on the bedroom floor. It still looked wet. Then she spotted the tear over the knee of her jeans.

My best Armanis. Cost me the best part of two hundred quid. I'll kill the wankers if I ever catch them!

Pulling away her stare she shook her head. *This is not doing any good. Focus! Get your arse in gear!*

She limped into the bathroom, turned on the shower and while waiting for it to warm up checked her face in the mirror. There had been the odd occasion when she had been told that she bore a striking resemblance to Taylor Swift, but no one would make that comparison this morning. The reflection staring back was not a pretty sight. Her mane of dyed copper red hair was knotted and clumped, and her normally intense hazel eyes were bloodshot and surrounded by dark rings – stark symbols of the few hours' sleep she had managed. Her left cheek was grazed and swollen; she could feel the soreness without even touching it.

At least there was no lasting damage, she told herself. Then, taking one last look, she stepped into the shower.

****

Twenty minutes later, hair dried and make-up applied, Scarlett examined her artistry in the dressing table mirror. There was still some swelling and faint evidence of bruising but she'd done a pretty good job with foundation and concealer. Satisfied with the result she chose a white cotton blouse and a pair of dark blue slacks from the wardrobe and made her way downstairs. In her galley kitchen she made herself coffee and toast, and with mug in one hand and a buttered round in the other gazed out through the French doors into the garden. Beyond her ghost-like reflection she could see the rain had stopped, but uniform grey clouds dominated the sky and everywhere was damp. The trees at the bottom of the garden still held their leaves, but this morning the autumn colours appeared only as a variety of dull browns. She was just thinking that her garden could do with tidying up the next time she had a day off when the sudden chime of the front door bell made her jump. She shot a glance at the wall clock. It was her lift.

Trotting down the hallway, clenching her half-eaten slice of toast between her teeth, she answered the door. Her colleague Tarn Scarr stood on the flagstone path looking dapper as always, his short fair hair styled with wax, and wearing a grey suit, white shirt and striped tie. In spite of his stocky build he looked more city banker than the front-line murder detective he was. An image flashed inside her head – her first day as a fledgling detective sergeant entering the office at Richmond CID. Tarn had welcomed her with a cuppa and shown her a vacant desk opposite his. That was four years ago, and since then they had become a formidable partnership; they had spent so much time together on investigations that they could virtually read each other's thoughts.

His blue/grey eyes lingered over her face for several seconds. Then narrowing his brow he dipped his head towards her. "That's new. Get that last night?"

Scarlett pointed to her left cheek and tightened her mouth."You've not heard what happened then?"

He returned a puzzled look while still examining her face. "Am I missing out on something here? The last time we spoke was in the pub last night. I said it was my round, went to the toilet and when I came back you'd gone. So how did you get the bruise then? Did you go on to somewhere else?"

She took on a disappointed look. "I hope you're not insinuating what I think you are?"

He offered a mischievous smile, "Well, you have got form."

She gave him a playful punch on the arm. "That was below the belt. I'm a reformed character now."

"Yeah, okay, I believe you."

She held his gaze for a few seconds. "One more word, DC Scarr, and you'll be getting a move you hadn't planned on."

He let out a hearty laugh.

She stabbed a finger towards the grazing. "If you'd like to know, I was frigging mugged last night."

"Mugged?"

"Yes, I know! Me of all people, mugged! And I'm pretty pissed off about it, I can tell you. And it especially doesn't help when your partner accuses you of falling down drunk."

Tarn met Scarlett's gaze and held up his hands in surrender. "Sorry."

With a flick of her head she beckoned him inside. "And so you should be."

Stepping into the hallway Tarn said, "Come on then, Sergeant, tell me all about it."

Walking back to the kitchen, she downed the remaining dregs of her coffee, and put the mug in the dishwasher. "To be honest I left early because I just couldn't face another drink. I was knackered and hungry, and I'd planned to grab a pizza and have an early night. But I'd only gone a couple of hundred yards from the pub when these two scrotes came from nowhere, decked me from behind and took my bag. My mobile, purse and warrant card was in it. I can do without my purse, but part of my life's in that phone and you know the issues regarding losing my warrant card?"

Tarn nodded.

"I was up until two this morning cancelling my cards and filling out forms in Richmond nick."

"Didn't catch them then?"

She told him about the chase and how it ended.

"Ouch! You eyeballed them though?"

Scarlett shook her head. "Both wearing masks! But I'll tell you one thing they weren't your average muggers. They were too big for the teenage gang members we have round here and too well made to be junkies."

"So you think you might be able to ID them?"

She pursed her lips. "I'm hoping so. There's CCTV dotted around the area, so I'm hoping we can track them to a vehicle or a house." She pulled her jacket from off the back of a chair and slipped it on, wincing as she put her left arm through the sleeve. "I'm sore as hell."

In the hallway she gave herself a final once-over in the full-length mirror, then, setting the house alarm and locking the front door, she followed Tarn down the path. "Anyway, did I miss anything? What time did you call it a day?"

"You didn't miss a thing. I think everyone else was in the same boat – it was the end of a very long day. I wasn't too long following you out. Half an hour tops, at the most. I finished my pint and left with George and Phil. There was only Ella and Gaz in the bar when we left, and they said they were finishing off their drinks and following us." Tarn popped the locks of his car and went around to the driver's side. He called back over the roof and pointed inside the car, "We made the front page this morning."

Opening the passenger door Scarlett spotted a folded copy of the *Richmond & Twickenham Times* on the front seat. She picked it up as she climbed in and after fastening the seat belt flipped it open across her lap. Emblazoned across the front page was the headline, "BRUTAL RAPIST CAPTURED". For the past two months the Homicide and Serious Crime Unit, of which she headed up Syndicate One, had been investigating a series of sexual assaults and three reported rapes involving female students attending Richmond University. The man they had dubbed the

Lycra Rapist, from the descriptions witnesses had given, had attacked at least half a dozen females over a two-month period, during September and into October, especially targeting lone girls walking through the college grounds in the early evening. On every occasion he had grabbed his victims from behind, dragged them into nearby dense undergrowth and while holding a knife to their throats carried out his attacks. For two of the girls the consequences had been devastating and they were unable to continue with their courses. Scarlett had spent hours trying to persuade them to change their minds but the girls were too traumatised, and so she had given them her personal mobile number and made them a promise she'd keep in touch.

After the third attack they firmly believed it was a male at or living close to the university, and initially they focussed on this aspect, questioning a couple of male students whose names had been put forward as well as a number of sex offenders in the area, but no one emerged as a central suspect. Then, because of the description, it had been aired that the rapist was someone posing as a jogger who might live close to the tree-lined grounds, such was the speedy nature of his disappearance after the attacks, and the enquiries were redirected. That was until something had struck a chord with Scarlett while examining one of the witness questionnaires, given by a twenty-year-old female student who, having been especially diligent because of the attacks, noticed that a cyclist at the Queens Road entrance to the park appeared to be in the act of repairing a puncture on two occasions over a three-day period and it had made her suspicious. Scarlett had thought this too much of a coincidence, and shared her findings at briefing, expressing to the team that they should set their sights on this unknown cyclist. Two nights ago her hunch had paid off – the rapist had been caught following a sting operation. Detective Constable Ella Bloom, posing as a student, had been pounced upon by him, and members of the squad, secreted around the grounds, had been on hand to apprehend him as he'd tried to flee. He had been revealed as twenty-six-year-old James Green from Twickenham.

She and Tarn had spent the majority of the previous day interviewing him. Over three probing interrogation sessions he had refuted responsibility for any of the assaults, denied being the cyclist seen repairing a puncture and denied ever being in the grounds, other than on the night of his arrest. When pressed for an alibi for each of the attacks he had repeated that he was a single man who lived alone. Coming to the part when he had attacked undercover detective Ella Bloom he had calmly replied that it was she who had approached him, offering herself, and he had thought her to be a sex worker, and being offended by her proposition he had "merely grabbed hold of her and pushed her away," insisting "he hadn't attacked her". She and Tarn had pressed and pressed but they had been unable to budge him from his story and mid-afternoon, drained and frustrated, they had led him back to his cell.

Scarlett had become even more frustrated when she had presented the evidence to CPS and requested a holding charge of attempted rape with an application for a remand to prison. The CPS lawyer turned it down without hesitation, and it had led to some intense debate, during which the lawyer told her if she could get some supporting evidence he would reconsider. Scarlett scrambled back to the office and allocated Tarn and the other members of her syndicate the task of poring back over the witness statements and video evidence, while she searched out the female student who had seen the cyclist by the campus gates. She finally tracked her down to her boyfriend's house in Richmond and sent a car for her, and while that was ongoing she hastily assembled a series of video mugshots for an identification parade. The twenty-year-old student viewed the footage twice, picking out James Green without hesitation. They had charged him yesterday evening and in celebration the squad had decamped en masse to the pub.

Suddenly feeling buoyed, Scarlett settled back into the seat and began to read the newspaper report as Tarn pulled away from the kerb to begin the journey into work.

Three

On the way to the station Scarlett and Tarn called off at a deli for a tall latte each before continuing on their way through Wimbledon on heavily congested roads. In steady bumper-to-bumper traffic Scarlett bemoaned her previous night's mugging again until Tarn interrupted.

"If it's any help, as soon as we get done on this job, I'll help you find your muggers, personally torture them and then dump their bodies in the Thames. Now, will that shut you up?"

Scarlett glanced sideways at her colleague. He was steering the car one-handed. In the other he gripped his cardboard cup of coffee.

"Am I going on?"

"Sergeant, you're going on."

"You want me to shut up about my mugging?"

"We've got a remand file to do for this afternoon's court appearance. And we've got a fair bit of evidence to go through. I think we've got enough to worry about."

Scarlett pulled back her gaze, fixed her eyes on the slow-moving traffic. After several seconds of silence she said, "I promise I'll not say another word about my mugging. And I'd be very grateful for your help when we've finished this job, but will you promise me one thing?"

"What's that?"

"You'll let me do the torture?" Out of the corner of her eye she caught Tarn cracking a grin.

****

The Homicide and Serious Crime Unit occupied the top floor of Sutton police station – a grand Victorian redbrick building on Carshalton Road. Two years ago the station had been renamed Patrick Dunne House in memory of a PC who was shot dead while following up the sound of gunfire in a street in which a nightclub bouncer had been murdered.

Tarn managed to find a slot in the rear yard to park his car, and still clutching their coffees he and Scarlett made their way up the back stairs to the office.

They entered a squad room exuding an atmosphere of unusual calm. The phones for once were silent. Scarlett noted that not everyone had made it in yet. Those that were in were chatting across desks, nursing warm drinks. No one had even booted up a computer. As she made her way to her desk she smiled to herself. She knew that in another half an hour all this would change, with everyone in full flow, each member playing their part in delivering justice.

Dumping her bag on her desk and slipping her outer coat off she thought she'd take up the initiative of being the first to start up a computer, but as she reached across to switch on her desktop a voice from the back of the room stopped her in mid-action.

"The DI wants to see you."

She recognised the voice of DS Gary Ashdown, her counterpart and supervisor of the other syndicate of detectives in the squad, but she still glanced over her shoulder to where he was seated. As usual, Gary's wavy mop of dark brown hair was fashioned Liam Gallagher style and the knot of his tie hung below an unbuttoned collar. He was reclining back in his chair, holding a mug two-handed against his chest. A wry smile was playing on his lips. "Said to tell you as soon as you came in, and he didn't sound best pleased."

She met his gaze. Something about Gary always made her shore up her defences. Sure, he was cheery enough and a good DS who got results, but there was this other side to him, this cocky air, as if he was better than everyone else, which grated on her. And he was always sucking up to the detective inspector, which she couldn't abide.

Scarlett dropped her bag onto her desk and rolled up her eyes, "When is he ever in a good mood?"

"You've not been up to anything, have you?"

"Nothing that you wouldn't do, Gaz." She returned with her own sardonic smile. Then, with a heavy sigh, she picked out a green elastic hairband from her top drawer, dragged back her hair from her face, gathered it into a ponytail and flicked the bunch over the back of her collar. As she strode towards the door she called back, "Best make myself presentable for Mein Führer."

Detective Inspector Hayden Taylor-Butler occupied an office two doors down from the squad room. As Scarlett approached she could see his door ajar. She stopped a metre before it and took a deep breath, trying to compose herself. She could feel her heart banging against her breastbone and she wasn't even in his office yet. She dreaded being in his company, especially on her own. It wasn't just that he was a bigoted, sexist, set-in-his-ways gaffer: they had history. The first time she introduced herself to the team he had made a snide comment about her being in the fast-track promotion system. She had occasionally experienced this during her time in uniform and in her early days in CID, and knew that to some, especially those in the latter years of service, her being groomed for early promotion was an irritation. Although it grieved her deeply that they should respond so bitterly she had learned to live with it. So when the DI had had his dig she had laughingly responded with, "We can't all be blessed with brains as well as beauty." It had been intended as light-hearted repost, but from the look on his face she knew she had pissed him off. Since then he had taken every opportunity to demean her and that had recently manifested into him sexually assaulting her. Four months ago, at Gary Ashdown's barbeque, which she had reluctantly agreed to attend, he had pinched her bottom and told her that he could help her get her next promotion. She'd reacted by throwing lager all down his shirt and pretending it was a drunken accident. Half an hour later he confronted her on the upstairs landing when she came out of the toilet, pressed her against the wall and leaned in close to her face, his drunken and stale tobacco breath assaulting her nostrils. In a menacing tone he made it quite clear he had the power to destroy her career should she ever make anything of it. There had been many days since when she had considered calling it a day, but she reminded herself she had joined the job for a reason, and she had reached her position not just because of her law degree, but because she was a bloody good copper.

She took another deep breath, held it for a good few seconds, exhaled slowly until she stopped shaking, and then stepped forward, rapping lightly on the DI's door.

Upon hearing a low muttered "Come in," she pushed the door open.

In the small narrow room, DI Taylor-Butler was seated behind his sizeable desk. It took up a good proportion of the room and was a desk quite the opposite of her own – neat and uncluttered – and every time she viewed it, it always made her wonder what he actually did on a daily basis, especially when a job wasn't running.

She stepped into his office, already beginning to feel claustrophobic. "You wanted to see me?"

The DI lifted his head slightly and gave her a scornful look. He didn't offer a seat.

Eyeing him carefully she couldn't help but think that his heavily lined moustached face and balding head, with its pelmet of greying hair, gave him the appearance of being older than his forty-two years.

He dropped his gaze to a piece of paper he was holding across his jotter. "I found this on my desk this morning. A copy of a report, by you, into the loss of your warrant card. You don't need me to remind you that losing your warrant card is a discipline offence."

She knew only too well the problems that could arise were it to fall in the wrong hands. "Of course. But I didn't lose it – it was stolen. In fact, if you've read my report properly you'll see that I was robbed."

He shot up his gaze. "I hope that isn't insolence, Detective Sergeant!" He flicked the sheet of paper. "Of course I've read it, that's why I wanted to see you." He locked eyes. "Is this really how it happened?"

She bit her lip. "What do you mean, 'Is this how it happened'? Of course that's how it happened."

"Not pissed up? You were out celebrating last night." He dropped his gaze back to Scarlett's memo.

"No I wasn't 'pissed up'! I only had two halves of lager. You can check with the team if you want. In fact, Detective Chief Inspector Harris was there – ask her if you don't believe me." She speared a finger towards the document he was holding. "That's exactly how it happened. And for your information I haven't been pissed up, as you put it, in years. That was a long time ago – unlike some of us."

His balding head shot up like a bolt. He fixed her with a vicious stare. "And what is that meant to infer?"

Scarlett wanted to mention the incident at the barbeque but knew that wouldn't be a good move. "Nothing."

"And it had better not be."

There was a few seconds of uncomfortable silence. The DI glared across his desk.

She saw his eyes drift downwards and felt that he was looking at her cleavage. She immediately felt uncomfortable. She pulled her waist-length jacket tighter and folded her arms protectively. "Now that we're settled this did happen, can I go?"

He returned his gaze to meet hers. "Can I go *what*, DS Macey?"

"Can I go, Sir?"

"That's better. You may be the blue-eyed darling following this latest job but just you remember your position in the team, Sergeant. And before you go back to the office tidy yourself up."

"Tidy myself up?"

He pointed towards her face. "What have I said about that muck you insist on trowelling on each day? This is a place of work, not the cosmetics department of Debenhams. Now go and make yourself decent and look the professional you're paid to be."

****

In the ladies washroom Scarlett gripped the edge of the vanity unit and stared into the mirror. She was livid. Her face and neck were covered in blotches and tears welled in the corners of her eyes. She fought back the urge to cry, taking a deep breath and holding it in, in an effort to regain her composure. Examining her reflection, she cursed herself for allowing that low-life shit of a DI get under her skin. Scarlett reminded herself again why she had joined this job.

Keep it together. Don't do anything silly.

Out on the streets she could easily handle the likes of Taylor-Butler, but his superior rank prevented her from publicly tearing a strip off him. And she knew if she reported him it might make things worse – it was her word against his.

What did Dad used to say? "Revenge is a dish best served cold."

Within a minute she could feel the calm returning. Releasing her vice-like grip and watching the colour return to her fingers she picked off a paper towel from the pile by the hand basin and dabbed at her lower lids. Then she returned her gaze to the mirror. Examining her face, it sometimes felt as if she was looking at another person. A little bit like Eleanor Rigby, from the Beatles song, "wearing a face that she keeps in a jar by the door".

And I'm buggered if I'm going to remove my make-up for that arsehole. He can just go and fuck himself!

She cracked a grin back at her image. Feeling sorry for herself wasn't going to get her work done. She had a complex court remand file to prepare and a pile of exhibits to sort out.

Four

Grazyna Sabalis awoke to the sound of music. Pop music. Muted. Distant. She could recognise the tune but didn't know the words. For a few seconds she lay there, staring up at the ceiling, letting the song wash around inside her head, then roamed her eyes around the room taking in her new surroundings; she'd been too tired last night. In fact, spotting her battered nylon suitcase propped against a wardrobe she realised that such had been her lethargy that she hadn't even had the energy to unpack. She mentally pictured the few possessions that were inside the case and hoped that new clothes came with the new job.

Grazyna continued surveying the bedroom. The limp curtains were translucent, allowing through a great deal of light, letting her see most of the room. There wasn't much in it: the single bed she lay in, a battered bedside cabinet, dressing table and wardrobe, a yellowing landscape print on the wall opposite, but at least the carpet was fitted, and it was much warmer than the room she shared with her two sisters and three brothers back home. The thought of her family instigated a slideshow of memories to run inside her head, provoking a sudden tinge of sadness. Nevertheless, she couldn't help but allow herself a little smile; if this was the luxury she was to experience, things already looked positive and it jolted her into reminding herself the reason why she was here, in England: not only to make a good life for herself but to be in a position to provide for her loving family back in her village.

For that she was grateful to Andrius. She wouldn't be here had it not been for a chance encounter with him and Henrikas.

****

Two months ago, she and her friend Kofryna had bumped into the two good-looking young men from the next village while out shopping in Alytus, the main town in Dzukija region of Lithuania. Andrius and Henrikas had quickly made an impression and followed them around for the best part of an hour, charming them into going for coffee. It had not been difficult saying yes, especially when they had offered to pay, and she and Kofryna had spent two hours in their company being captivated by their stories of travel through Europe, especially of how they had found work in London, England, and made themselves a small fortune. They had been so enthralled by the pair that they had missed the last bus home, throwing them into a panic. Andrius had been so kind and offered to give them a lift home in his Mercedes. She had returned to her remote farming village feeling like a princess. It had been such a special moment, and before he had driven away he had given her his mobile number and told her to give him a ring. That night, as she lay in her shared bed, listening to the soft snores of her brothers and sisters beside her, she toyed with the piece of paper Andrius had written his phone number on and replayed the stories that he and his friend Henrikas had regaled them with. She had been unable to shake his vision from her head and became overwhelmed by a sensation she had never felt before. Her stomach had turned-turtle so many times that night and she ached to see him again. Not only was he handsome, but far more wealthy than any other person she knew, and his lifestyle had sounded so idyllic in comparison to the future she had before her. After a restless night she met up with Kofryna and while toiling in the fields talked of nothing else but their meeting with Andrius and Henrikas. She hadn't been alone in her feelings. Kofryna was also smitten with Henrikas, and so after finishing work that day she made the call and arranged to meet up with them again.

****

The following Saturday, Grazyna took her time getting ready, bathing herself for longer and sneaking away a little of her mother's "special" perfume before donning her best cotton dress. She was embarrassed about her scuffed shoes but she couldn't do anything about them – they were the only "best" pair she had. She rubbed them against the back of her calves, trying to put a shine onto the toes, hoping that Andrius wouldn't notice them.

She met Kofryna on the edge of the village, looked her up and down and told her how good she looked, especially how much she liked her cardigan. Kofryna repaid the compliment about her dress, and with big smiles the pair linked arms and excitedly skipped their way along the dirt track the half mile to the metalled road where the bus stopped.

As usual it was late and overcrowded, and they had to squash themselves into the aisle and remain standing throughout the three-quarters-of-an-hour journey into Alytus.

Despite being stiff, hot and flustered, as Grazyna alighted from the ageing ramshackle bus in the main terminus of Alytus she told herself it was all worth it as she caught sight of the bustle of people all heading towards the stores.

She and Kofryna joined the throng of shoppers and found their way to the coffee shop they had previously visited. They peeked inside but there was no sign of Andrius or Henrikas so they hung around, eyeing the shoppers and chatting together. It was good ten minutes before their young men turned up.

As Andrius and Henrikas ambled towards them, hands in pockets, Grazyna couldn't help but notice how Andrius appeared even more handsome than before. He was wearing a polo shirt and jeans and his short dark curly hair glistened. He was unshaven but the couple of day's stubble made him look sexy. Her stomach fluttered as if a thousand butterflies were taking flight inside.

He greeted her with a big smile, displaying a mouthful of pearly white teeth, and pulled her towards him and kissed her on the mouth. Her first kiss. It wasn't a lingering kiss, but it was longer than a peck and it felt as if a charge of electricity was running through her.

She watched as Henrikas did the same with Kofryna and as they parted she caught her friend's gaze. Her grey eyes were sparkling and a huge grin stretched across her face. Grazyna knew from that look she was experiencing similar feelings.

"Coffee, ladies?" Andrius said, opening the café door for them.

They took up a table towards the back of the shop and Andrius ordered four coffees and two pieces of cake. In between mouthfuls they chatted and laughed; Andrius was especially funny. Grazyna couldn't believe her luck. She had to pinch herself as she stared into his warm brown eyes.

As they finished their coffees Andrius said, "What do you fancy doing now? Doing some shopping?"

Grazyna looked across at her friend. Kofryna displayed an uncertain look.

As if picking up on her trepidation Andrius added, "Our treat."

With that Andrius paid the bill and led them outside. Hooking an arm across Grazyna's shoulders he hugged her close and kissed her cheek. "Let's shop till we drop," he said softly into her ear.

They visited several department stores, many of which she and Kofryna had only ever browsed in. But now, thanks to the young men's generosity, they were here as shoppers.

In the ladies department they separated as couples, and Grazyna, with encouragement from Andrius, scoured the dress rails. For the best part of twenty minutes she looked at a number of different styles and then finally Andrius selected a short black figure-hugging dress with an expensive label. She was unsure at first when she saw the price, but he shrugged his shoulders and told her to try it on.

It fitted perfectly. She looked at herself in the mirror from various angles before finding the courage to leave the changing room and show Andrius.

She was so glad when she saw his face light up.

Crooking his arm he formed an "O" with his finger and thumb. "You look beautiful," he said." It makes you look like a young woman."

Hearing those words made her feel as if she was walking on air – only her parents had told her that before.

As Andrius paid for the dress Grazyna couldn't help but notice the large bundle of money he had pulled out of his jeans pocket. She had never seen anyone with so much money.

The shopping didn't end there. He also bought her lipstick, eye shadow and eyeliner – her first make-up. And he made her blush when he suggested she needed some new shoes. But the embarrassment hadn't lasted long as she tried on half a dozen pairs before finally settling on a pair of black court shoes.

An hour later she and Andrius met back up with her friend and Henrikas, and laden with carrier bags they made their way back to the coffee shop, where they drank and chatted some more before Andrius and Henrikas walked them back to the bus station. Here, once again Grazyna received a gentle kiss from Andrius as they said their goodbyes.

That evening, as Grazyna and Kofryna travelled home together on the bus, showing each other glimpses of their gifts, they found themselves competing for airspace as they exalted about their new-found boyfriends.

Five

Grazyna and Kofryna spent many more shopping days with Andrius and Henrikas.

With each meeting Grazyna's kissing with Andrius had become longer and more tender, but she hadn't gone all the way with him. She had told him she was a virgin and he hadn't pushed her. He had been a proper gentleman.

Three weeks ago Andrius had dropped the bombshell. He told her he had work to return to in England and didn't know when he would be able to come back home. She had tried hard not to cry but found herself unable to hold back the tears. For the best of five minutes she had sobbed while Andrius held her gently in his arms. After she had stopped shaking Andrius had dried away her tears, and then taken her by surprise by asking if she would like to travel with him to England and work there herself. He told her that he had contacts and finding work wouldn't be a problem. She had never even contemplated leaving her village, never mind Lithuania. She told him of her trepidation and he put her mind at ease by telling her he would speak with her parents. If they agreed then he would make all their travel plans. When she had broken her exciting news to Kofryna, she learned that Henrikas had made the same proposition to her. Within days Andrius and Henrikas had approached and spoken with their respective parents and been granted permission to escort their daughters to England on the understanding that the two girls would have regular phone contact.

Since then, talk of their new life had dominated every waking moment together and it had been the talk of the village. They had found it so difficult to concentrate on their labouring of the fields, and each day she and Kofryna had ticked it off as another last day of drudgery.

Two weeks ago she and Kofryna had spent the best part of a day travelling to and from Vilnius to arrange their passports and book their flights to England. It was her first visit to the capital and although exhausting it had been so exciting. It was a place she had only ever previously seen on TV, and she had trawled the streets looking in wonder at the architecture and how much traffic occupied the streets and how many people there were. Andrius had told her that this was nothing – London was even busier. As she jostled her way through the crowds she couldn't imagine anything being busier than this.

She had glanced sideways at her best friend Kofryna, arm in arm with Henrikas, and meeting her gaze exchanged a happy smile.

And then yesterday the day she and Kofryna had waited so long for had finally come. They had set off mid-morning to drive the few hours to Vilnius, breaking their journey on the outskirts of the city, where they stopped off at a large old house and were introduced to Andrius's cousin Morta. She had cooked them cepelinai, and served up the potato dumplings with pork and mushrooms, and as they ate hungrily she shared with them that she had worked many years in England, earning the money to buy the house she now lived in. During the meal Grazyna swapped looks so many times with Kofryna, seeing in her glistening eyes that she was as excited as herself about the future.

Then it had been on to the airport, and despite a two-hour delay, her time with Andrius had been magical. They had talked endlessly about what she could expect life to be like in England and he had treated her and Kofryna to their first alcoholic drink – a glass of wine each. Grazyna had boarded the plane in high spirits.

The only dampener to this wonderful experience had occurred upon their arrival at Heathrow Airport. Andrius had told her he had to make a phone call and following a short conversation ushered them through to a coffee lounge where he introduced them to a shaven-headed man called Skender, telling them he was his Albanian contact for work. He had arranged for Skender to put up her and Kofryna in his home for a short time while a job was sorted out. Andrius said that he and Henrikas had to go straight on to the hotel where they both worked to begin their shift and that they would see them again in two days. He had kissed Grazyna gently on the cheek, given her a reassuring hug and whispered in her ear not to worry – everything would be fine.

Being left with Skender was not what she had expected.

Under normal circumstances the shaven head, striking blue eyes and strong jaw with dimpled chin – handsome characteristics – should have made her feel at ease, but his muscular build and the disfiguring scar that travelled across the bridge of his nose onto his right cheek gave him a menacing appearance and made her nervous and uncomfortable.

Nevertheless, she had tried to come to terms with it as she and Kofryna had loaded their bags into the boot of his four-by-four and journeyed to the house where they were now staying.

Where that was, Grazyna had no idea. She only knew that it was somewhere outside of London, because she had followed the signs.

****

As Grazyna pushed herself further up the bed she spied the chair she had jammed beneath the handle of the door, provoking thoughts from last night.

They had pulled up outside this large two-storey house shortly after ten p.m. – she had noted the time on the dash of Skender's four-by-four. Getting out of the car, she had noticed the lights were on in most of the rooms facing her, and once inside, in the brief spell she stood in the hallway, she heard lots of different voices and noises around the house. In one of the rooms above she had heard shouting and it made her nervous to the point of being scared. She had moved closer to Kofryna for support.

Skender had said nothing. With their bags in his hands he had nodded for them to follow him up the flight of stairs. Stopping on the landing of the first floor he had handed over Kofryna's suitcase and directed her into a room, where, as soon as she had gone inside, he had closed the door behind her, preventing them from bidding one another goodnight. Then she had been guided up a further flight of stairs to the top floor of the house and been shown into this room.

Before he closed her door she had nervously told Skender she needed the bathroom. With a grumpy sigh he had shown her along to the end of the corridor. There she had swiftly locked the door, used the toilet and then cleansed and refreshed herself by washing her hands and face. When she had come out Skender was waiting for her. Not just waiting, but standing in the middle of the landing, partially blocking her way back to the room. She had approached him cautiously but he did not budge and she had been forced to brush past him. She had felt his hot breath on her neck as she squeezed by and it caused her heart to race and her stomach to churn. Upon the bedroom door being fastened she had spotted the dressing table chair and secured it beneath the door handle.

Undressing in the dark, she had climbed into bed knowing she didn't want to stay here more than a minute longer than she had to. As soon as she saw Andrius again she would tell him she wanted to leave.

As she contemplated what the day ahead held she caught the sound of distant footfall. Someone was coming up the stairs. She hoped it wasn't Skender.

Six

It was Skender. He shouted for her to open up after making two quick unsuccessful attempts to push open the door. The action made her jump and she braced herself back against the headboard. As she watched the chair judder for the third time her mind began to race.

"Open door now!" Skender yelled in broken English.

She could sense from the tone in his voice that he was angry and the hairs on the back of her neck began to prickle. Realising that she couldn't go anywhere she called back shakily, "One moment."

Throwing back the duvet, she remembered she only had on a T-shirt and knickers and she sought out where she had dumped her clothes the previous night. They were draped over the bottom of the bed.

Picking up her skirt, she slipped it on, adjusted it around her hips and fastened up the zip. "One moment," she called out again. She couldn't stop the nervous inflection in her voice and as she padded towards the door she could feel her heart beginning to pound faster.

Removing the chair she stepped back. "It's open."

Skender pushed open the door.

He seemed even bigger in daylight. Grazyna noted that there was only a few inches gap between his shaven head and the top of the door.

For a second he stared at her, then switched his gaze to the chair she was still holding. "Why you do that?"

"I–I wasn't dressed properly. I felt scared."

He smiled, narrowing his eyes.

"You do that no more," he said, stepping towards her.

She released the chair and edged back, catching her legs against the bed. "What do you want? Where is Kofryna?"

"She is in her room getting ready. It is time for you to get ready. You work for me soon."

A sudden confusion engulfed Grazyna. After a few seconds' silence she said, "Work for you? I don't understand. Andrius is getting me work."

He guffawed. "Andrius is gone. Gone back home."

Her head went into a spin. "Gone back home? I don't understand. Andrius is at work. He has a job at a hotel. He said he was going to sort out work for me and Kofryna and then come back for us."

Skender's mouth curled up. "You think Andrius is your boyfriend, yes?"

"Of course Andrius is my boyfriend. He is looking after me."

Skender fixed her gaze for several seconds then with a sneer said, "Andrius is not your boyfriend. You and your friend Kofryna belong to me now."

His words were like a blow to her stomach. She felt her chest tighten. "What do you mean belong to you?" she gasped.

"What I say: belong to me. I pay five thousand each for you to come here. Now you have to pay me back by working for me."

The nervousness she had felt minutes earlier disappeared and changed to anger. "You are lying. I am not working for you. I want to see Andrius and I want to go home." She jammed her hands onto her hips. "Right now."

Without warning Skender lashed out, back-handing Grazyna across the face. The blow knocked her onto the bed.

A split second later he was on top of her, clamping a hand around her jaw. "You work for me now, you understand? You make no more trouble. If you do I hurt you. You understand?"

Tears welled in Grazyna's eyes. Her jaw felt as if it was going to pop out of its joints. The pain was nothing like she had felt before. She managed to nod her head and he released his grip.

"Good, we understand one another, yes?"

Fighting back further tears, she nodded again.

"Good." He stroked her face with the back of his hand. Looking into her eyes he said, "You are virgin yes?"

Grazyna's stomach emptied. She felt sick.

Skender's eyes tightened. "Answer me. You are virgin?"

"Yes – yes," she managed to stammer out. Her throat was dry.

"Good, that is what I was told. I don't care anyway. I already tell people you are virgin." He fixed her with a threatening stare. "If anyone asks you tell them you are virgin. Understand?"

She couldn't believe what she was hearing. Licking her lips she said, "Please, I want to go home."

Skender broke into a mischievous grin. "You go home when I say you go home." He drew up a knee and straddled it across her thighs. "Now I try the goods."

He reached a hand beneath her skirt and Grazyna tried to squirm free but he pushed himself down more firmly and squashed her further into the bedding.

She wriggled even harder. "No, please no."

He hooked his fingers through the waistband of her knickers and yanked. Her knickers snapped.

"No," she cried out louder.

Skender viced her jaw again. "Scream, and you fucking die!"

Seven

"I think James Green is more calculating than we give him credit for." Scarlett was addressing members of both syndicates who were clustered around her and Tarn's desk. DI Taylor-Butler was among them. He had drawn up a chair and had his daily journal open across his lap. He was fiddling with his pen and unlike the other members of the HSCU his face showed no emotion. She continued, "I thought at first his attacks were impulsive, in as much as he cycled around, especially through the university grounds, until he spotted his victim, checked it was quiet, then dumped his bike, hid among the trees or bushes and struck as they passed." Pausing, she checked a few faces. The DI's face still bore a dead-pan look. "As I say, that's what I first thought. Now I believe that's not the case."

"What makes you say that, Serge?" Ella Bloom asked. Slightly built with short white-blonde hair and elfin-like features, she had the appearance of being a lot younger than her twenty-six years, making her a no-brainer for the undercover work.

Scarlett replied, "Since we charged him I've been going back through the evidence, especially the video interviews. If you recall, our first two victims were just groped by him, in as much as he ran up behind them and grabbed their breasts and then fled. But the third girl" – she glanced down at some notes she had made – "twenty-one-year-old Adelle Harrison, was also grabbed from behind, but on this occasion he put his hand over her mouth and dragged her towards some bushes. Thankfully, she managed to fight him off by back-heeling his shins – something she'd learned in self-defence classes. As he let go she screamed and he took off." Scarlett looked back up. "Although the light was fading she managed to get a glimpse of him and she said in her interview that she thought she had seen him before, although she couldn't place him." Scarlett gazed down at her notes again. "And then we have the two rapes, both girls again grabbed from behind, their mouths covered and dragged into bushes. On these two occasions they both had knives put to their throats and were told to be quiet or he would kill them. The first girl, twenty-year-old Claire Ridgewell, froze completely and kept her eyes shut throughout the whole ordeal. She's one of the girls who has been unable to carry on with her courses and gone back to her home in Maidstone. The second girl, nineteen-year-old Penny Wilkins, got a good look at him, and although he had a scarf covering his mouth she also thought she had seen him somewhere before." Scarlett paused again, taking in the thoughtful expressions on some of the faces. "If you also remember, although Claire kept her eyes closed she thought she heard clomping sounds as he ran away afterwards. When we arrested Green, following his attack on Ella, he was wearing cycling shoes with cleats attached, which you will recall gave off a clomping noise as he walked. And finally, we have our witness, Emma Caroll, who saw a cyclist on two occasions at the main entrance, who she describes as being in the act of repairing a puncture. On the second occasion she was very suspicious, because she thought he appeared to be looking around rather than working on his bike. This is the witness who picked out Green from the video identification parade."

DI Taylor-Butler spoke, "As you've pointed out DS Macey, we know all this. And so, your point is?"

Scarlett could feel her heart starting to race. She drew in a breath and held it briefly. Letting it out slowly and keeping her composure she said, "I think he stalked his victims." She focussed her gaze on the DI. He gave back an empty stare. "Two victims thought they had seen Green previously before the attacks." She deliberately paused a few seconds then continued on a stronger note. "I think they had definitely seen him before. Because he chose and targeted them." She pulled her eyes away from the DI and returned them to her team members. "This is where we need to do some extra work. Speak with those victims again and see if we can narrow it down to when and where they had seen him. It may well have been just a chance meeting – in a pub somewhere, for instance – but after that I'm convinced he targeted them." She paused again, gathering her thoughts. "We've got Green on remand for seven days on a holding charge of attempted rape following his attack on Ella. We all know that's a flimsy one and the likelihood is it'll be reduced to sexual assault, but it gives us the opportunity to do a thorough search of Green's flat. We've recovered the clothes he was wearing when he attacked Ella, but the cycling shirt in particular is a different colour according to two of the witnesses, so let's see if there are anymore. Also, strangely, he didn't have a mobile phone with him. Let's see if that's at his flat, then we can track his movements. Also see if he has a computer and check if he's on social media. With a bit of luck there'll be some incriminating evidence. I also want to know if he owns a vehicle. And whether he has a girlfriend." Scarlett paused, dipping her head, looking at the list she had compiled and mentally going over it. Satisfied that she had ticked each point she looked back up and roamed her eyes around. "I want to find out everything about James Green. I want every detail of his life examined. I've just got a hunch these aren't his only victims."

Eight

Beneath the bedclothes Grazyna hugged herself tighter into a ball. She had given up crying hours ago.

Now she was alone and her thoughts were roller-coasting. She couldn't stop thinking what Skender had said about Andrius. He had to be lying. The Andrius she knew was kind, thoughtful and gentle. Andrius would come soon and rescue her. She just knew he would.

And she could not stop thinking what had happened to her. The images of what Skender had done repeatedly played themselves out inside her head, plaguing her consciousness and making her feel sick. It was as if she was living a nightmare. She tried to tell herself that at least she was alive.

A sudden creak on the stairs pricked her ears and she could feel her chest beginning to tighten again. She balled her hands into fists.

The creak became distinguishable footsteps that stopped on the landing outside her door.

Grazyna caught her breath. Her head screamed, *Please, go away.*

She caught the sound of a key turning in the lock – she hadn't realised she had been locked in.

I'm being held a prisoner!

The door opened slowly and Skender stepped into the room.

For a few seconds he just stared at her, not speaking. Then he said, "Now you make phone call to your mother, yes?" He strode towards her holding out a mobile phone.

"I put in your mother's number. You now ring her and tell her you are okay. If you say anything wrong or make trouble I hurt you, you understand?"

Grazyna remained in a tight ball, though she had lifted her head from her pillow.

"You understand?" Skender snapped.

Grazyna jumped. "Yes."

"Good." He passed her the phone.

She uncurled herself and took it.

Fixing her eyes he thrust a piece of paper towards her. "You say to your mother that you have job, and everything is good and you tell her this is where you are living." He shook the piece of paper.

"You read out to her the address I have written down there. You tell her you will ring her again in a couple of days. You understand?"

Skender narrowed his eyes as Grazyna hesitantly took the piece of paper.

"You do as I say and everything will be okay. If you do not, not only will you get hurt but I will make sure the same thing happens to your sister."

Grazyna's eyes widened. Her stomach emptied again.

"Your sister is fifteen, yes? And she is also virgin."

The inflection never changed in Skender's voice but Grazyna sensed an underlying threat.

Skender leaned forward, towering above her. "I am right, yes?"

"Yes." Her response quavered.

"Good. I think we understand one another. Now you call your mother. And you be very careful what you say. I put phone on speaker so I hear. I know Lithuanian."

Pushing herself up, yet still cowering to keep some distance from the Albanian, she viewed the number on the phone and then hit the call button. Listening to the dialling tone, a chaotic thought raced into her brain despite Skender's threats. Something was telling her to fight back. To tell her mother to call the police the moment she answered, but as the dialling tone prolonged she caught herself. If it was true what the Albanian had told her about Andrius, then the same could happen to her sister.

After a few seconds her mother answered. The sound of her voice caused a surge of emotion to wash over her. She almost let out a cry and at first she couldn't speak.

"Hello?" her mother called again.

She had to hold it together. Not just her own life depended upon it but her sister's as well. Grazyna swallowed. "Hello Mama, it's me."

"Hello beautiful, I was just thinking of you. How are you?"

"I'm fine, Mama."

"You don't sound fine. Is everything okay?"

Grazyna looked up. She caught the threatening look on Skender's face. His eyes were drilling right through her. She gulped. "I'm fine, Mama. Just tired." After taking another deep breath she followed Skender's script, only slightly expanding on what he had told her to say. She mentioned that she had a job, that everything was good, and then she read out the address from the piece of paper he had given her. Then as she told her that she had to go she could feel her voice beginning to break. "Speak to you soon, Mama," she finished on a brittle note. As she ended the call tears welled in her eyes.

Skender held out his hand and Grazyna handed him back the phone.

He reached towards her face and she sharply pulled back her head, catching the headboard. She winced.

With the back of his hand he stroked her cheek. "That is good. Now we are friends." He turned away and made for the door.

Hearing the key turn in the lock, she began to shake uncontrollably. Then she sobbed.

Nine

Half asleep, Grazyna heard the sound of screams. At least she thought they were screams, because as she flashed open her eyes and awoke, there was only silence. She strained her ears for the best part of a minute. Nothing. It made her wonder if she had been dreaming.

For a few seconds she began to study the confines of her room, wishing that all this really was a dream. Without warning, ghost-like images of her ordeal burst into her inner vision again and she snapped shut her eyelids, squeezing them tight, attempting to shut out the horrific mental pictures, but they hung on in there, refusing to budge.

Will this torture ever end? I don't deserve this. I'm not a bad person.

Then another scream forced her eyes open. This time she knew it wasn't a dream. It had come from somewhere below and it sounded like Kofryna.

Kofryna! A vision of her own ordeal came to her again.

Grazyna drew up her knees and covered her ears, but the action didn't block out all the noise and she picked up the sound of a door slamming followed by heavy footsteps running up the stairs.

She started to shake. *Please God, not again.*

Withdrawing her hands, she heard the key in the lock. The door flew open, crashing against the edge of the wardrobe, making her jump.

Two men stormed into the room. One of them was big and bulky with a shaven head like Skender. He had so much fat below his chin that it gave him the appearance of having no neck. The other was slim but well toned like an athlete and had an army-style crew cut. They were both dressed in T-shirt and jeans.

In a state of panic she started to push herself up into a sitting position, but they were on her in seconds, grabbing at her wrists and restraining her.

A feeling of dread and despair overcame her. She stiffened but didn't resist, and turned away her head and closed her eyes.

After a few seconds when the mauling didn't continue she slowly opened her eyes. Her two attackers weren't even looking at her. They were focussed on something the overweight one was holding. At first she couldn't make sense of the object. Until the burning smell, which she associated with that of an iron, assailed her nostrils. Then she realised what the big man was pushing towards her.

As the soldering iron made contact with her right shoulder she began to scream.

Ten

On the way home from work Scarlett got Tarn to drop her off in Richmond town centre; she needed something for her evening meal. At M&S she bought an oven-ready chicken, mushroom and mozzarella pasta bake and a bottle of Soave, then walked the short distance home, occasionally looking back over her shoulder, still unable to shift the thoughts of her mugging, even though it had now been the best part of a week since her encounter with the two thieves.

Entering her home, she deactivated the alarm, toe-heeled off her shoes in the hallway and made her way into the kitchen, turning on the oven and cracking open the wine. Pouring out a generous measure she took a swig, tilted back her head, swilled it around her mouth to activate her taste buds and then swallowed slowly. Savouring the sharp fruity tang she could already feel herself beginning to unwind as she tore away the outer sleeve of the pasta bake. Then, sliding it into the warming oven, she set the timer and made her way into the lounge, where she snatched up the remote and activated the TV. The opening moments of *X-Factor* emerged onscreen as she flopped down onto the sofa.

Mindless viewing – just what she needed after the day she'd had.

In actual fact, it wasn't just that day she was unwinding from. For most of that week she had endured a hectic schedule and an intense workload. She had supervised the search of James Green's council flat, though the evidential pickings and information from that had been minimal. The search team hadn't found any form of computer or his mobile, though they had found a charger for one, which had led to frustration. And despite emptying every drawer of every sideboard and cupboard and rifling through his wardrobe they hadn't discovered any other cycling or Lycra-type clothing. Similarly, they had established very little out about him, other than what they already knew. Scarlett not only found this strange but also very disturbing. Door-to-door enquiries had not helped much either. Surprised and shocked by the news, neighbours described him as a very pleasant man who kept himself very much to himself, though one neighbour had informed them that she had seen him on a number of occasions recently burning what she thought to be rubbish in an old metal bin beneath the flats.

Following that revelation, she and Tarn had hot-footed it down to the refuse area, where they had found a battered and rusted oil drum, the inside of which was heavily sooted, half full of burnt detritus. Sifting through it they found blackened and shrivelled remnants of Lycra, and although nothing of significance could be gleaned forensically from them, it did confirm Scarlett's thoughts about the type of villain James Green was. Particularly, how forensically aware he was. And as she bagged the burnt nylon pieces it quantified, in her head, that she and her team had a long way to go before they could put the case before a court. But rather than be down-hearted about the lack of evidence, she had returned to the office in a determined frame of mind and drawn up an action plan. Two days ago, together with Tarn, she had returned to the university with the purpose of determining if there were any more victims who, for whatever reason, had so far not reported their attacks. Inside the beautiful Gothic-style building, the pair had met with the head of the university, and then briefed department heads, teaching staff and student union reps on the current status of their investigation. From there they had sought approval and gained access to lectures, where Scarlett had delivered a heartfelt plea to the female students. During these appeals she had drawn on her eighteen months' experience of working with Sapphire Command, the Metropolitan Police's rape and serious sexual assault unit, highlighting some of the cases she had previously worked on, with special emphasis on the care and support she had provided to victims. Scarlett had delivered the requests to packed theatres but no one had come forward. Then, a day ago, they got a breakthrough. Overnight, a girl had left a message anonymously on the incident room helpline asking if she could meet DS Macey and had left her mobile number. Over the phone, Scarlett had spoken briefly with a very nervous-sounding young woman who was willing to give scant details about herself and what happened but did not want to talk about her ordeal at a police station, and so Scarlett arranged to meet her that morning in a coffee shop by Richmond Bridge, overlooking the Thames. It was a place she had been to many times before, its interior warm and welcoming, and although popular she knew there would be enough space between tables for a private conversation.

Shortly after ten a.m. she and Tarn entered the coffee shop. They saw that a few tables were taken, and briefly scanning the room, they spied the only girl of the age they were looking for tucked away in a corner, hunkered over a large white mug, staring into space. Nineteen-year-old Claudette Jackson had a glowing tawny complexion and glossy black shoulder-length braided hair. Her attractive face bore an anxious look. Making eye contact, Scarlett issued a reassuring smile and approached slowly. Pulling up a chair opposite, Scarlett softly introduced herself and Tarn and sat down. Tarn followed, pulling himself closer to the table and resting his arms. Ordering three fresh coffees, Scarlett opened up by telling Claudette that she was really glad she had been brave enough to contact them, and went on to explain that although James Green had been remanded to prison, it may only be temporary, that they were still some way off getting enough evidence to put him before a court. She added, "That's why, Claudette, it really is important that you tell us your story. With your help we can put him away for a very long time." In between sips of coffee, Scarlett drew on her training to put her at ease, spending time asking her about the course she was doing at university, about her family background, and whether she was going home for Christmas. Claudette said she was going home, though she didn't know what she was going to say to her family. She had not told anyone about what had happened. Scarlett saw this as her opening. "You've made a big start contacting us. We can support you through all this. You don't need to be alone and suffering. Trust me, I've spoken to many girls who've gone through what you've gone through and they've come through it and become much stronger as a result." Keeping eye contact and studying her features she finished the last of her coffee. Then, putting down her cup, she said, "Do you feel able to talk to us about the attack?"

At first Claudette just stared. For the best part of thirty seconds she was silent. Then she spluttered, "I can't help think I'm somehow to blame for what happened to me."

Scarlett hadn't expected that response. She probed, "What makes you say that?"

"Well, he bought me drinks, didn't he, and was nice and I just fobbed him off and flirted with some other guys I knew."

Scarlett straightened, "You knew him then?"

Claudette's nut-brown eyes drifted a second and then returned. "Not exactly knew him in the sense of his name and everything. He came into the bar where I worked."

"Which bar is that?"

"The Red Cow."

"I know that pub." Scarlett scrutinised Claudette's face, trying to recall if she had seen her there. Her mind was blank. She continued, "The team I belong to regularly go in there, but I can't remember seeing you there."

She shrugged her shoulders. "I work behind the bar. It's not regular hours. I fill in when they're short. Occasionally I do weekends."

"And it was there you first met James Green?"

"I didn't know his name. I've since found out his name from the piece in the papers. He came into the pub a couple of times. One night when it was quiet he just started chatting, asking me what I did. I told him I was a student. He said he'd been a student at the university and that he now worked in the city in banking."

Scarlett responded by shaking her head. "He's unemployed, Claudette."

"Well I wasn't that convinced to be honest. He didn't dress well enough for someone in banking. But you get all sorts chatting to you when you're behind the bar, so I just let him rabbit on and he paid on a drink for me, so I was nice to him and listened."

Scarlett interrupted, "When was this, Claudette?"

Her forehead screwed into a frown. She thought about the question for a couple of seconds and then answered, "Probably about a month before he attacked me. I remember it was Thursday evening. Quiz night. He didn't do the quiz, that's why we were chatting. It wasn't that long, to be honest. I got serving again and that was the end of it. Until the following week, that is. He came in again, didn't do the quiz and we chatted on and off while it was on." She paused. "I say chatted. He really did the talking – said he'd had a busy day and then started waffling on about this multi-million deal he was involved in. To be honest, I switched off, just pretended I was interested. He was a bit of a bore and not my cup of tea. Anyway, he paid on a drink for me, I thanked him and then I got busy again. This second time, before he left, he made a point of coming up to the bar and saying cheerio to me and said he'd see me again. I just said cheerio and nodded and that was it. He turned up the following week, but this time my room-mate and some friends were in. I told them to stay close, that I thought he fancied me, so they hung around. He bought his usual lager and stayed at the end of the bar. In between serving, whenever I glanced up, I could see him watching me. It made me feel uncomfortable, and when I served him again and he asked me if I wanted a drink I turned him down, thanked him and told him some friends had paid on a couple for me. After that I spent as much time as I could with my friends and pretended to flirt with one of the guys. Just jokey stuff to put him off. When I looked up again he'd gone." Claudette's face changed. Her lips tightened and her chin quavered. "The Thursday after, that's when he raped me. I finished in the bar just after twelve, walked back to the university and he was waiting for me near some trees." She took a deep breath. "He grabbed me from behind and put a knife to my throat! Said he was going to kill me if I screamed or struggled!" Claudette's eyes started to glisten.

Scarlett reached across and touched Claudette's hand, "Try and relax Claudette. Talking to us like this has got the hard part over with." She patted the back of her hand. "And let me tell you, none of this is your fault. James Green is a rapist. Full stop. You know from the papers that you're not the only one he's done this to and if we hadn't had caught him there would have been a lot more girls like you who he would have attacked. Telling us this now will help us put him behind bars for a long time. A very long time." Scarlett gently squeezed her hand. "Before we finish talking, Claudette, can I just take you back a bit. I just want to get something clarified. Are you absolutely sure that the man who raped you was the same man who chatted with you at the bar? I'm not trying to dissuade you, but the university grounds are not that well lit and you did say he was waiting behind some trees."

Claudette nodded. "I know it was him. He had a scarf covering his mouth and nose, trying to hide his face, but we weren't that far from one of the paths, which are quite well lit, so I got quite a decent look at him. And I recognised his voice." She held Scarlett's gaze. "Anyway, you'll be able to tell if it's him, won't you?"

Scarlett threw her a puzzled look. "How will we? I don't understand."

Claudette squeezed back Scarlett's hand, "I put the clothes I was wearing, when he attacked me, in a plastic bag and I've kept them under my bed. I've watched CSI and I'm right in thinking you'll be able to get his DNA from them, aren't I?"

Scarlett's eyes lit up, she shot a sideways glance at Tarn. He was displaying a wide grin. She could have punched the air.

The rest of that day had been spent video-interviewing Claudette at a victim and witness suite and then she had been examined by a female force medical examiner. After that they had driven Claudette back to her room at the university and recovered her bagged clothing from beneath her bed, leaving her in the company of her room-mate for support, before returning to the office late that afternoon, where they had delivered the good news to the squad. The week's hard work had paid off and consolidated their enquiry. Now all she wanted to do, especially tonight, was chill in front of the television, get a good night's sleep and then rejuvenate herself tomorrow morning in the gym. She took another mouthful of wine and sank back against the cushions. Dermot O'Leary was introducing contestant Sam Bailey, a prison officer. She'd heard her sing twice already on previous episodes she had recorded and thought she stood a very good chance of winning the competition this year. She glanced at her watch – she should just have enough time to listen to her before the pasta bake was ready.

Abruptly her BlackBerry rang. She diverted her gaze to the coffee table, where she eyed the brightly lit screen of her work mobile. This usually meant only one thing: a call out. Her shoulders sank. "No!" she groaned. Reaching across she set down her glass and snatched up the phone. She glanced at the screen before she answered but there was no name, only a mobile number, and although she couldn't put a name to it she was familiar with the line of digits.

Narrowing her eyes, racking her brains as to who it was, she answered, "DS Macey."

"It's me," said the male voice.

She recognised the voice. Her face lit up. "Hello, It's Me."

"I've been trying to get hold of you since Thursday. I've left umpteen messages on your phone. I didn't know if you'd changed your mobile or not so I contacted your work. They weren't going to give me your number so I had to tell them I was your cousin and I needed to get hold of you urgently."

She pushed herself back on the sofa. "Oh sorry, Alex. My mobile's been nicked. I was mugged last Friday night. I've lost all my contacts."

"Good job I'm resourceful."

"Resourceful! Someone's got a bollocking coming Monday morning. They shouldn't release this number without my permission first."

"Now, now, Detective Sergeant Macey, I don't want you throwing your weight around. I'm a very persuasive man and you know that."

She let out a laugh. "Well this better be good, Alex King, I've got a glass of wine that's ready for topping up, a pasta bake for one in the oven and *X-Factor* on the telly. What more can a girl want on a Saturday evening?"

"Well I think I might just be able to better that."

"Oh yes, and what might that be then?"

"I think I've found your sister."

Her head went into a swirl. Her hand tightened around the phone. "Rose! Where?"

For the next few minutes she hung on to Alex's every word. When he ended the call she found herself shaking.

Eleven

Following the phone call Scarlett had not been able to eat her pasta bake. She'd managed a few mouthfuls, but mostly she'd pushed it around the plate, her mind in a daze. She had managed to finish the bottle of wine, though, and although she knew she shouldn't, she opened another, refilling her glass, dwelling on what she had just been told.

Alex had possibly found her younger sister after all these years!

It was something she had managed to avoid thinking about for these last couple of months, thanks to work, but in the space of a few minutes the news had resurrected all her pent-up anxieties again. As she sipped on her replenished drink her thoughts went into a tailspin and flashes of ghostly images from her past leapt around in the deepest recesses of her mind. Especially imagery from that fateful night, almost eleven years ago, when she had learnt that her parents had been killed – murdered, more specifically – and her younger sister had fled the scene. She had been wanted in connection with their deaths ever since.

Swallowing another mouthful of wine, a feeling of guilt overcame her. Scarlett pulled away the glass and stared at the contents. She had been drunk that night – the fifteenth of February 2002. She still wore the date like an ugly wound cauterised into her grey cells. It was her second year at university, studying law, and she and a group of friends had hit the bars in Covent Garden celebrating Valentine's night. She had been dating a guy in his final year and they had staggered back to the flat he shared with four other students. There they had polished off the remains of a bottle of vodka and collapsed into bed just before two a.m. She had been awoken three hours later by the incessant ringing of her mobile. It was the police, who said they needed to know where she was. She knew it had to be serious, but not for one moment did she think just how bad the news was going to be. Ten minutes later two cops were banging at the door giving her the news of her parent's death. She had viewed the remainder of that day through a woozy fog, nursing the worst hangover she had ever had.

Detectives did interview her, initially in an off-hand manner, but once they had confirmed she had been with at least a dozen other people at the time that her parents had met their deaths, they told her what they knew of the circumstances.

She learned that earlier that night, her mother, Carran, and her father, John, had also been celebrating Valentine's with a meal in a restaurant when they had been interrupted by a phone call from the police. Rose, who had then been sixteen, had been detained by officers called to a fight near Covent Garden station involving two women. When the police had got there they had found Rose grappling with an older woman. She was drunk and refused to calm down and so they had detained her. The older woman didn't want to complain but because Rose was so inebriated they had taken her to hospital. Her dad, who was a detective sergeant in Lewisham CID, knew the officers who had escorted Rose, and had persuaded them to leave it with him. He and her mum had driven straight to the hospital and collected her, still in her drunken state, from the A&E department. Half an hour later a young couple driving home from a nearby pub had come across their crashed car, embedded in a tree, on an unlit country lane. Their phone call had brought out all the emergency services and it was determined that this was no ordinary accident. Her father had been found lying in undergrowth only yards from his car, covered in blood and in a critical condition. Paramedics discovered within a minute of examining him that he had been stabbed in the stomach and the chest. Firemen and traffic police attending to the car found her mother dead in the front passenger seat. She had taken the full impact of the collision when their car had hit the tree. Her dad had been rushed to hospital and taken directly to theatre. Sadly, he had died while undergoing surgery.

At first the police at the scene hadn't realised about her younger sister Rose, until Scarlett had mentioned her being missing. Then they had carried out a search. It wasn't long before they found bloodstains and tracks leading away from the scene into the copse of trees beside the lane, prompting an even wider exploration. But despite the search parameters being extended and tracker dogs being used they did not find Rose. She had disappeared and a murder hunt was launched.

Initially, the detectives interviewing Scarlett never actually said that Rose was a suspect, but the implication was there, such was their line of questioning, and Scarlett still felt guilty about how she had responded during those early days of the investigation. After all, it was she who had revealed Rose's problems.

Her younger sibling had always been difficult. Scarlett could remember that as a young child Rose would say and do the most hurtful things and would regularly throw a tantrum before sinking into days of depression where she wouldn't communicate with anyone. She could recall, after one bad outburst, her father locking Rose in the bedroom, shouting at her that she was just an attention-seeking, spoilt little brat. As a teenager the temper tantrums worsened. During one of her manic bouts she assaulted two teachers at her school and was excluded. That was when her parents took Rose to the doctors. She was referred to a psychologist but no definite diagnosis could be made. From then on her behaviour deteriorated. At the age of fourteen Rose began drinking and hanging out with older teenagers. She could remember her father having to go out many a night to bring Rose home. More often than not she would be in a drunken stupor.

And through those early days of the enquiry, albeit Scarlett fought her sister's corner vehemently, telling the detectives that despite Rose's bad behaviour she couldn't believe for one minute that she would kill their mum and dad, having no other independent witnesses, and no other information to hand, she had been circulated as a suspect.

After that her life changed irreversibly; the event had shaped her life and her career. In the year following, Scarlett gave evidence at her parent's inquest, in which the verdict of "murder by persons known or unknown" had been recorded against her father and an open verdict against her mother. She had overseen their burial and completed her law exams, where in spite of the distraction she gained a 2:1. She had celebrated attaining her degree by getting drunk alone and falling early into bed, sobbing her heart out.

For a while she had wondered how she was going to carry on with her life. Everything she had dreamed of lay in ruins. Then it had come to her one night in a half-drunken state. Her father had been a detective, and she'd grown up on a TV diet of *Prime Suspect*, *Cracker* and *A Touch of Frost*. Joining the police seemed the most natural thing in the world. And she knew it would give her a way in to do her own digging. She had kept in touch with one of the detectives involved in her parent's case. He had provided her with regular updates, from which she had made notes, and she had compared those alongside the many and different newspaper reports, studying and dissecting the information. But no matter how hard she tried to pick between the lines everything still led back to her sister.

And those were the reasons why, instead of being a lawyer, like her father had wanted her to be, she had joined the Metropolitan Police. Since then she had worked tirelessly behind the scenes to uncover the truth and track down her sister Rose. She had been waiting a long time for this news.

Twelve

Grazyna didn't know how long she'd been out for. When she came to, the first thing she noticed was that the curtains had been drawn back, bathing the room in a warm ambient light.

And she was alone.

A feeling of relief washed over her.

On the bedside cabinet she saw that someone had left her a sandwich and a bottle of water. Despite the sick feeling in the pit of her stomach the sight of it made her realise just how hungry she was. The last time she'd eaten had been on the plane and that was well over a day ago. She reached over to grab the sandwich and in doing so caught the top of her shoulder. A sharp pain shot down her arm. The jolt reminded her of what the two men had done to her and glancing down she saw the burn marks the soldering iron had made. Heaving herself up, Grazyna took another look. Lingering along its outlines she delicately traced a finger over the tenderness. The shape of the ugly red mark reminded her of a crescent moon and star. She would be left with a permanent scar.

Why are they doing this to me?

For what seemed like the hundredth time she re-ran everything that had happened to her inside her head and once more her chest began to tighten. She took a long deep breath and held it. She needed to stay focussed if she wanted to come through this. Nevertheless, even as she tried to control the release of the captured breath she felt it reverberate up through her throat as the anxiety remained. She took another slow breath, and as she did so she caught the sound of the stairs creaking.

Ten seconds later the key clicked in the lock and the door opened. Skender stood in the doorway.

Grazyna froze with fear.

He stepped into the room alternating his gaze between her and the bedside cabinet.

"You need to eat and drink. You need your strength."

He walked towards her and she cowered away, pulling the duvet up towards her chin. She watched Skender's mouth take on that jackal-like smirk of his. It filled her with fear.

He sat on the edge of the bed, picked up one half of the sandwich and pushed it towards her. "Here, you eat."

Grazyna eyed him nervously. She didn't know if she could stomach it. She felt sick again.

He held the sandwich at arms length, jabbing it towards her face, glaring. Nervously she lowered the duvet and reluctantly took it from his grasp. As she bit into the bread and cheese he pulled away his gaze and levelled it upon the branding on her shoulder.

Chinning towards her he said, "I do that to protect you." He pulled back his eyes and met hers. "People know you now work for me. They not touch you." He pushed himself up. "Now you eat up, and then you bathe and get dressed. We go in a few hours." As Skender strolled back towards the door he picked up her suitcase. "You not need this anymore. I give you clothes." He flicked his head towards the wardrobe. "You wear something in there after you bathe. I come up in one hour. You be ready or trouble."

With that, he left the room with her case, this time not closing the door.

****

Grazyna did manage to force down the cheese sandwich and gulp down the water while staring out through the barred window. It was the first time she'd done so. The road below had a steady flow of traffic passing along it and she got the impression that although they weren't on a main street, because all she saw was an endless row of houses with tiny low-walled gardens, she still thought they must be on a busy thoroughfare. From up here she got a partial glimpse of the inside of the vehicles that passed, and as she watched one lady making a call on her mobile, she wished that could be her. As the car passed she spotted a young woman pushing a buggy, crossing the road, directly beneath. For a brief moment she did contemplate smashing the window and shouting for help. But as she toyed with the idea her heart missed a beat, as a disturbing vision of the consequences flashed inside her brain – not just her but for the young woman and her child and she wavered against it. She also remembered the threats Skender had made against her younger sister. With a feeling of despair she stepped back and determined it would be best if she took the bath Skender had ordered her to take.

With a heavy heart she undressed slowly, wrapped a towel around her and apprehensively made her way along the landing to the bathroom. Standing before the mirror she stared at herself. She looked as awful as she felt. Her shoulder-length straw-coloured hair was a tangled mess and had lost its usual shine. Behind dark-ringed eyelids her pale blue eyes were lifeless and bloodshot. And then there was the angry-looking burn marks to her right shoulder.

No young man will ever want me again.

She couldn't believe Andrius had betrayed her like he had. She so much wanted to believe that Skender was lying, but she knew deep down that wasn't the case.

Grazyna ran the bath as hot as she could bear without the water scalding her, and lay in it scrubbing at her skin until she was red and sore. Upon finishing she wound the towel around her lobster-pink flesh and returned to the bedroom.

Recalling what Skender had said, she pulled open the wardrobe door. It had a rack full of clothes but they weren't of a style she was expecting. Shiny black PVC trousers and skirts, skin-tight metallic dresses and crop-tops filled every hanger. Below was an assortment of differently sized footwear consisting of patent-leather boots and high-heel sling-back shoes. Trashy clothes.

Grazyna gulped. She had a bad feeling about this.

I have to escape.

For five long minutes she stared at the rack of clothing, wishing there would be something there that wouldn't make her look like a tart. A feeling of despair enveloped her as she realised no amount of wishing was going to change her situation.

From below Grazyna heard a door bang. Her heart leapt. Footsteps clomped up the stairs and she caught her breath.

He said one hour!

The footsteps stopped on the landing below and a door was opened. Then it closed. She released a long sigh, but the activity had caused an element of fear to rise within her and it burst her into action. Grazyna dove her hands into the wardrobe and began rummaging through the clothes again, checking most of the garments at least twice for size before finally selecting a pair of shiny black leggings, knee-length patent leather boots, a red crop-top and a short leather jacket. She knew it made her look cheap and tarty, but her appearance wasn't as bad as it could have been in some of the clothing she'd dismissed. She just hoped Skender would approve.

Finally, not wanting to feel his wrath again, she tiptoed back to the bathroom, brushed her hair, cleaned her teeth and applied a little of the make-up which had been left on the dressing table.

As she checked herself again in the mirror she wasn't happy with what she saw, but she had no choice – especially if she wanted to survive.

Making her way back to the bedroom Grazyna stopped for a moment on the landing and peered down the gloomy staircase. She listened, hoping to pick out Kofryna's voice in the rooms below, but not a sound came back. In fact, except for the sound of a television playing out somewhere downstairs the house was quiet. She cast her gaze over the banister to catch a glimpse of the entrance hallway. For a second she thought about making her escape, and tried to judge how far down she had to run and how long it might take, but from here up she couldn't see if the front door was unlocked. She thought that more than likely it wasn't and rubbed away the thought.

With a sense of dread Grazyna returned to the bedroom and dropped down onto the bed.

And waited.

Thirteen

She didn't need to wait long, catching the sound of creaking wood. The footfalls on the stairs were heavier than normal and the big man with no neck who had branded her earlier appeared in the doorway.

"You have to come with me," he said, with a backward flick of his bulbous head, turning on his heels.

Pushing herself up off the bed Grazyna followed him onto the landing and then began a disquieting descent down the stairs. On the landing below, standing beside Skender, she met Kofryna. She took one look at her and couldn't believe it was the same friend she had arrived here with. Kofryna's nutty brown hair had been pulled back from her face into a pony tail, revealing hollow cheek bones and dark-rimmed eyes. A gash of bright red lipstick scarred her usual cheery smile. The clothing Kofryna had on was even more whorish than her own outfit. She had on a silver Lurex top, black leather miniskirt and black and silver sling-back high heels. The expression she wore was sorrowful and as they exchanged glances Grazyna saw that she had suffered the same horrors as herself.

Grazyna offered up a meek smile. It was reciprocated but there was no emotion behind it, as if the lifeforce had been sucked from her friend. She stepped forward to give her friend a hug.

Suddenly Skender thrust out an arm knocking her back. He shook his head and shot Grazyna a disproving look. "Arjan here is taking you to another house. You be good for him or bad things will happen, understand?"

Grazyna and Kofryna dropped their gazes to the carpet. Neither of them replied.

"Understand?" Skender repeated sharply.

Both girls jumped.

"Yes," they responded, one after the other. Their voices were shaky.

"Good." He pressed his head towards them. "Don't forget what I tell you about your families. And don't forget what I tell you if they ask if virgin." Pointing the way downstairs to the hallway, he added, "Now you go with Arjan."

Under escort, Grazyna and Kofryna trooped downstairs and were shown out through the front door into the street. Skender's four-by-four was parked directly in front.

Arjan popped the locks and yanked open the rear door. He indicated with a nod of his head for them to climb in.

Grazyna shuffled in first, followed by Kofryna.

Pressing herself back against the leather upholstery Grazyna shot a glance out through the windscreen. She got her first full view of the area from street level. Similarly styled two-storey houses stretched for some two hundred yards. Dotted along sporadically, both sides of the road, were autumn-leafed trees. Up ahead, a crepuscular light touched the rooftops – it was turning to dusk. She looked for life, anyone she could exchange glances with, but she saw no one. Pulling back her gaze she swapped another weak smile with Kofryna and tentatively reached sideways and squeezed her hand.

Arjan climbed into the driver's seat. The car dipped sideways with his bulk. He fired up the engine and engaged gear. Without turning around he said gruffly, "You not talk. You be quiet or there be trouble, okay?"

Grazyna caught Arjan's eyes in the rear-view mirror looking back at her. She nodded towards him.

"Good." He pulled his eyes back to the road and heaved on the steering.

As he pulled away from the kerb Grazyna breathed a sigh of relief. Skender wasn't coming with them. They left him standing on the pavement, hands in pockets, wearing that evil smile of his.

Driving slowly along the road Grazyna began to take in the surroundings, storing them to memory. At the junction ahead they stopped. It looked to her as if they were entering a busy thoroughfare; a steady ribbon of traffic threaded past the front of their car.

Arjan went for a gap, screeching away from the junction, slotting in behind a blue van and breaking sharply to match its slow speed. A car at the back of them sounded its horn. He groused over his shoulder, shaking his pudgy hand in a threatening manner.

A hundred metres later they stopped at another junction. Upon turning right, Grazyna spotted a road sign: Brentford 5.

Is that kilometres, or was it miles in England?

The traffic moved at snailpace on this road. And bumper to bumper. Grazyna listened to Arjan chuntering and saw him tapping the steering wheel in frustration.

She felt a hand flick her thigh and turned to face Kofryna.

Kofryna blazed open her eyes and canted her head towards Grazyna's door.

Grazyna's heart began racing. Was Kofryna indicating the door lock? Was she signalling her to jump? She flashed a quick glance towards Arjan, and seeing his concentration was on the traffic ahead flipped back her gaze. She mouthed the word "escape" and Kofryna nodded. Her stomach leapt and she felt sick.

Wide-eyed, Kofryna dipped her head towards Grazyna's door. This time her action was more urgent. Then without warning she launched herself forward, flinging her hands around the driver's seat headrest, slapping them across Arjan's face.

Arjan yelped. The car lurched sharply and a split-second later there was a loud bang as they smashed into the van in front.

Grazyna was flung forward, banging her chest and the side of her face against the back of the passenger seat. The blow knocked the wind out of her and for a few seconds she desperately fought to catch her breath. Beside her she saw Kofryna frantically scratching and pulling at Arjan's head and face. Defensively, he was swinging his arms wildly attempting to halt the attack while simultaneously trying to grab a hold of her friend's flaying arms. Grazyna finally caught her breath, took in a great gulp of air and leapt to Kofryna's aid, throwing in a punch at Arjan's head.

In Lithuanian Kofryna screamed, "Run, Grazyna, run!"

It took only a second for Kofryna's cries to register and for Grazyna to make her decision. She threw another quick punch at Arjan, then reached for the door release and shouldered it. The door sprang open so easily that it took her by surprise and she almost fell out. She staggered as she hit the pavement, adjusted quickly and set off running even before she could straighten herself. Behind, she could hear horns blaring, followed by the sound of screeching tyres, but she never looked back. She just kept on running.

Fourteen

Scarlett awoke with a thunderous headache. She dragged herself out of bed and into the bathroom, where she laboured under a cold shower, willing her body out of its lethargic state. Inside her head she berated herself; she knew she shouldn't have drunk that second bottle. Drying herself she came to the decision she needed something a lot tougher than the gym to get herself out of this languid mess. A run beside the river always did it; once outside she always pushed herself harder than on a treadmill in a warm gym.

Downing a full pint glass of water she pulled on her running leggings, a T-shirt and running vest and added a hooded top before grabbing a bottle of water and taking to the streets. For the first half-mile the pace was slow, warming up and stretching the muscles, but as she turned onto the track which took her riverside, she kicked up her heels. For the next three miles she pounded along the embankment of the River Thames, pushing herself to her limits, grasping for every breath, feeling that her lungs were about to burst through her chest. Then she eased off into a pace which, although still fast, was more comfortable. The last half-mile of her six-mile run she finished at a gentle jog. At the front door, grabbing back her breath, she stretched out her aching legs, and checking her watch for her running time, she entered the house in far better shape, both mentally and physically, than she had left it thirty-four minutes earlier.

The second shower was more comfortable and invigorating and she emerged feeling refreshed. She even had time for a bowl of porridge before getting ready to meet Alex. From her wardrobe she chose a pink tight-ribbed V-neck jumper and skinny jeans, because those would fit under her biking leathers – she had decided while running that she would give herself an added injection of adrenalin this morning by taking her motorbike for a blast.

Snatching up her keys and grabbing her helmet out from under the stairs, as ever, before leaving the house, she gave her appearance the once-over in the hallway mirror. Canting her head, she thought she looked pretty good for someone who only two hours ago had been suffering a wrecking-ball headache.

Locking the front door she ambled round to the side of her Victorian terrace, where she kept her motorbike chained up beneath heavy-duty plastic, and whipping off the sheet she checked over the classic 1967 black Triumph Bonneville. It had been over a fortnight since she'd last ridden her, yet the chrome and paintwork still shone.

As a young teenager, Scarlett could remember her father bringing it home one summer's evening, declaring he had bought it from a colleague at a bargain price, much to her mother's disgust, berating him for bringing home a death trap. Excitedly, he had begged her and Rose to go outside, where he had proudly shown off the rusted heap, spouting off one technical detail after another to them. It had bored Rose and she had disappeared back inside the house to watch the telly, but Scarlett had been fascinated and over the next eighteen months she and her dad had lovingly restored it. When it was finished he had asked her to choose a name for the bike and after mulling over a few names she had finally come up with Bonnie. He had repaid her by taking her out on pillion for its first maiden run following restoration. "This is how a bike should ride," he had shouted back over his shoulder as he'd opened it up on the dual carriageway. And as she gripped the sides of his jacket, he had added laughingly, "Just don't tell your mum." It had been her first adrenalin rush. Since then she had passed her motorbike test and repeatedly ridden the bike alone. Following her father's murder she had taken ownership, caring for it in the same loving way he had.

Bunching back her hair she slipped on her helmet and straddled the Triumph. Kick-starting it, it fired first time and she tweaked the throttle, listening to the throaty roar of the 649cc engine. Two minutes of warming the engine later and Scarlett freewheeled it from the side of the house and onto the road. Then she gently opened the throttle to begin her journey. She had decided to take a long route to the pub where she was meeting Alex and so she headed out towards Chertsey, joining the M3 before switching onto the M25, where she really wound the bike up. Half an hour later, her adrenalin rush sated, she pulled off the motorway and headed back to Teddington and the Anglers pub. The peaceful riverside pub had been a regular meeting place of theirs when they had dated, and even though they were no longer a couple, it was still a place they came to whenever they wanted to catch up with one another. And it was a place where they could play "spot the celebrity"; the pub was close to Teddington Studios and therefore a magnet for film and TV drama stars.

It was just before twelve-thirty p.m. when Scarlett entered the car park. There were a few cars around but the place wasn't choc-a-bloc like it was in summer. Pulling off her helmet she scoured the car park. No sign of Alex's Range Rover Sport.

Good.

It would give her enough time to smarten herself up.

In the toilet she stuffed her biking leathers and helmet into her knapsack, replenished her make-up, ensuring that the bruising to her face was suitably disguised, and finally shook out and straightened her hair before stepping back into the bar. Quite a number of the tables were taken, mostly by families out for Sunday lunch, but she spotted a couple of empty ones by the far wall and she reserved one by dumping her bag in the middle of the table before making for the bar. There she ordered a J2O orange and returned to her chosen table, where she picked up a menu and settled down onto a chair. Scarlett had already determined she fancied something different from the traditional Sunday lunch.

The mussels with cider, leeks and bacon definitely sounds tempting.

"Have you ordered already?" Alex's voice made her jump. She dropped her menu and diverted her gaze upwards. His handsome face was lit up with a smile. A tingling sensation travelled down her body.

"No, I've only just picked up the menu. I haven't been here long."

He leaned in and she half rose and offered her cheek. As he planted a kiss she caught a whiff of his musky eau-de-cologne. It stirred a memory.

"You look nice." He pulled away his gaze and settled his glistening blue eyes upon her drink. "I'm just going to the bar, can I get you anything?"

She shook her head, "No, I'm fine thanks."

He dragged out a chair, took off his jacket and draped it over the back.

Seeing Alex standing there, his well-toned chest, shoulders and arms straining his rugby top, reminded Scarlett of what had attracted her to him in the first place.

"I'm just going to get a beer and then we'll order shall we?"

As she watched him stroll to the bar, right hand dipping into his jeans pocket, she felt her heart flutter. That spark hadn't gone away even though their relationship was over. The decision to split had been made nine months ago and for her part she still felt guilty over it. Guilty, because it had been so full-on, especially physically, unlike anything else she had ever experienced, and yet selfishly she hadn't given everything to the commitment side. It wasn't just her; they had talked about it. Many times. The bottom line was that they were both dedicated and committed to their work, frequently cancelling dates because one or the other had a job running. And so the decision to call it a day had been made. It had seemed so right and sensible at the time, yet nevertheless she still had moments, like this, when she questioned herself for coming to that hasty conclusion. Eyeing him, making his order to the girl at the bar, and watching her face light up, she couldn't help but feel a pang of jealousy creeping upon her. Her eyes remained glued to him and as he made his way back, sipping the head off his beer, Scarlett wondered if he was seeing anyone. Watching him take up his seat she tried to dismiss the thought from her head, but she knew it wasn't going to go away. She was so thankful that they had remained good friends and still spent some time together.

Alex took another drink. "So, you said on the phone you'd been mugged."

It broke Scarlett's day-dreaming and dragged her back to the moment. She took a sip of her own drink and then told him her story.

Giving her a lingering look as she finished, he said, "I'm sure, knowing you like I do, you'll catch up with them sooner or later."

"And boy when I do they'll know about it."

Shaking his head he smiled, "Still the same Scarlett, I see."

"That's what attracted you to me, wasn't it?

"Actually, it was the long legs and nice arse."

Scarlett soft-punched his arm. "Alex King, you are so shallow."

"Ooh, Scarlett Macey, you can talk. I used to catch you drooling over me in the gym."

"Drooling! Drooling! Oh, you are so vain. I'll have you know that was sweat that was."

They both laughed.

Changing her expression she said, "Anyhow, you said on the phone that you think you've found Rose."

"Not exactly hundred per cent sure. Her hair's not the same, but it's fair just like the photo you gave me and she certainly has your eyes."

"Where did you see her?"

"Just inside the entrance of the subway to Charing Cross. She was with a guy." Alex paused and pursed his mouth. "They were begging."

Scarlett took on a serious look. "When did you see her?"

"I've spotted her there twice now. I first saw her last Monday evening. It was purely by chance – I normally don't use that entrance to the Underground, but I'd just finished meeting with a client and went for a coffee on the Strand. As you can imagine, spotting her was a real surprise, but I didn't want to hang around too long in case I spooked her so I noted the time and then caught the tube home. I had some time on Wednesday so I decided to check out the tunnel again and there she was – in the same place and with the same guy. It was just after half four. I couldn't believe my luck. I dropped them a couple of quid so that I could get close enough to double-check her likeness. I'm pretty sure it's Rose. I wasn't able to get there on Thursday or Friday because I had meetings."

"When you say begging does it look as though she's sleeping rough?"

Alex shrugged his shoulders. "Hard to tell. To be honest she didn't look too bad. Her clothing was a little shoddy but she certainly looked well. As I say, I only hung around for a brief look. I didn't want her to clock me." He took another sip on his beer and licking his lips added, "Anyway, how are you fixed tomorrow? I've nothing pressing for the next few days. I've got to go to Germany this week but that's not until Thursday, so what you say we meet up and you can check for yourself?"

Scarlett raised her eyes to the ceiling, recalling what she had on at work. After a couple of seconds she returned her gaze. "I've got a rape enquiry on at the moment, but I'm close to wrapping that up. There are some loose ends to tie up and some paperwork to sort but I should be able to get away early if I crack on first thing tomorrow and nothing else comes in."

"Okay, that's sorted then. I'll give you a call mid-afternoon and if everything's cool we'll meet at the front of the National Gallery at four."

Scarlett picked up her glass and took a lengthy drink, her thoughts going into overdrive. After all these years, was she finally going to catch up with her sister?

Fifteen

Scarlett could feel her eyes getting heavy. She finished the paragraph she was reading, folded down the page and placed Horace Walpole's *The Castle of Otranto* on the bedside table. It had been a long time since she had read a classic but she had been gifted the book by the head of the university as a thank you for her sensitive approach and support to the students in the course of the rape enquiry and she had promised faithfully to read it. Well, she'd started it, but it was heavy going. Alex King's revelations had tormented her thoughts all that afternoon and they were still distracting her. From the moment he'd told her about Rose she had not stopped thinking about her. She couldn't even remember eating lunch in the pub or anything she and Alex had said to one another following his shock disclosure. All day it had been as if she and her thoughts had been wandering around surrounded by a fine mist. The reading had probably done her good; even though she had not immersed herself into the story it had certainly made her feel tired.

Checking the alarm was set on her BlackBerry she turned out the light and snuggled beneath her duvet. For several minutes she lay with her eyes open listening to the sounds of the house settling and thinking about tomorrow. She really hoped it was Rose. She needed some answers.

Scarlett closed her eyes.

A dream visited her. It was the dream she used to have as a young girl. It hadn't visited her during her teenage years but had reappeared following the murder of her parents. With counselling it had disappeared again and so for the last seven years her subconscious had been undisturbed by the terrors. Now it was back.

As always, it began with her walking along a corridor lit by old flickering gas lamps which gave off only a dull glow. Heavy panelled doors lined either side for as far as the eye could see. She could never see the end of the corridor. The building she was in was old and decrepit and for some reason she knew it was Victorian Gothic, though she didn't know why, because her only view of it had always been among the corridors and the rooms behind the doors. Moving along at a slow pace, a familiar feeling of dread overcame her for she knew what was going to happen next. It was always the same.

Ahead she heard the creak of a slowly opening door and stepped forward tentatively. To her right the door was ajar, though the gap was not wide enough for her to see what lay beyond, and as she pushed the panel inwards fear rose within. The room she entered smelt fusty and looked cluttered. She tried to pick out the shapes in the gloom but everything appeared to be covered in dark dust sheets. Although nothing inside the room was discernible, the surroundings reminded her of an old Victorian parlour. Heavy drapes hid windows, woollen rugs covered a polished wood floor and the walls were adorned with Christian artefacts. She walked to the centre of the room and someone whispered her name. She froze. Before her, in the left hand corner, was a rocking chair, slowly rolling to and fro. Someone was sat in it, though she couldn't pick out any features, only a shape. She couldn't even tell if the silhouette was male or female. Her name was called again but she was confused. The voice that called her contained a mixture of sounds from her father's and mother's mouths. And there was another voice among them. Hearing it speak chilled her to the core. Her eyes searched within the dimness. Someone else was in here, hiding in the shadows. She turned to run and she felt a presence stir. Then it was if she were stuck, as if someone or something was holding her back. She fought to free herself, willing her legs to move, but they were like lead and a feeling of panic and dread overcame her. Her heart began to pound against her chest as she exerted more pressure and finally she was free and back in the corridor again, running for all she was worth. Doors clattered behind her. At the far end a light appeared. It was getting brighter.

Scarlett flicked open her eyes and found herself in her bedroom. She heaved a sigh of relief.

Sanctuary. The demons hadn't got through.

She saw that the duvet was half on her, half hanging over the bed and she was covered in sweat. She took in a deep breath and let it out slowly. She began to shake.

The thought of Rose had stirred the haunting again.

Sixteen

It was lunchtime before Scarlett's languor had dissipated. The half a dozen cups of coffee and the two Pro Plus tablets had helped by giving her the hit she needed to challenge the fatigue from her restless night.

Despite her weariness and her thoughts continually drifting to that evening's plans she had managed to make a dent in her paperwork. The four hours she had spent rooted at her desk, without interruption, had enabled her to make some in-roads into the Lycra Rapist investigation, especially with the preparation of an updated remand file, adding the rape of Claudette Jackson to the list of charges. Other pieces of information she had gone through had focussed on James Green himself, though the feedback and findings from her colleagues had disturbed her. Despite a search team and Forensics going through his flat with a fine-toothcomb and extending house-to-house enquiries, they had uncovered very little about him, especially his past. It was that part which especially concerned her. She was no further forward in knowing when he'd arrived on their doorstep, where he'd lived previously or even where he'd worked. On that score she had left enquiries with the Housing and Benefits departments, but no one had come back to her yet. It was on her list of chase-up calls. Thankfully, they had Claudette's clear identification of Green to back up the charge, and Scarlett had tasked her partner Tarn with logging the clothing recovered from Claudette's room and bagging them for forensics, in the full expectation that a positive DNA match would be made affirming that James Green had carried out the attack. Holding those thoughts, she glanced up from her keyboard to catch Tarn's attention only to find him levelling his gaze at her.

"What?"

Tarn tapped his watch. "Lunchtime. Do you fancy going out for a sandwich?"

Pushing herself back in her chair, she teased out the stiffness in her spine and gazed across her desk, locking onto Tarn's enquiring gaze. Tarn was probably the best partner she had worked with. He not only shared her enthusiasm and tenacity for hunting down criminals, but matched her professionalism as an investigator.

Their first job together had been a series of robberies on lone women leaving railway stations late at night, the offender being a fifteen-year-old boy already hooked on cocaine. He was caught because he got sloppy. Three of the attacks were at a station close to his home in Fulham and she and Tarn had spent a couple of nights on stake-out there, catching the BMX-riding youth as he targeted a young woman just walking to her car in the car park. Tarn had a brought him down, bike and all, with a neat rugby maul. He was currently doing four years in a young offenders' institution. Since then they had also worked together on a number of murder enquiries, complementing their individual skills. When she had been offered the DS's post on the HSCU two years ago, and there had been a gap in her team, she had immediately thought of Tarn. It hadn't been difficult persuading him to join and since then he'd been her regular working partner.

"Under normal circumstances I'd say yes, but I want to get this file ready for court tomorrow. If you're going for one can you bring me something back?"

"What's the rush? You've got all day."

"I need to get a flyer."

Arching his eyebrows he said, "Got something on?"

She hadn't told him about her meeting yesterday. In the past she had confided in him about her younger sister Rose, but as she'd climbed into his car that morning she had decided that it would be best if she left him out of it for now. That way he would be protected. Especially given that Rose was still officially circulated as a suspect in her father's murder. "Let's just say I need to get away early."

His frown tightened."Very mysterious."

"Not really. I've just got some personal stuff to sort out."

"So personal you can't share it with a friend?"

Scarlett threw him a scolding stare.

He held up his hands in surrender. "Okay, okay, this interview is terminated."

She smiled. "Good. And as you've got nothing better to do, I'll have a ham and salad on brown."

****

By three-thirty p.m. Scarlett had finished her work for the day. She printed off her documents and after checking that the numbered pages were in sequential order, tapped them together neatly and dropped them into her pending tray. Then, lifting her coat off the back of her seat she waved a hand to catch Tarn's attention, and with a flick of her head towards the door she mouthed him a silent goodbye and left the office.

Twenty minutes later she was at Richmond railway station catching the train to Waterloo. There she alighted, crossed the bridge and caught an overground train to Charing Cross, where, jostling with commuters making their way home, she fought her way up the escalator and along the corridor towards Trafalgar Square. She emerged from the exit facing Nelson's Column and cast her gaze around. As usual the square was busy and she noticed that in the short time she had been on her journey day had given way to evening and the weather had changed – dark, brooding, pregnant rain clouds filled the sky. She pulled up the collar of her coat and headed towards the National Gallery.

Passing the fountains she spotted Alex at the top of the steps leaning against the balustrade. He gave her a wave and skipped down to greet her.

"No problem getting away then?"

"No, although I had to be a bit discreet getting away from the office. Tarn is the only one who knows I needed to leave early but I didn't tell him why. The fewer who know, the better."

"Okay then, are you good to go?"

She eagerly rubbed her hands together. "You bet."

He lifted up a carrier bag he was holding and delved into it, pulling out a lightweight outdoor jacket. "You need to put this on." He handed over a Gore-Tex coat. "It's reversible, just in case we need to do a couple of sweeps past our target."

Scarlett threw him a look. "Alex! What do you mean target? The target might be my sister. She's called Rose."

He met her gaze. "You know what I mean." He fished a hand back into the bag and withdrew two woollen hats. He handed one over. "You might need this as well."

As Scarlett pulled the grey coloured hat down over her ears she glanced at Alex and smiled. From their relationship she had learned he was a former senior non-commissioned officer in

71

Military Intelligence, specialising in global terrorism. He had once been attached to the SAS, involved in the targeting of terrorist groups in Iraq and Afghanistan. Now – so he had told her – he was employed by a London-based specialist security company advising international organisations and Third World countries on their security measures. As she watched him pull on his own hat she couldn't help but think, from the look on his face, how much he was revelling being back in action, organising and playing his part.

As Scarlett pulled on her jacket Alex reached across and tucked in some loose strands of her hair. "You've got to hide that red hair. You'll stick out like a sore thumb." Then looking her up and down he added, "This might be daft question but have you done surveillance stuff before?"

"Watched a few villains from the back of an unmarked van many a time."

"But have you followed anyone before?"

She shook her head.

"Right, pin back your lug-holes, Scarlett Macey, I'm going to give you a crash-course in foot surveillance. Fortunately for us this shouldn't be too hard. Our target" – he paused, smiled and continued – "sorry, Rose, is more than likely going to be static, so it'll just be a matter of getting yourself in a position to observe. But what you mustn't do is hang around too long or you'll draw attention to yourself and blow it. Okay with that?"

Scarlett nodded.

"Right, what we're going to do is split up at the top of the escalator and head down to the platform. I'll go first and do a recce and then pull away and tuck myself to one side. You'll follow up and see if you can get a good look at the girl and see if it is Rose. Don't do anything if it is. Join me and we'll plan our next move. And if you're not sure and need to do another sweep, reverse the jacket and take off your hat."

"But then my hair'll be a mess."

He shot her a disbelieving stare.

Scarlett returned a scolded little-girl look. "Only joking."

"You'll be the death of me, Scarlett Macey."

She swiped a hand down in front of her face. "Serious head on now, Alex. I'm ready for the off."

"Okay, we're going down the same entrance I've used the last couple of times when I've spotted her."

With that Alex set off, taking Scarlett by surprise. She quick-stepped after him, falling in beside as they marched past the statue of Sir Henry Havelock towards St Martin's Place, where they crossed over the road to the tube entrance by the South African High Commission. Here they descended the steps and took the white-tiled tunnel towards Charing Cross.

A hundred yards in Scarlett felt the atmosphere warming up and she picked up on the rumbling, echoing sounds of the trains trundling through the station below.

Alex slowed his pace. Softly he said, "I saw her just after I got off the escalator, she was to the left in front, okay?"

Scarlett nodded as they stepped onto the down escalator. She could feel her stomach flipping over and for a couple of seconds she was overcome with nausea. She took a deep breath.

"I'll flick my head if she's there," Alex said, picking up his pace.

By the time Scarlett had reached halfway Alex was leaping off the bottom. She closed in behind a man wearing a large overcoat, almost breathing down his neck. She stiffened as her view of the bottom began opening out. A couple of seconds later she spotted the pair Alex had mentioned: a young man and woman, resting back on their haunches, backs pressed against the wall. On the floor between them was a cap with coins inside. Scarlett zoned in on the girl. Because she was crouching it was difficult to judge her height, and the green combat-style jacket she was wearing disguised her size, though she could see she definitely wasn't of a big build. Although straggly, the girl's hair was fair, the same colour as her own before she had dyed it, with a centre parting. It framed a thin pale face, without make-up, and as she drew nearer she noted the girl's eyes were ringed with dark rims, a distinct sign of exhaustion – or drug abuse. The girl was reaching out a begging hand to passing commuters.

Scarlett was so focussed, drawing on her memories, trying to determine anything familiar in the girl's features, that she missed the man in front of her stepping off the escalator and her body jarred into the ground, causing her to stumble forward as she was dumped off the moving staircase.

The sudden movement caused the girl to divert her gaze and she locked onto Scarlett. Scarlett knew from the returned look she had been clocked.

The girl's reaction was instantaneous. She launched herself up and a split second later she was bolting for the southbound platform.

Scarlett wasn't far behind but found herself meeting headlong a wall of rush-hour commuters all coming towards her and in only a matter of seconds she had lost sight of her quarry. She clawed herself forward, squirming and pushing between disembarking passengers who cursed after her. As she rounded the bend onto the platform she faced a standing crowd of people all waiting for the next train. She drew to a halt and began probing a sea of faces before her and beyond. It was hopeless. She couldn't even see if Alex was among them, never mind the girl. Through gritted teeth she let out a note of frustration. Then she stepped forward into the foray and slowly began weaving her way left through the crowd. Within thirty seconds she heard a loud rumbling noise and felt a rush of warm air brush her face, heralding the approach of the next train. A couple of seconds later she saw the engine come thundering through the tunnel up ahead. It swept past, giving off a long metallic screeching sound as it lurched to a halt. Then there was a hiss and the doors of the train opened. The throng of commuters began to edge forward, brushing their way past as they made for the carriages. Scarlett stood her ground and began scouring the sea of faces. For a few seconds her sight was overwhelmed by the numbers moving onto the train. She could feel herself getting anxious. Her chest tightened. Finally the platform cleared and she began searching the carriages, breaking into a jog, heading towards the back of the train. This was no better. Every coach was full to bursting.

Too many heads to count. Too many faces.

She had just reached the second-to-last coach before the tunnel when she picked out the face she had been looking for. For a couple of seconds she zeroed in on the girl but it was two seconds too long; as she stepped forward to board the train there was another loud hiss and the doors slid shut before her. Spurred into action she leapt forward and attempted to prize them open, but to no avail. The train lurched forward. In a panic she began running beside the moving carriage, peering intently through the glass doors, willing them to open, her face a mask of agony. She caught sight of the girl and watched on helplessly as she stared back at her, a self-satisfied smirk stretched across her face. The girl gave her the finger, but just before she disappeared from view Scarlett saw that her expression had changed. For a brief moment she thought she saw a look of recognition. Then her view of the girl had gone. Scarlett stopped running and in an act of embittered defeat banged the side of the departing train with her hand.

Seventeen

In a coffee shop on the Strand, Scarlett nursed a mug of coffee while staring out through rain-streaked windows. Bumper-to-bumper traffic meandered past and her gaze was settled on the glaring reflections of headlights and tail lights shimmering back from the rain-sodden road.

Suddenly, a hand flashed in front of her, making her jump. She felt a light tap on her forehead.

"Penny for them."

She brought her attention back to Alex sitting opposite. "Sorry."

"Thinking about the girl?"

She nodded.

"You think it's Rose?

She rocked her head. "Part of me is saying it was her. I only got a brief glance, and it is such a long time ago since I last saw her, but it was just a look she gave me from the train. As if she recognised me." She set down her mug sharply. It clattered onto the table.

"That's good then."

"It is if we find her again."

"We've found her once, we'll find her again. We're all creatures of habit, stick close to the surroundings we're familiar with. She's obviously living in the London area if she's using the Underground, and that'll not be the only section she'll be begging in. She'll more than likely lay low for a couple of days but I'm guessing she'll be needing the money, so she'll back again. Not the same place, granted, but she'll more than likely be operating in at least half a dozen places on the network. She'll turn up."

Scarlett picked her mug back up, rolling it backwards and forwards in her hands. She stared at the remaining lukewarm contents. "I'm gutted! So near and yet so far."

Alex reached across and touched the back of her hand. "No point beating yourself up over it." On a lighter note, he added, "Anyway, what's to say she'll not come back there again? If she has recognised you then maybe she wants to be found."

Scarlett lifted her eyes and met Alex's stare. "Somehow I don't think so. She's still a suspect in my dad's killing, remember."

"You don't think that though?"

She shrugged her shoulders. "It's not what *I* think though is it? It's what others believe. It still niggles away at me: if she is innocent, why hasn't she come forward?"

"Could be lots of reasons. From what you've told me about their killings only your sister knows why that is. You know your sister best though."

"I thought I did. I used to when she was younger. But then I'd listen to Mum on the phone, when I was at university, getting upset when she told me the things she'd been up to."

Alex scraped his chair back. "Well, nothing we can do now. The main thing is we've found her."

"Someone we think is her."

"Well, we don't give up because of this. When I get back next weekend we'll have a day out and run around the Underground. What do you say?"

Scarlett returned a meek smile. "That'll be good."

He pushed himself up and nodded down at the mug she was holding. "Well that coffee looks as though it's cold. What you say I take you for a real drink? And then we'll go for some food. I know a great Indian."

Scarlett examined the contents of her mug and briskly set it down. "Let's have that drink first and take it from there."

Eighteen

Scarlett awoke with a start to the ringtone of her BlackBerry berating her ears. She rolled over and threw out a hand, scratching around in the darkness to search it out on the bedside cabinet. Within seconds she had clamped her fingers around it, lighting up the screen.

Pushing herself up in bed, simultaneously hitting the answer button, she said gruffly, "Hello, DS Macey." She swallowed hard. Her mouth felt as if it was lined with cotton wool. The events of last night flashed into her thoughts. She knew in the taxi on the way home that she shouldn't have drunk those two large glasses of wine after the curry, especially after the two pints of lager.

Why do you do this to yourself, Scarlett?

"Scarlett, time to drag that backside of yours out of that nice warm bed."

The voice of Detective Chief Inspector Diane Harris brought her thoughts back.

"Boss?"

"Didn't I promise you would get the next murder?"

"You did, yes."

"Well right now I'm on the banks of the Thames with a body that's got your name written all over it and I'd like you to join me." There was a slight pause before the DCI added, "And that's not an invitation by the way, that's an order."

Breaking into a smile, Scarlett threw back the duvet and swung a leg out of bed. "Where do I need to be?"

"I'm in your neck of the woods. Down near Glover's Island. You know it?"

"Roughly. It's a long time since I've been around there. Where do I need to be exactly?"

"I'm sending you a text with the location. Oh, and Scarlett…"

"Yes, boss?"

"I'd get wrapped up if I was you, it's enough to freeze your tits off down here. And bring some wellies – I'm up to my ankles in mud."

****

78

Twenty minutes later Scarlett was locking the front door of her home feeling distinctly excited. She'd been waiting to take the lead on a murder enquiry for months.

Zipping up her leathers, she roamed her eyes along the tree-lined road, taking in the early morning peacefulness as well as the weather pervading the surroundings. It was damp and drizzly, and icy cold, and the last thing she wanted to do was take out her bike, but it would be easier and quicker to go direct to the scene, rather than go to the station to pick up a pool car. So for the first time she had sought out the black sports bag she had stored under the stairs. In it was everything she required for attending a crime scene. She had put it together following her last appraisal with the DCI, after being told that as part of her development the next murder was hers. As she strapped it to the back of her Triumph she was already running through in her head the list of priorities from her Professional Investigation Programme training.

Within ten minutes of leaving home Scarlett was nearing the rendezvous point, buzzing with adrenaline. Approaching a hazardous bend she spotted a liveried police car, off road, blocking the entrance to River Lane, and easing back on the throttle and gearing down she turned off the wet metalled highway, mounted the footpath to get around the unmanned patrol car, and edged onto the minor road leading down to the banks of the River Thames. She caught sight of a uniformed officer in a high-visibility jacket, hands in his pockets, directly in front of a line of blue-and-white crime scene tape fixed across the road. She squeezed on the brakes and coasted towards him.

Parking the Triumph she removed her helmet, placed it on the seat, and stepping towards the officer, who she didn't recognise, lowered the zip of her leathers and pulled out the lanyard securing her ID.

"DS Macey," she announced flashing her card.

Snapping his hands out of his pockets he pulled out a clipboard tucked beneath an armpit and wrote down her name in his scene visitors log. Then, with his pen, he pointed the way down the street.

"My colleague PC Devlin's down near the bottom of the lane with the witness who found the body," the officer said, adding, "She'll direct you. Can you keep to the left-hand footpath, Serge?

That's the established route to the scene and it keeps you away from some tyre tracks halfway down that they want to keep preserved. Could belong to the suspect's car. You can't miss them, there are some cones protecting them."

Scarlett couldn't see beyond twenty metres, everywhere was enveloped in a fine damp haze, reminiscent of a sea fret. She asked, "Who's here already?"

The officer glanced at his log and then returned his gaze. "A DCI Harris, a CSI supervisor called Gregory, my sergeant and PC Devlin. I've heard on the radio that they're requesting the Marine Search Unit, Forensics and the pathologist. Oh, and the helicopter will be up once this weather's cleared."

Acknowledging his reply with a nod she returned to her bike and took out her forensic protection suit from her holdall. Putting on the white all-in-one was a real struggle. It was a tight squeeze and awkward because of the resistance in her leathers but after several minutes she managed to pull it on. Then, red-faced and puffing loudly, she picked out two pairs of disposable gloves and a face mask and began making her way along the narrow pavement, keeping as close to the various boundary walls as possible. She remembered from her previous jogs around this area that the first section of the side road was residential, containing a small number of exclusive and expensive homes within sumptuous grounds surrounded by high walls. Some of the walls she passed were well over ten feet tall so she couldn't see beyond. However, passing a couple of the ornate metal gates securing their entranceway she took the opportunity to take a look along the driveways, scouring the frontage of the houses to determine if any of them had CCTV. She identified two homes with their own personal system and made a mental note for later. A hundred yards down she came across the cones the officer had referred to, on the opposite side of the narrow road next to some wooden fencing. She paused to check out the tyres tracks. They were at the very edge, where it abutted a grass verge, and it looked as if whatever vehicle had made them had done so avoiding a good-sized pothole. She could see that a lot of the lane's stone chippings had been churned up and the soil beneath had a series of deep ruts gouged into it. The marks looked to be reasonably fresh and the rain had not disturbed them. The forensic team would be able to get a good cast made of the tracks so as to identify the make, model and size of the tyre. If they did belong to the suspect's car then it was a good start.

Another twenty metres down and the lane's geography changed. Opposite was a hedgerow of trees and beyond that a huge field. She knew this to be Petersham Meadows; she'd jogged past it enough times along the riverside towpath. To her left was the beginning of a copse which, in spite of its lack of leaf cover, she had difficulty penetrating because of the fine mist shrouding everything. Drifting between the skeletal trees it gave the wood an ethereal appearance.

Another fifty metres along Scarlett finally began to pick out signs of life. First, as silhouettes, but a couple of steps further and the shapes became more distinct. She picked out a female officer in a fluorescent jacket standing beside a police-liveried Volvo – PC Devlin, she said to herself. She had the passenger door partially open and was using it as support while looking inside the car. She lifted her head as Scarlett approached.

Scarlett announced herself.

"Morning, Serge," replied the officer, stepping back, straightening and almost coming to attention.

Scarlett took a good look at her. Once again the officer wasn't a familiar face. Fresh-faced PC Devlin, who Scarlett deemed to be in her early twenties, was shivering and did not seem too impressed to be here. She couldn't help but feel a tinge of sorrow for the officer. Scarlett remembered the numerous times, during her uniform days, when she had been given the job of guarding a crime scene and knew what it felt like.

Scarlett shot her a friendly smile and flicked her head back up the lane. "Your colleague said you were down here with the person who found the body?"

The PC sprung the passenger door fully open, giving Scarlett a clear view inside. She got a glimpse of a man wearing a heavy-duty waterproof and khaki-coloured woollen hat. He swung out his legs and poked out his head. His clean-shaven face was drained of colour and displayed a stunned look.

"I still can't believe it. I never expected to find that this morning, I can tell you. It was a real shocker!" His accent was broad East London.

Scarlett stepped toward the police car. The man started to haul himself out from the passenger seat. Raising her hand Scarlett brokered for him to remain, and he returned to his sitting position, though he left his legs planted outside the car as he faced her.

Scarlett said, "Morning, I'm Detective Sergeant Macey. You are?"

"Linane. Michael Linane."

"Do you want to tell me what happened Michael?"

Pursing his lips he shook his head. "I'll never forget this, you know. Until my dying day, I tell you. I've never seen anything like it in my life."

Scarlett was still unaware of the circumstances of how the body had been discovered, and though she knew it was somewhere inside the thicket behind her, and had been found close to this section of the Thames, that was the fullness of her knowledge. She remembered her cognitive training; she needed to lead this crucial witness with open questions. "I can see this has been a bit of a shock for you, so just tell me in your own time what happened."

He took a deep breath. "Well, I was on my usual walk this morning. Set off from home, like I normally do, round about quarter to seven. Came up the trail past Buccleuch Gardens." He thumbed backwards indicating the wide expanse of fields. "Then I crossed over here and went into those woods." He gestured beyond Scarlett. "You've seen what the weather's like. It was thicker than this an hour and a bit ago and I was keeping my eye out for Jackie, who'd run off. I was wondering where she'd got to."

Scarlett arched her eyebrows. "Jackie?"

The man dipped his head.

Scarlett followed his line of sight and in the footwell of the car she saw a black and brown Jack Russell terrier looking up at her with wide-open brown eyes. She re-engaged with the man and gave him a nod of clarification.

"I spotted her fussing round this tree on the banking. I thought she'd found a rabbit hole or something like that, and walked past her at first, but when she wouldn't come when I called I went back to have a look at what she was fussing at. That's when I saw this suitcase just below the banking. It was a big thing and I could see it had got itself wedged in the roots of the tree. I mean, you do see a few things floating in the river. Once found a couple of cats in a bin liner that some bugger had drowned." He paused and shook his head before continuing. "But I've never seen a suitcase before. I thought it was a bit suspicious. Wondered if might be full of stolen goods, from a burglary or something like that, know what I mean?"

Scarlett nodded.

"Anyway, I decided to pull it out and take a look." He took another deep breath. "If I'd have known what I was going to find I wouldn't have done, I can tell you. Especially as it took me a fair while to lug it up. It weighed a ton."

Scarlett wanted him to move on. "But you managed to get it out?"

"Yes, eventually. Dragged it up the banking. I could see it was in fairly good nick, to say it had been in the Thames. I also saw it wasn't locked and so I opened it up." He visibly shuddered. "There was all this plastic wrapping inside. I pulled a bit of it back and that's when I saw there was a body in there. Didn't half make me jump back, I can tell you! I only saw part of it, but it looked to be naked. I tell you I've never seen anything like it before. Proper shocked, I was. I didn't even look to see if it was a man or a woman. As soon as I saw what it was I rung the police."

Scarlett reached in and rested a hand on his shoulder. "You did the right thing, Mr Linane. Now I can see this has been pretty traumatic for you, but I need you to hang around for just a while longer. I'm going to arrange for someone to take you to the police station, where we'll get a statement from you." Then, switching her gaze, she made eye contact with the policewoman. "Now, I need to take a look at what we've got and make contact with my DCI."

The PC extended an outstretched arm toward the coppice. "They're about fifty yards in, Serge. We've set up an inner cordon around it. And, there's a line of tape to lead you in. Just keep to the side of the main path."

Scarlett nodded a thank you and set off into the mist-shrouded belt of trees.

Nineteen

It was almost four p.m. before the briefing got underway in the Major Incident Suite. In the thirty-foot-square air-conditioned room the two syndicates of the HSCU sat on identical padded chairs, resting their major incident notebooks on attached side tables, facing a state-of-the-art interactive whiteboard. Standing before it on a raised rostrum was Detective Chief Inspector Diane Harris. Fussing with her light-brown hair to restore it back into a pony tail – a style she'd been forced to resort to, having been turned out straight from her bed that morning – she looked jaded. She had been on the go now for almost nine hours and had had very little opportunity to do anything with her appearance, except apply a little eyeliner and lipstick to add some colour to her tired-looking face. Her white blouse was rumpled and dark-blue slacks heavily creased. She finished coaxing her hair into an elastic hairband and shuffled her gaze among her seated team. Diane Harris deliberately and loudly cleared her throat.

The detectives' excited chatter died away and a hush fell across the room.

"Good afternoon, everyone. Sorry it's taken so long for this briefing to get off the ground, but this is not one of our normal run-of-the-mill murders. All will become clear very soon." She pointed a hand-held remote up towards a projector hanging from the ceiling and an image flashed up on the whiteboard behind her. "The scene of our murder." Taking up half the screen was an aerial shot, consisting of a section of river running from the top middle of the image down to bottom left. Above the top-left bank of the river was a strip of land incorporating trees and houses. In the middle of the river was a tiny rectangular island, comprising wholly of trees, and from the bottom bank of the river down to the right-hand corner of the picture was an area of woodland, a large field and a few large detached houses in their own grounds. A track separated the woodland from the fields. "For those who are not familiar with this area, or not yet had the opportunity to go to the scene, what you are looking at is an area of Ham. The island you can see is Glover's Island and these woods at the bottom of the picture, which will become highly relevant in a few seconds, are accessed via River Lane, which is off the A307. Just so you can get your bearings, to the left-hand side of these woods is Ham Polo Club." Diane Harris caught sight of a number of nodding heads. "Okay. At approximately six-fifty this morning, a witness walking his dog in these woods came across a suitcase wedged beneath a tree by the banks of the Thames, here." She aimed the remote toward the projector again and the image contracted. Within a few seconds the view homed in on a section of the wooded copse and part of the river. Individual trees could now be picked out and what also became clear for the first time, close to the river bank, was a blue tent with five white-suited people dotted around it. "This shot was taken by the force helicopter at nine a.m. this morning. Inside that tent is the suitcase the witness found. And inside the suitcase is our body." DCI Harris paused and scoped the room. She had everyone's attention. "That body was wrapped in clear heavy-duty plastic sheeting similar to the type used by builders, and when forensics removed that sheeting they found that our body had been placed inside the suitcase naked. This is our body." She clicked the remote and the picture changed. On screen, the shot was of an opened dark-blue suitcase with layers of clear plastic sheeting hanging over the sides. Squashed inside was a naked body, minus its head. The image was laid so only one arm was on show and that had no hand. It had been severed at the wrist. The flesh was waxen-like and wrinkled.

Diane heard someone exclaim "Wow!"

"Wow exactly!" she responded without looking back. She pointed to the screen. "The pathologist has made a cursory examination of the body at the scene and identified that it is female. He is unable to give a time of death at the moment but has said that he does not believe that the body has been in the water longer than forty-eight hours." She turned back to face her team. "As we yet don't know the cause of death." She paused, and smiling added, "And I don't want anyone stating the bleeding obvious – you know what I mean. The post-mortem is fixed up for seven o'clock tonight. Myself and Scarlett will be attending." She exchanged glances with her DS and gave her a nod. "Before I move onto our priorities I want to bring you in, Scarlett. You've interviewed the witness who found the body. Tell us what you've got."

Scarlett pulled herself up from a slouch and viewed the room. In a clear, confident voice, she said, "I video-interviewed a Michael Linane this morning. Mr Linane is sixty-seven, a retired teacher who lives on Friars Style Road, about a quarter of a mile from the scene. Eighteen months ago he lost his wife, and since then has had difficulty sleeping, and so he has a regular habit of going out walking with his dog each morning at around 6.30, taking the same route." She glanced up at DCI Harris, who replaced the shot of the headless corpse with that of the previous aerial shot of the scene. "This morning Mr Linane set off at roughly the same time." She pointed to the top right of the screen. "Leaving his home he crossed over the main A307 to the lane beside Buccleuch Gardens, and there he entered the track which runs beside the river and Petersham Meadows and headed towards the trees. His normal route is to keep to the towpath, cross over River Lane, enter the copse and carry on towards the ferry crossing near Eel Pie Island. There he turns around and walks back the way he came. Same route – day in, day out. I asked him if he ever met anyone on his walks, and he told me that on the first part of his journey, going towards the ferry crossing, he very rarely does, but coming back he sometimes comes across a couple of other dog-walkers who he usually just passes the time of day with. This morning, however, was different. This morning he met two young men on the towpath just before approaching Glover's Island. He's pretty sure they were young men, although he didn't get a good look at their faces, because they had on hooded tops and they didn't look up as he passed. He says that although he was surprised to see them, there was nothing about them that made him suspicious. They didn't appear to be in any hurry or anything. Just simply walking along the towpath with their heads down. And he never gave it any thought about the hoods covering their faces because, as we know, the weather was horrible. He said there was nothing about them which raised any alarms, especially as they acknowledged him when he bid them good morning." She paused and waited a couple of seconds before continuing. "He describes them both as being IC1, and of medium height and build. One was wearing a light-grey hoody and the other a dark-blue one. He thought there was a logo across the front of the dark-blue top, though he can't recall what that logo was. He can't remember much else about them. He said good morning to them, and the one in the grey top mumbled good morning back, but neither of them looked up, and they both walked past him. Mr Linane continued along the path, crossed over River Lane and into the woods, where, as we've all heard from the boss, he discovered the suitcase." Wetting her lips she said, "Regarding Mr Linane's journey, the towpath is narrow and besides the entry from Buccleuch Gardens it has no other access points until River Lane, where, as we can see on the map, there is a large parking area at the bottom. It slopes down into the river and is occasionally used by canoeists as an entry and exit point. I asked Mr Linane if there were any vehicles parked there this morning or if he had heard any vehicle on that lane and he hadn't." Pursing her mouth, Scarlett added, "Michael Linane is not known to us and I'm pretty happy with everything he's told me at the moment. He appears to be simply another 'dog-walker finds body' statistic." She gave a smile, saying, "That's it," and nodded toward her DCI, indicating she had finished.

"Right," Diane Harris said, clapping her hands. "Thank you for that, Scarlett." She shuffled her gaze from one detective to another. "As you can all appreciate things are still pretty much in their infancy, so there aren't many actions at the moment, but it is imperative we discover who these two men are that Mr Linane saw this morning. Besides him, for now, those are the only other people we have around the scene where the body has been found. Following Scarlett's interview with Mr Linane we have extended our cordon to include the towpath, and besides the Marine Search Unit, I have a Task Force search team joining us tomorrow." The DCI focussed her gaze upon DI Taylor-Butler, the designated incident room manager. "Other actions I want instigating are house-to-house. I know there aren't many on River Lane, and given the grounds some of those are set in, and the height of the walls protecting them, I don't expect anyone to have seen anything, but we have found some good fresh tyre tracks on that lane and as we can see from the aerial video it does provide good vehicle access to the river. As yet, we haven't identified how, or where, the suitcase containing the body went into the Thames. Until we find that out we make attempts at tracing the vehicle which made those tracks. Scarlett has told me that a couple of the houses have their own CCTV systems fitted, so let's see if they have a view of that lane; we might just get lucky. It's too late today for all this so we kick things off tomorrow morning. By then the HOLMES team should have everything up and running, so everyone back in for eight a.m. briefing. I'll bring back the findings of the PM and anything else we find out about our headless body."

Twenty

The naked, marble-like, headless and handless female corpse lay on her back on a steel gurney. A Y-shaped stitched incision stretched from the neck down to the pubis area.

"Our victim," exclaimed DCI Harris, pointing with the remote to the image on the interactive whiteboard. Today she was back to her old self, looking refreshed and smartly dressed. Her shoulder-length hair had been straightened to a bob, and her high-cheekboned face, as usual, had just enough make-up to camouflage the incipient crow's feet around her pale-blue eyes, which had their sparkle back. She wore a tailored two-piece grey trouser suit with white cotton blouse. "The pathologist puts her at between eighteen and twenty-five. She would have been approximately five foot seven and as you can see she is very slim. She had been dead between twenty-four and thirty-six hours. Her stomach contents consisted of the partly digested remains of a cheese sandwich. Cause of death cannot be determined, and as the head is missing, injuries to that are expected to be the most probable cause. She was certainly dead when her head and hands were removed and there is no water in her lungs, so she wasn't drowned." Pausing momentarily she surveyed the room. The majority of her team's eyes were focussed on the screen behind her. "There is extensive bruising to her back, stomach and legs, indicative of being kicked, punched and even stamped on, and there are marks to her upper arms. Probably finger marks, signs of her being restrained. What is clear is she took a hell of a battering prior to her death, though none of those injuries would have caused her death." Tightening her mouth she added, "And either she engaged in pretty rough sex shortly before her death or she had been raped." The majority of gazes were now upon her. "Anally and vaginally. From the pathologist's findings I'm more inclined to think the latter." She pointed back. "Without doubt this young lady suffered horrendously prior to her death. And even after death she was treated no better. Her killer, or killers, dismembered her quite crudely. The flesh around her neck and wrists has been hacked in places, suggesting that the knife that was used wasn't that sharp, and the bones have been separated by a grinder. The pathologist believes it's one of those small hand-held ones." The picture changed. "And he has also discovered this." On screen was a blown-up shot of a shoulder and upper arm. On the waxen-looking shoulder was a distinct crescent moon mark and inside that a shape that looked like a star. The symbols were in the form of raised pink scars which appeared fresh.

"The pathologist said that these are burn marks. They were done while she was alive. More than likely twenty-four-hours before she was killed. I have to confess I thought it was part of her beating until the pathologist pointed out that he had seen similar markings before on two females he had carried out PMs on around Christmas time last year. Two young women who'd died in a house fire. He thinks in Camden Town. He's sure the detective investigating the case told him that the fire had been in a brothel and he believes the women were of Eastern European origin." She paused. "He says on that occasion the marks were deliberate brands, like that on cattle." Shaking her head she continued, "The pathologist is going to get his secretary to go through his records this morning and find out those details. In the meantime we have our own priorities." She pointed to the screen. "Our victim. We need to identify her. Someone will be missing a wife, daughter, sister – check missing persons. Not much to go on, granted, but let's make a start. We've got her height and build and DNA." She aimed the remote at the projector and changed the picture. "The suitcase she was found in. Large, blue canvas. It certainly doesn't appear to be new and doesn't have any details as to the make but let's see if we can trace its origin. The plastic sheeting she was wrapped in, the type builders use. That's currently with Forensics to see if it has any prints on it. I know it's been in the water for some time but we might get lucky." She drifted her focus toward DI Taylor-Butler. "The two men our witness saw on the towpath. At present these are our only TIE's. I want these two traced, interviewed and eliminated as a main priority. Arrange for e-fits to be done, and see if we can narrow down what that logo was on one of the hooded tops, to give us a better opportunity of identifying them. Let's see if we can get something good enough for circulation. And I want the pathologist's secretary chasing up. Get what details you can of the two females who died in that house fire in Camden Town. And track down the officer who was in charge of the investigation.

Speak with whoever it was and arrange to get a copy of the file. I want to know the location of that fire and the circumstances." She caught the DI nodding back as he scribbled notes in his notebook and she returned her eyes to her team. "And everyone else, if you haven't got a priority enquiry its house-to house and liaison with the search teams at the scene." Clicking the remote she returned the image of the headless woman onto the screen. "It's imperative we catch whoever did this to this young lady – and fast."

****

Seething inside, Scarlett was multitasking. She had her eyes set on her desktop screen and the phone trapped between her shoulder and ear. Jiggling with her mouse and tapping the keyboard one-fingered, she was slowly adding sentences to the Lycra Rapist file while speaking with the CSI supervisor, making arrangements for someone to visit Michael Linane, so that a composite e-fit could be compiled of the two young men he had seen on the towpath. Five minutes earlier DI Taylor-Butler had dramatically slapped an action form down in front of her, partially covering some of the documents scattered across her desk and barked, "The e-fit is yours."

Stabbing a finger at the paperwork she had sharply replied, "But I've got some more work to do on the James Green remand file. CPS have requested that I put in more evidence about the attack on Ella, when he was arrested. He's due back at court this afternoon."

"That's not my problem, DS Macey," he had snapped as he turned his back on her.

As he had marched away she had remembered the words of the Bon Jovi song and mumbled back sarcastically, "Have a nice day" beneath her breath. She knew he had heard her because he had paused momentarily in mid-stride and looked back over his shoulder. She had met his glowering eyes with a fake charming smile.

Finishing her conversation and setting down the handset she glanced over in the DI's direction. He was staring over his reading glasses back at her. She met his gawp and issued another false smile. "E-fit sorted, Sir," she mouthed across the room and returned to the Lycra Rapist file.

Half an hour later, with the task completed, she clicked her mouse and scooted her chair away from her desk. On a table opposite a printer whirred into action and began spewing out sheets of paper. She watched her document churn out, counting each leaf inside her head as it was delivered into the printer tray, and just as the last one exited her desk phone rang. Sighing, she snatched it up.

"DS Macey, Homicide and Serious Crime Unit."

"Scarlett." It was DCI Diane Harris. "Can you nip down the corridor to my office? I've got a job I want you to go out to."

"Two secs, boss." She hung up, picked out the dozen or so pages of the remand file, skimmed through them, checked they were in sequential order and fastened them together with a paper clip. Then, dragging her coat off the back of the chair and picking up her bag, she strode across the room and dropped the bundle over the lowered head of DI Taylor-Butler. It landed in front of him on top of the document he was concentrating on with a loud slap, making him jump.

Scarlett bit her lip and forced back the urge to smile. She said, "The Lycra Rapist update. As I said earlier, he's due back in court this afternoon for a further remand. Can you check and sign it please before it goes to CPS?"

Over the rims of his glasses he looked up at her with enquiring eyes.

"The boss wants me to go out on some job." She shrugged her shoulders, an indication that she had no idea what it was for, before adding, "The file needs to be with CPS by lunchtime." With that she tucked her coat and bag under her arm, turned on her heels and left the room.

Scarlett rapped lightly on Diane Harris's door and pushed it open.

The DCI was writing away at her desk. A pile of papers lay in front of her. Poising her pen she looked up and beckoned Scarlett to come in. "That was quick." She set down her pen. "I've got a job I need you to do. I need you to go out to Ham House and liaise with the Task Force inspector. His search team have found a stolen BMW sports car dumped in the car park there. Looks as though someone's tried to set fire to it. It's only a quarter of a mile from where our body was found. You can probably guess what I'm thinking."

"Those two hoodies our dog walker saw."

The DCI nodded. "I've got forensics on their way. I need someone to supervise. Can you go out there for me? I'd go myself but I've got a stack of paperwork to get through and the assistant chief constable has called a Gold meeting at eleven-thirty for an update." She issued a weak smile. "Are you okay with that?"

"Yes, no problem, Boss. I've got my urgent paperwork out of the way."

"Smashing! When you find out what you've got at the scene give me a call and update me. Text me, I'll have my mobile switched on."

Scarlett was just about to turn and leave when the DCI said, "A little bird tells me you've had a run in with the DI recently?" Diane Harris bent forward, rested her elbows on her desk and made a pyramid of her hands. She looked over the tops of her fingers. "Is everything okay between you?"

Scarlett met her gaze. She could feel her face and neck getting warm. She knew she was colouring up. She gave a meek smile. "Nothing I can't handle, Boss. He got the wrong end of the stick about the loss of my warrant card. You know how he is sometimes."

"I do, and I know you two don't exactly see eye to eye. That's why I asked if you're okay. I think deep down he's pissed off because he missed the link with the cyclist from the last job and you spotted it."

"I just got lucky with that witness form."

"It was something he should have picked up on and everyone knows it. You've embarrassed him, Scarlett, and he doesn't like it. I also know he can be a bit of a dinosaur at times." She held Scarlett's gaze. "You get my drift?"

Scarlett felt a lump emerge in her throat. She swallowed hard and nodded. "Everything's cool. You've no need to worry about me."

"You sure?"

"I'm absolutely fine, boss."

The DCI released her hands and rested them across her paperwork. "Good, glad to hear that. You know where my door is if you ever need to talk."

Scarlett issued her a reassuring smile. "Sure do. Thanks, boss."

As she turned to leave, the DCI finished, "Please don't give him any excuses, Scarlett. I need you on my team."

At that moment Scarlett felt an overwhelming urge to cry. She was so glad she had turned her back on her boss. Feeling her eyes beginning to water, she nipped together her eyelids and took a deep breath before stepping out into the corridor.

Twenty-one

In the time it had taken Scarlett to drive out to Ham her anger toward DI Taylor-Butler had waned. Now, as she pulled off the main drag and headed down the narrow road towards historical Ham House and Gardens, she just thought he was a wanker.

Driving slowly, she checked each side of the road for a car park sign. She was almost at the entrance to the house and grounds before she saw the first notice, and spotting it she picked up her speed and headed down the lane. The opening to the car park was only another hundred yards beyond the public entranceway, but she could go no further – a barricade of fluorescent cones and a "Police Stop" sign barred her access. Braking, she steered to the side of the road and pulled up.

She opened the door to a cold wind. It caught her unawares and sent an icy shiver cascading through her. She snatched up her coat from the passenger seat and hauled herself out of the car. Slipping on her Barbour jacket, belting it tightly around her and pulling up the collar, Scarlett looked skywards at the leaden clouds and preyed the rain would hold off while she got her job done. Then she went to the boot, took out her forensic clothing and began dressing herself for her scene visit.

Entering the car park, the Task Force inspector she had been expecting to meet was nowhere to be seen. The only uniformed officer she saw was just walking out of view, heading in the direction of where they had found their dismembered corpse. However, she did spy two white-suited forensic specialists hovering around a black BMW 530d M Sport with a 2010 plate. It was the only vehicle parked in the large gravelled area. For a moment Scarlett took in the surroundings. The car park abutted a riverside path and beyond that was the Thames. It was in full flow and looked as steely grey and cold as the sky above. To her right the path wended its way between the trees to Hammerton ferry landing, where a public ferry regularly crossed over to the opposite bank. Quarter of a mile ahead was where they had found their victim.

She gathered her thoughts. Inside her head she made a checklist of what was required and then, satisfied she knew what she was doing, headed towards the forensics guys.

The taller beer-bellied one, writing on a paper-filled clipboard looked her way. Stopping what he was doing, he stepped away from the black BMW and pulled down his facemask. It was Mason Gregory. Mason was an aged detective sergeant who had specialised into the forensics field many years ago and was now a CSI supervisor. When she'd first met him six years ago at a stabbing at a pizza takeaway, the first thing he'd said to her when she'd identified herself was, "I used to work with your dad. Great detective. Great guy." Since then he'd always been her first port of call whenever she'd needed not only a crime scene investigator but a professional job done to boot.

Scarlett made a beeline to him. Offering a beaming smile she said, "Hi Mason, what have you got for me?"

He returned a smile. "They've given this one to you then?"

Wide-eyed she nodded. "I suppose you could say that."

"Well I'd best make sure I do a thorough job then. Have they discovered who the vic is yet? I was off yesterday so I'm catching up."

Scarlett shook her head. "Not yet. It's one of the main priorities." She chinned towards the BMW. "Think the car's linked? The SIO says it's nicked."

"Not sure yet. It was taken two nights ago in a two-in-one burglary. The thieves broke into a house in Hounslow and took the keys from the kitchen. This car belongs to the wife. The owners disturbed the two burglars and they fled in the car. A patrol car came across it half an hour later in Twickenham and pursued it but they managed to get away."

Scarlett stepped towards the car, pulling up her face mask. "I was told they'd tried to fire it?"

Mason also fixed his mask. He pointed towards the rear nearside with his clipboard. "Tried to, but failed."

Scarlett saw that the fuel flap was open and a piece of charred rag was hanging from the aperture. Dropping her gaze she saw the further remains of scorched rag lying near the rear wheel surrounded by an oily blackened patch.

"They've started to fire it alright but they've obviously not hung around to see if it took hold. The combination of the damp weather yesterday and hardly any fuel in the tank has resulted in this." Mason dipped his head toward the fuel cap. "What they also haven't realised is that this is diesel and that's a lot harder to ignite. We've got lucky."

"So if this is linked and it was used to transport the body in the suitcase you should be able to tell."

"Any fibre cross-match will light up like a Christmas tree."

Scarlett caught Mason's watery grey eyes twinkling and guessed behind the mask he held a joyful smile.

"What's to do now then, Mason?"

"A low-loader is on its way. We're going to get the car back to a drying room, give it twenty-four hours then begin our work on it. You should have a result by tomorrow afternoon as to whether the suitcase was transported in this or not."

Scarlett touched him lightly on the shoulder. "Anything I need to do?"

Before Mason had time to answer her BlackBerry rang. Brokering a halt in the conversation with her hand she reached into her pocket and slipped out her phone. Turning away she answered. It was her partner Tarn.

"Listen, I've just got back into the office. CPS have been trying to get hold of you. The prosecutor for our case is at the Magistrate's and she says she hasn't got your update for this afternoon's court. She's says that the court is sitting in half an hour and she wants to know what we're doing."

Scarlett gasped. "Did you tell her we're going for another remand?"

"Yeah. I've told her there is an additional charge of rape"

"Good."

"But what about the update? Have you got the file there with you? I've searched your desk and trays and can't see it anywhere. She says she needs it urgently."

"Tarn, I gave it to Taylor-Butler before I came out here. I asked him to check it was okay and I told him CPS needed it for this afternoon's court. Is he there?"

"No, he's gone with the gaffer to the Gold meeting with the ACC."

Pulling the phone away Scarlett exhaled sharply. "Fuck, he's done this deliberately!" she growled. Taking a deep breath she raised her eyes to the sky. Her thoughts were racing. Replacing the phone to her ear, she said, "Tarn, do me a favour. Ring the prosecutor back up and tell her I'm on my way to court. I'll get access to one of the computers at the Magistrates and print off another copy." Raising her voice she shouted, "I'm setting off now." Then she ended the call.

Not forgetting Mason Gregory she spun around. He and the other forensic officer were in the process of pulling a protective blue tarpaulin over the BMW. Waving a hand and calling out to him that she had to go and she would catch up with him later, she sprinted back towards her car, tugging off her white protective suit as she ran.

I'll fucking swing for Taylor-Butler.

Twenty-two

At home Scarlett downed the first glass of wine without taking a breath and poured herself another. With her second glass she took two paracetamol. She had a thumping headache and inside she was a screwed up ball of fury.

Hours earlier, she had broken the speed limit to get to Richmond Magistrates Court, where, struggling to find a parking place nearby, she had abandoned her unmarked car next to Richmond Green and dashed on foot back to the court building, arriving just as the magistrates had begun their afternoon session. Fortunately the Crown prosecution solicitor had been granted a one-hour adjournment, enabling her to get another copy of the remand file printed off. She had sat at the back of the court trying her best not to look agitated as the prosecutor had presented new details of the rape of Claudette Jackson and argued for a further remand in custody of James Green. The application had been successful giving her and Tarn one whole month to gather the remaining evidence and compile a full court file prior to his first Crown Court appearance.

She knew she should have felt relieved as she'd left court but the session had only succeeded in infuriating her, those feelings being exacerbated further upon returning to her car and discovering a parking ticket affixed to the screen. She had torn back to the office and stormed into DI Taylor-Butler's office, confronting him angrily, demanding to know why he hadn't submitted the Lycra Rapist remand file when she's specifically asked him to.

His face had flushed, but as calm as anything he had glanced over his glasses and replied, "You asked me no such thing, DS Macey. If I recall, you asked me to check if the file was okay. Then you said – and these were your exact words – that CPS required the file by lunchtime." Slowly removing his spectacles, he had raised his tone, "I assumed by those comments that you yourself would be submitting the file. If you had wanted me to do that then you should have asked me to." Then he had got angry, thrusting his glasses toward her, rattling them like a sabre. "Who on earth do you think you are? You come in here blaming me for your own incompetence." Then he had deftly turned the exchange of words in his favour, tearing her off a strip about her attitude and her lack of respect towards him, demanding that she apologise or he would be requesting her immediate removal from the department. She had locked eyes with him. She was livid, but he had the upper hand. She was not going to win this argument. Standing before him, balling her hands into fists she had recalled what Diane Harris had said to her that morning. And so, through clenched teeth she had yielded, apologised and left the room burning with rage.

By the time she had got to the office her head was thumping and she felt nauseous. Apologising to Tarn that she couldn't carry on she had gathered up her things and left.

That had been an hour ago. Since then, before opening the wine, she had rang DCI Diane Harris and given her an update about the car. She had told her about having to attend court but decided not to tell her about her head-to-head with Taylor-Butler. She mentioned her headache and apologised for leaving early. The DCI comforted her. "No problem. There's not much happening this end anyway. You get an early night and I'll see you at morning briefing."

Scarlett took another hit of wine. This second glass was having a calming effect; she could finally feel herself beginning to uncoil. She pulled her bag onto the kitchen work surface, fished around inside and brought out her work phone. It beeped when she switched it on. Checking the screen she saw she had two missed calls. Same number. It was Alex. She hit the redial button and he answered on the third ring.

"Hi Alex, you're back then. Did you have a successful trip?"

"Very, thank you. Got back yesterday afternoon." There was a short pause. "I've been trying to get hold of you."

"Yes, sorry, I've been in court most of the afternoon. Is it anything important?"

"I found Rose again yesterday evening. Or the same girl at least. Well, to be honest I found her then lost her again. She clocked me and did a runner."

Alex's voice trailed off. It was replaced with his measured breathing. She knew he was waiting for her to respond. She said, "That's a good result isn't it? At least she's not gone to ground."

"She might do now, though." There was another short pause. "I have got some other good news though."

"What?"

"All in good time. What say I come round? You provide the food and I provide the wine and information. Unless you've got a better offer?"

She guiltily looked at the glass of wine she was holding. *Surely another couple of glasses wouldn't hurt.* Thinking quickly, it wasn't hard to come to a decision. She smiled. "That sounds good, Alex. I've got some steak in the freezer, and some colcannon mash and green beans."

"A home-cooked meal? That'll be a first."

"Cheeky swine! I'll have you know I rustle up a real mean gravy."

"Cube or packet?"

She laughed. "Damn! You've caught me out again."

"That's sorted then. I'll grab a quick shower and I should be with you within the hour."

As she ended the call she felt suddenly cheered. Alex's company was just what she needed after the shitty day she'd just experienced.

Twenty-three

Alex turned up on the doorstep forty minutes later holding out a bottle of Merlot and flashing his usual toothpaste ad smile. He pecked her on the cheek and she caught a whiff of his aftershave as he brushed past her into the kitchen. It brought back another nice memory. She still held it as she sloped away into the lounge and put on Paloma Faith's *Fall to Grace*, a CD he'd bought before they had split up. She cranked up her music system a couple of notches and joined Alex in the kitchen. He had removed his jacket and was leaning against the breakfast bar displaying his toned physique in a baby-blue Ralph Lauren polo.

He picked up the wine she'd opened earlier. "I see you've started without me."

"Rough day." She took out a glass from a wall cupboard and handed it to him. "I'll tell you about it later." She watched him pour himself a decent measure and then held out her own glass.

He replenished it and they clinked glasses.

"Come on then, tell me your news. Tell me about Rose. Was she in the same place? I've not been able to get anywhere; I've been so busy. We've got a murder running."

"Yeah, I saw it on the front page of the *Evening Standard*. Headless body in a suitcase isn't it?"

Scarlett pulled the wine glass away from her lips. "Bloody journalists! I didn't release they'd got hold of the story. They must have got to our witness."

In exaggerated fashion Alex tut-tutted. "When will you cops ever learn? Shouldn't hide things from the press. They're like bloodhounds once they get hold of a story." He met her gaze. "And pick your bottom lip up, it doesn't suit you." He sipped on his wine. "They might have done you a favour. If the report is anything to go by it seems to me the killer was expecting that body to be at the bottom of the Thames. They might slip up now."

"Yes, I suppose you're right."

"I always am."

She looked at him and lightly punched his arm. "Smart arse." Then she added, "Come on then, tell me about your encounter with Rose."

"You keep saying it's Rose. It might not be."

"I'm telling you it's Rose. I saw the way she looked at me."

He shrugged his shoulders. "Whatever." He finished his wine and poured the last of the bottle into his glass. "Well she wasn't in the same place. I had a bit of time yesterday afternoon so I zipped about a bit. I found her, and that guy she was with before, at Edgware Road, but as I say, she clocked me almost straight away and was on her toes. She's a bloody fast runner."

"I thought you were a surveillance expert," Scarlett smirked.

He shook his head. "You know what they say about sarcasm?" He took another sip of wine. "Do you want to hear my story or what?"

"Go on. I'm listening."

"Well, after I'd lost Rose I decided to go back and see if the guy was still around. Fortunately, I caught him just packing up, so I switched my jacket and changed my hat and decided to see where he went to. He got on the tube and got off at Notting Hill Gate. I followed him a little way, but he kept looking round – really suspicious, he was. I didn't want to spook him as well so I backed off."

"So you didn't see where he went?"

Alex shook his head. "No I didn't."

"So we're no further forward to finding Rose."

"Well we might be, if that's the normal stop for them. All we have to do next time is plot up around the Notting Hill Gate exit and see if either of them comes out there. Then we follow them to where they're holed up." In a high-pitched quirky voice he finished, "Simples."

Scarlett's face lit up. She took a long drink of her wine. "You're not just a pretty face are you?" Then she set down her glass and turned to the cooker. "Now, how do you like your steak...Medium isn't it?"

Twenty-four

Scarlett stared at the macabre image of the headless torso on the large interactive screen. Beside it were two blown-up digital e-fits of the two hoodies the witness, Michael Linane, had seen on the towpath, near to where the body had been discovered. She turned back to face a full incident room, though she deliberately avoided eye-contact with DI Taylor-Butler, who was seated on the back row.

"These are the e-fits compiled by our witness. Unfortunately, as you can see he's not been able to come up with any striking or recognisable features with regards their faces, other than to describe them as being male, both IC1 and clean-shaven. And the only age range we can get out of him is that he believes they were both early twenties. However, thanks to some prompting from the CSI girl who did the e-fits, he has been able to better describe their clothing." She glanced backwards and then returned her gaze. "One of them was wearing a dark-blue full-zip hoody with an orange Vans logo across the chest. He had on jeans and blue-and-white canvas-type shoes. His mate, as we can see, was wearing a grey fleece-type hoody with black arm stripes. We're convinced from the description it's an Adidas make. He also had grey Adidas-type jogging pants and black trainers." She picked out a couple of friendly faces from the front row. "We've already had a result with these two e-fits." She glanced behind her. The stolen black BMW sports car appeared onscreen. "This car was discovered by the search team yesterday, abandoned in the Ham House public car park. Attempts had been made to fire it but they were unsuccessful. The car was stolen during a two-in-one burglary in Hounslow three nights ago, where the thieves were disturbed by the occupants. Although the occupants didn't get a good look at their faces, they were able to describe the clothing the pair were wearing. Guess what?" She jabbed a finger towards the two e-fits. "Fits the pair seen on the towpath to a tee."

DCI Diane Harris took a step forward. "Thanks for that, Scarlett. Couldn't have put it better myself."

Scarlett stepped off the rostrum and took up the seat next to Tarn. The DCI waited while she settled then said, "The car was removed yesterday lunchtime and is presently in a drying room waiting to be forensically examined. I've spoken with CSI this morning and they've also confirmed that those tyre tracks found on River Lane fit the front offside wheel of this car." She rubbed her hands together, "That means we can place this car very close to the scene where our body was found, and we can also place two identically dressed men as the thieves who took it, only a couple of hundred yards from the body. This is too much of a coincidence. I've spoken with the ACC and we're going to run with this at a news conference this afternoon." She offered a cheery smile. "The positive news doesn't end there." Another image appeared on the screen. It was the branded crescent moon and star on the corpse's shoulder. "Remember I told you that the pathologist said he had seen similar marks on the bodies of two girls who had died in a house fire. Well his secretary came back to me yesterday afternoon with those details and I was able to get hold of the detective who investigated that case." She paused, surveying the room before continuing. "It was a house fire which occurred in Camden Town, in the early hours of the second of December last year. The seat of the fire was the downstairs front lounge and was believed to be accidental – more than likely caused by a cigarette down the side of an armchair. The two girls who died occupied a bedroom in the loft space of the house. They died from smoke inhalation. Three young women who occupied bedrooms in the floor below managed to get out and it was those three the detective interviewed." She paused again. "Or at least tried. None of them were forthcoming at all. The detective told me that neighbours said the house was a brothel and that numerous complaints had been made to the council. He also learned that the people running it were Eastern Europeans, and he suspected the girls were illegal immigrants so he took them into custody. With the help of interpreters he eventually coaxed out of them that two were from Slovakia and one from Lithuania, and that the two dead girls were Lithuanian. That's as far as it went. The girls gave him first names, but he suspected these were false and even though he went back and searched the house he couldn't find anything to confirm the names they had given or identify them. Custody handed them over to immigration officers the next day and that's almost where his involvement ended. Except to say that he did eventually track down the owner of the house – an

Albanian, though he can't recall his name at the moment. Because the fire was accidental, he passed everything on to the Coroner's Office for the inquest." She pointed back to the close-up of the branded shoulder. "The detective has confirmed that both the dead girls, and the three handed over to immigration, all had crescent moon and star scars, and although they refused to say how they had got them he learned from Interpol that this is a typical branding used by Eastern Europeans, who mark their sex workers to display ownership. Apparently they are ancient Turkish celestial symbols of power. He told me that at that time Interpol were interested in speaking with the girls and so he e-mailed over a copy of his report to them. I've also requested that report." Diane Harris clapped her hands. "Right, actions!" She tapped a forefinger against her palm. "The three girls involved in the house fire in Camden Town. It's an outside chance but they just might know our victim, or if it not, at least be able to point us in the direction of the people who carried out their branding, which will give us a link. I want Immigration contacted to see what happened to those girls. It's almost a year ago now, and I'm guessing they'll either have been sent back to their country of origin or released back into the community. I want them tracing. I also want copies of their files. They'll have been interviewed, fingerprinted and photographed. If we haven't got current addresses I especially want their photographs for circulation. And get those over to Vice as well, just in case they're back on the streets." She clasped her hands together and flicked her head back at the screen. "And we also focus on our two suspects. As I've said, I've fixed up a press conference this afternoon in which I'll be releasing those images and offering a reward." Tightening her mouth she finished, "We're going to be cranking things up today and the pressure is going to be on these two young men currently at large. Either they'll go on the run or give themselves up. Hopefully we'll get an early result."

Twenty-five

Scarlett took out a carton of orange from her fridge and pinched back the top. She was about to pour out a glassful when her BlackBerry rang. With a sigh she set down the carton and picked up her phone. She cheered up when she saw who it was.

"Hi Alex. This is a surprise."

"Nice surprise, I hope."

She held back her answer but nodded to herself.

He said, "How's your day been?"

"Up to my neck. Still not found out who our victim is. Got a couple of leads maybe."

"And two suspects, I see. It was on the local news."

"Missed it. Been out most of the day, following stuff up."

"Snap!"

"Snap?"

"Rose's friend."

"You found him again?"

"It was just like I said. I hung around by Notting Hill Gate and lo and behold out he came late this afternoon. Just like I thought."

"Was Rose with him?"

"No, it looks like she's still laying low."

"Did you see where he's living?"

"No. I followed him for a couple of hundred yards. He stopped a few times to look in shop windows. And he had a good look around every time he set off; he's obviously still nervous, so I hung back a fair distance. He didn't suss me and so when he turned left into the backstreets I decided not to follow. But now I've seen the turning he took I can take a different approach next time."

"Gosh, Alex, that's great. Are you able to go back soon?"

"I've got a four day break before I have to shoot off again, but I could do with some backup. How are you fixed for tomorrow?"

She raised her eyes to the ceiling. She recalled that she and Tarn had been given the job of travelling down to Dover to liaise with Immigration. "So sorry, Alex, can't do tomorrow, but I should be okay for the day after."

"Okay, day after it is. I'll text you with the meet and fill you in." With that Alex hung up.

Scarlett ended the call and stared at her BlackBerry. A flutter of butterflies took off inside her stomach.

Twenty-six

DCI Diane Harris strolled to the front of the Incident Room, her face lit up by a healthy smile. Stepping up onto the low stage she said, "Our suspect!" Behind her, onscreen, was a head and shoulders mugshot of a scowling, heavily acned, brown-haired young man. She continued, "Jamie Hill, twenty-four years, from Southall, part of a gang who are currently targeting homes where there are high-performance or expensive cars. They force their way in while the occupants are asleep, snatch the keys and then drive off with their car. Following last night's news we received seven phone calls naming this man – five of those were from cops. Apparently Jamie and his crew are pretty well known to detectives at Southall nick. They are responsible for quite a number of this type of offence and are currently being targeted by the Intelligence Unit there." Still joyful she steered her eyes around the full room. "Ten days ago, Jamie and another man, Dane Rolletts, also from Southall, stole a Mercedes sports car from a house in Ealing and got into a chase with traffic. They crashed the car in Wembley and were both arrested. Guess what Jamie was wearing when he was nicked." The image zoomed out, opening up the mugshot to his chest. Jamie Hill had on a blue hoody with an orange Vans logo emblazoned across the front.

"Bless him. He couldn't have made things easier for us if he'd tried." She dropped the smile. "Unfortunately, Jamie Hill does not fit the profile of a killer. But that's not to say we're going to dismiss him. He's certainly in the area where our victim was dumped, so he's got a few questions to answer. And we've still not got back the full results from forensics on the BMW found at Ham House car park. I spoke with the supervisor yesterday and he tells me they have quite a number of fibres from the driver and passenger seats, but they're not confident this car has carried the suitcase our victim was found in. Apparently, the boot contained the owner's sports bag and the contents of that had been scattered all over the boot. If the suitcase had been put in the boot, without a doubt, it would have squashed everything, and there are no indentations on any of that stuff." The DCI took on a studious look and fixed her eyes on Scarlett. "Scarlett, I know I wanted you and Tarn to go to Dover today and liaise with Immigration, but I want to change that. I want you to put together an operational order and arrange for early morning knocks for Jamie Hill and his team. Liaise with Southall CID and they'll provide all their details. Until we've completely eliminated him and his cohorts from this enquiry we put things on hold." Diane Harris pulled back her gaze and settled it on the squad. "We still don't know who our victim is. This is now day four, and although we've had a few calls come in regarding missing people, none of those seem to fit the physical profile of our victim. And, given the branding to the shoulder, and what the detective told me, I am more inclined to believe our victim is from another country and more than likely an illegal. Therefore I want fresh actions to involve contact with Interpol. Give them what we've got and see if they come back with anything. And I also want some background into the gangs who bring in the sex workers. See if we have any local names or addresses." Clenching her hands together she finished, "Lots to do team. Let's do it well."

Almost simultaneously, the squad closed their journals and noisily rose from their seats.

Twenty-seven

Immediately after briefing, Scarlett tasked Tarn with gathering photographs of all of Jamie Hill's crew. She was particularly interested in seeing a mugshot of his accomplice Dane Rolletts. She hoped that he might be the one in the grey hoody who the witness saw on the towpath.

While he engaged in that she threw herself into her work, making the many phone calls requesting background details of everyone involved with Jamie, including up-to-date addresses. The DCI had invested her faith in her to lead this operation and she wanted to make sure that her homework was thorough. She didn't want any cock-ups. She especially didn't want to give any excuse to DI Taylor-Butler to criticise her.

In the midst of her work she texted Alex; the operation wasn't being conducted until first light tomorrow and she knew she would have the paperwork finished by mid-afternoon. That meant it would give her a good few hours that evening to conduct her own personal operation into finding Rose.

****

Lifted by the sight of the recent mugshot of Dane Rolletts, identifying him as being the second suspect on the towpath, it only took Scarlett a couple of hours to compile the operational order for the next morning's raids on Jamie's and Dane's addresses. Leaving Tarn with the job of swearing out the magistrates' warrants for their arrests, she nipped to the locker room, hurriedly changed into a pair of jeans and a jumper, dashed to the Underground, and by four-thirty p.m. she was standing inside a rare records shop in Notting Hill Gate, pretending to be a shopper, meddling through a rack of eighties vinyl albums, and although her head was lowered her gaze was set on the main thoroughfare outside. In the time she had been in the shop daylight had gone and a fine rain had visited the street, though its wetness hadn't diminished her view – quite the opposite, its reflective quality had enhanced the brightness of the street lighting. Added to that, the record shop she was in was protected beneath a concrete canopy from the flat above, helping keep the store window she was looking out of clear. She had stepped in here fifteen minutes ago as the first drops of rain had begun to pepper her face. Since then she had lost sight of Alex, though she knew he wouldn't be too far away. Before they had separated he had told her he would eyeball the Underground entrance and as soon as he clocked either Rose or the man he had tailed to this location, he would text her.

Scarlett picked out an album. She was getting bored. She was anxiously waiting for her phone to ping so she could leap into action.

"Can I help you?"

The voice made Scarlett jump. She spun around to face the man who had been behind the counter when she'd walked into the shop. She had been so focussed on her surveillance of the street outside that she hadn't been aware of him leaving his domain.

"Looking for anything in particular?" He stuck his chin forward, eyeing the album she was holding.

Gathering her thoughts quickly she said, "Just browsing." She couldn't help but notice the black T-shirt he had on – the words "I'm here to help" stretched across it.

She pasted on a false smile. *I don't need any help, please bugger off I'm busy.*

"Anything special you're looking for or interested in?" He met her gaze. "I see you've chosen the Boomtown Rats."

She lifted the album. It was the first time she had noticed what she'd picked out from the rack.

"The Fine Art of Surfacing – probably their best one. "I Don't Like Mondays" – a classic."

The last thing she wanted to do was get caught up a conversation about eighties pop bands. She responded, "I'm looking for something for my dad for Christmas. Like I said, just browsing." Turning her back, Scarlett returned the album and leafed through a couple more, pretending to scrutinise.

"Okay, you know where I am if you need any help."

She heard him pad back to the counter, mumbling some song as he went, and she returned to her vigil.

Less than a minute later her phone pinged in her jeans pocket. Scarlett prised it out and looked at the screen.

Alex had texted. "Target coming. Black hat, camouflage jacket."

112

A nervous energy, like a bolt of electricity jolted her into action. Pulling out another album she lifted it in front of her face, hiding her features, though leaving just enough space to see over the top edge.

A minute later a young man wearing a black beanie and a dark-green army-style coat slipped into view and began walking past.

Scarlett dipped her head and took a step back. She needn't have worried. She saw that his chin was tucked deep into his jacket and he had his hands jammed into his pockets, protecting himself from the elements. As he disappeared from view she dropped the album back into the display rack and counted to ten. Then, shouting back over her shoulder, "Thank you," to the guy behind the counter, she swiftly left the shop and stepped out into the street. The biting cold took her by surprise and it was spitting with rain. At that moment it felt like her face was being pricked by dozens of icy needles and she quickly dipped her head. December was only a week away and winter was making its mark.

Raising her eyes she saw that her target was a good thirty yards in front and appeared to be in no particular rush. She glanced behind her, taken aback by how many people were following, many of them sheltering beneath shiny black umbrellas, shielding themselves from the slanting rain. She could see no sign of Alex among them. Returning her gaze forward she stared in disbelief as the man she had set out to follow was now nowhere to be seen. In just the few seconds she had taken her eyes off him he had disappeared.

Shit!

Scarlett put in a sprint to the end of the shops where the road split into a side street. There she stopped and peered round the corner. He was there, head still tucked into his coat and ambling along just ten yards away. She heaved a great sigh of relief and took a quick step back out of sight. *Thank God!* She would never have lived it down if she had lost him in such a short space of time. Counting to five, she poked her head around the corner just as he was passing beneath a street lamp. A warm yellow light edged his silhouette and she could see that a good enough gap had opened between them for her to pick up his tail again.

Turning the corner she deliberately took the pace out of her stride and tucked herself against the low front walls of the houses as she headed further into the street. She still couldn't see any sign of Alex and it made her feel edgy.

Up ahead the man came to a T-junction. A high wall was directly before him and behind the wall loomed two blocks of redbrick maisonettes. Here he stopped and for the first time looked behind. There was a road opening to her left and without altering her pace she turned into it. After taking another half a dozen steps and confident she was out of his line of sight, she dashed back to the corner.

Once again he had disappeared. This was so frustrating. Where was Alex? She put in a jog, trying her best not to make too much sound, which was proving difficult as her rubber-soled boots splashed through standing water. Nearing the junction at the top of the road she slowed. The sign in front read Kensington Place. She logged it in her memory. She stepped into the street, looking quickly left and right.

The road was empty.

Where had he gone? It was along straight stretch of road. He couldn't have just vanished.

She was about to head off left when she heard a loud "Psst!" and she spun around to see Alex emerging from a dark entranceway ten yards along. He beckoned to her and she joined him.

"He's gone into those flats up there." Alex flicked his gaze behind him to the second block of maisonettes.

"Aren't we following him?"

"You are doing no more following. He's already seen you back there before you turned off. If he sees you again, that'll be it."

"Then what are we going to do? We can't just leave it at this."

"No we're not. He's not seen me, so I'm going to do a recce of those flats and see what I can see. You stay here, and if you don't hear from me in half an hour call in the troops."

With that Alex set off toward the maisonettes.

****

Scarlett was beginning to feel nervous. It was coming up to twenty minutes since Alex had left. The last thing she wanted to do was call in the police. What would she say to them? She had just started to run through a number of scenarios when he emerged up ahead. She was so relieved.

He jogged back to her.

Joining her he said, "Think I've found them. Flat on the fourth floor. There's a black anarchist flag hanging out of one of the windows."

Scarlett stepped out from the entranceway and began walking.

"Where are you going?"

She stopped and stared back. "To give them a knock."

He shook his head. "Scarlett! If you were running an operation, would you go in on your own, all guns blazing, with no intelligence?"

After a couple of seconds she answered, "Well, no."

"Exactly. And that's exactly why we aren't doing anything further tonight. I know someone who works with the council. I'll make some enquiries tomorrow and then we'll take it from there."

Scarlett was about to say something when Alex leaned forward and pressed a finger firmly on her lips.

"No arguments, Scarlett. Let's see how the land lies before we do anything else."

Twenty-eight

After calling a halt to their surveillance, Scarlett and Alex jumped on the train, got off at Richmond and called into the pub opposite the station for a much-needed drink. As they sated their thirst they discussed the next steps of their plan to snare Rose. They weren't planning for long, both of them deciding they could also do with some food. They finished their drinks and, re-energised, left the pub and yomped up Kew Road to seek out a place to eat. They settled on a Chinese restaurant they had been to previously. As they chose from the menu Scarlett told Alex about the next morning's raids. She added, "I'm afraid I'm going to have to do a disappearing act once we've eaten."

Glancing over the top of his menu he said, "I can take a hint, you know."

Smiling, she replied, "I don't mean it like that. It's just that I need to be up for five. I'm co-ordinating the raids."

He half laughed. "I'm only joking. To be honest, Scarlett, I could do with an early night myself."

****

By eight-thirty they had finished their meal, split the bill and with an embracing hug parted company.

Scarlett walked the short distance home mulling over the evening's events. The more she thought about the outcome the more she could feel frustration creeping up on her. By the time she had reached home she needed another drink. Slipping off her shoes and coat she made for the fridge, where she took out a half-drunk bottle of white wine and poured herself a glass. Then she run herself a hot bath and languished in it with her eyes closed while sipping her chilled wine, trying her best to put the evening's disappointment behind her. By the time she had finished the glass she could feel herself beginning to relax, and by the time she climbed into bed she could feel sleep catching her up. Setting the alarm for five a.m. she crashed out.

****

Scarlett awoke with a start to the sound of her alarm. She'd slept like a log. Following a quick shower, she got dressed, made up her face and even found time to make herself a coffee before Tarn arrived to pick her up. As she climbed into his car she was surprised at how fresh she felt.

They had arranged to meet everyone at Norwood Green nick, where the Neighbourhood Policing Team worked from, and the drive across there was an easy one – the roads hadn't yet started to fill up. As Tarn drove, Scarlett read over the operational order and checked the warrants for the morning's busts. By the time they had arrived she had rehearsed what she needed to say at the briefing.

Scarlett and Tarn entered a ground-floor room where the raid team were waiting. Bouncing her gaze from one person to another Scarlett noted that they appeared relaxed, nursing warm drinks and talking in hushed voices, but at the same time she could sense an air of expectation within the room.

Someone had set up a whiteboard displaying mugshots of Jamie Hill and Dane Rolletts next to their digital e-fits. Also added were blown-up sections of A–Z street maps showing the locations of both target's addresses.

Scarlett unfurled her papers and strolled to the whiteboard. "Morning everyone," she said, facing the team. Beside Tarn and DCs Ella Bloom and George Martin from her syndicate, she recognised a number of faces. There were four detectives from Southall CID, a couple of officers from Ealing Intelligence Unit and a dozen officers from Task Force. She rapped her knuckles over Jamie Hill's photograph. "Our targets of this morning's raids." She continued by introducing each of the villain's backgrounds and detailing their convictions and gave an update into the murder enquiry. "Though there is as yet no evidence to link them to the killing of our victim they are certainly in the vicinity of where she was discovered five days ago, having dumped a vehicle they had stolen from a burglary only a few hundred yards away. We can forensically place that stolen vehicle in the lane that leads down to where the body was found, and it is therefore imperative that we determine what they were doing in that location on the morning of when she was found." Scarlett pointed to the e-fits. "This is the clothing we believe the pair were wearing that morning. A priority is to find that and seize it." Scarlett went on to explain how the body was butchered after death. "We also haven't found the location where the victim was killed, and although these two live with their families, and you wouldn't think something of this nature would have been done in their own homes, stranger things have happened. So we are also looking for any unusual and unexplained blood splatter at these addresses, a large serrated knife and a hand-held electric grinder." Scarlett wrapped things up by placing the officers into two teams, giving each a target address and identifying individual members' roles once inside the premises. Finally, she checked the time with each team and coordinated the busts for eight a.m.

****

Scarlett was with Tarn driving to Jamie Hill's home. Two detectives from Southall CID in their own unmarked car led the way; they had had previous dealings with Jamie and knew where best to park so as not to spoil the element of surprise. Backing up the convoy were half a dozen officers from Task Force.

Hill's address was on the sixth floor in a block of flats. She, Tarn and the two CID officers rode the cranky lift while Task Force took the stairs. They met at the end of the corridor and soft-shoed their way along to Hill's front door.

Scarlett hammered several times on the wooden panel. The sound echoed along the bare corridor. Within thirty seconds a female voice shouted out a grumpy "Hello?" from inside. Scarlett lowered herself, lifted the letter flap and called through, "Police, Mrs Hill, open up." A few seconds later she heard a couple of bolts being drawn back and a key turn in the lock before the door opened.

Mrs Hill was a thin, scrawny woman with crimson-dyed spiky hair. Her face was heavily lined and had a weary look. The dressing gown she was wearing was in need of a wash.

Scarlett knew from their intelligence that Mrs Hill was only in her mid-forties, but as she scrutinised her face she thought she looked older.

Mrs Hill held the door half open. She scowled at Scarlett and then cast her sight over her shoulder at the rest of her team behind her. "What the fuck do you lot want, banging us up at this time of the morning?" Her London accent was broad.

Scarlett held back a grin. "Good morning, Mrs Hill. Is Jamie in? We'd like a little word with him."

"What the fuck about? He was here all last night."

"I've no doubt he was Mrs Hill, but it's not about last night. It's about something that happened a few days ago." Scarlett stepped over the threshold, fanning the warrant at her.

Mrs Hill locked gazes with Scarlett for a few seconds and made a weak attempt at offering a hateful stare. Then she huffed loudly, stepped back and turned on her heel. Shuffling away she mumbled, "Fucking harassment, is what this is. He gets blamed for everything that goes on round here."

Scarlett stepped after her, beckoning back over her shoulder for her team to follow. She directed Tarn and the two Southall detectives up the stairs.

Abruptly, Mrs Hill stopped, lifted her head to the ceiling and shouted, "Jamie, get yourself up. Old Bill are here." With that she peeled left through an open doorway and disappeared.

Scarlett could make out through the gap that it was the kitchen. She heard the kettle being switched on and the sound of several cups clinking together. She stepped past the kitchen door and strolled through into the lounge. A rank smell of stale food and cigarettes greeted her. The place was a dump. Various items of clothing littered the floor and the furniture. Spread out over a small coffee table in the centre of the room was an array of polystyrene cartons, some of which contained gelled remnants of food. It looked like a cold Chinese takeaway. There were empty cups and glasses everywhere. A faux-leather sofa, in front of the large window, had a tear in one of the back support cushions and foam poked through.

A scuffling noise upstairs brought back her attention. It was soon followed by cries of protestation.

"What the fuck do you lot want? This is a fucking joke, you muppets."

It was a young man's voice. Scarlett guessed that Tarn and the Southall detectives had found Jamie.

The same person shouted, "Alright, I said I'm getting up. Hold your fucking horses."

There was a moment's silence and then a loud yelp went up and Scarlett picked out the sound of more scuffles above her, followed by heavy footfalls. She went back out into the hallway just as Jamie Hill appeared at the top of the stairs in handcuffs. He had on a T-shirt and jogging pants, though the jogging pants looked as if they would fall from his hips at any moment. He was scrawny just like his mother.

Jamie was yelling, "I said I was coming, didn't I? There's no need for the fucking rough stuff!"

Tarn, and one of the Southall detective's had hold of Jamie's arms and he was making a feeble attempt at shaking himself free.

Mrs Hill appeared in the kitchen doorway, clutching a lighted cigarette. She aimed it at Tarn like a loaded gun. "If he's marked, you'll pay. Anyway what's he supposed to have done?"

Scarlett saw Mrs Hill meet her son's gaze.

Jamie's eyes widened. "They say they want to talk to me about a body what's been found in the Thames."

Mrs Hill's shocked look ping-ponged between her son and Scarlett. "A body! What body?"

"The body of a young woman was found in the Thames at Richmond," Scarlett answered.

"That body that was on the news?"

Scarlett nodded.

Mrs Hill focussed on her son, who was just stepping down off the bottom stair.

He said, "That's not me, Mum! Honest! I haven't killed nobody. This is a stitch-up."

Mrs Hill pushed her way past Scarlett and stormed towards the lounge. She called back, "I'll get onto Mr Campbell, Jamie. Don't you say nothing 'til your brief arrives." Then she went out of view.

As Tarn and the Southall detective led Jamie towards the front door, Scarlett picked up the sound of items being tossed aside coming from the lounge.

Mrs Hill's voice shouted back, "Don't say fuck all, Jamie. I'm on the phone right now."

Twenty-nine

In an interview room at Ealing Custody Suite, Jamie Hill stared defiantly across the table at Scarlett and Tarn. Sitting next to him was his solicitor. Trevor Campbell was a balding, overweight man in his late forties, with a tanned complexion that looked recent. His pen was poised over a legal pad.

Scarlett introduced herself and Tarn and went into the customary interview preamble. She told Jamie Hill that the interview was being video recorded and cautioned him. Before her, in two neat piles, she had her interview notes and a number of sealed exhibits. Among them was a blue hoody with an orange Vans logo across the chest; Task Force officers had found it in a pile of dirty clothing in the bathroom.

Jamie's house was still being searched. As was Dane Rolletts's, who was currently in the interview room next door with DCs George Martin and Ella Bloom.

Scarlett said, "Jamie you have already been told the reason why you are here?"

Jamie folded his arms defensively and leaned back in his chair. "Because you're accusing me of killing a woman and dumping her in the river."

"You're not being accused of killing anyone, but we do want to talk to you about a woman's body that was discovered on the banks of the River Thames five days ago. But before that I want to talk to you about the offence for which you have been arrested this morning. You have been arrested for burglary at a house in Hounslow where a car was stolen. Namely a BMW 530d M Sport."

"Yeah and when was this supposed to have happened?"

"Six days ago."

"I was at home in bed that night. Ask my mum."

"I never said the burglary was at night." Scarlett watched Jamie's acne-peppered face colour up.

"No comment."

"That BMW was involved in a car chase with traffic police in the early hours of the morning following the burglary, and it was found abandoned in the public car park at Ham House. What do you know about that?"

He shrugged his shoulders. "No comment."

"Someone tried to burn that car with rags and petrol. What do you know about that?"

He again made no comment.

"Well after they tried to fire the car, the two offenders walked along the towpath where they were seen by a witness who was walking his dog. In fact one of those offenders said "Morning" to him. Ring any bells?"

Tight lipped, he said, "None."

"Well the witness described to us what those two young men were wearing and gave us e-fits. One of those young men was wearing a blue hoody with a Vans logo across the chest. And the owners of the house that was broken into in Hounslow also gave e-fits of the two offenders who took their BMW. And, surprise, surprise, one of those was wearing a blue hoody with a Vans logo across the front." Scarlett picked up the exhibit bag containing the blue hoody and slid it across the table. "And lo and behold, this morning we found one exactly like that in your bathroom. Don't you think that's some coincidence?"

He shrugged. "So?"

"So, we also recovered the rag that was used to try and burn the BMW. I already told you that it failed to burn properly. Well, because of that we were able to get DNA from the rag, which by the way was a torn piece of T-shirt, and guess what? Surprise, surprise again, it had your DNA all over it." Scarlett broke into a smile.

Jamie Hill didn't immediately answer. Instead he stared across the table. Several seconds later he snarled, "No fucking comment."

Scarlett held Jamie's gaze for a while. "Look Jamie, I'm not going to beat about the bush here. There is a reason why I said we wanted to talk to you about the body in the Thames. The body was discovered not far from where you and Dane dumped the BMW you stole from the house in Hounslow. It was found on the banks of the Thames near a jetty at the bottom of River Lane. That's about a quarter of a mile from where you left the BMW. On River Lane we found tyre marks that match perfectly with the front offside tyre of the stolen BMW, so we know that car was on that lane. We also have a witness who describes seeing and talking with two young men only a hundred yards from where the body was discovered. Two young men who fit you and Dane to a tee! Do you see where I'm going with this Jamie?"

Suddenly, Jamie Hill leaned forward. "Me and Dane killing a woman? You have got to be kidding!"

Scarlett never flinched. "Do I look like I'm kidding?"

Jamie pointed a finger. Scarlett noticed his dirty fingernail.

"Look it's not me and Dane you need to be talking to. It's that geezer with the four-by-four who was there that morning."

Scarlett froze for a second. "What did you say?"

Jamie broke into a wry smile and wagged his grubby finger. "That's got you hasn't it, Miss Smart Arse? You didn't know about him did you? Trying to stitch me up instead."

"Jamie, tell me who you saw on River Lane. This is important."

"Ha! Treating me different now aren't you?"

Sternly, Scarlett said, "Jamie, just tell me about the man you saw on River Lane the night you stole the BMW."

He rubbed his face vigorously and took a deep breath. He let it out with a prolonged "Harrumph." Then he said, "Look, alright, me and Dane did nick that BMW. And, like you say, we did have a bit of fun with the traffic cops and had a bit of a chase. But that's what it was – a bit of fun, nothing else. You're also right about trying to fire it." He sighed, "I can't really deny that seeing it was my T-shirt. But we had nothing to do with dumping any body. Fuck me!"

"Just tell me what happened that night, Jamie. Especially about who and what you saw on River Lane."

"Well, after we had that chase, we decided we should dump the car, so we drove around looking for a good place to leave it. That's when we came to that lane. Dane knew the area and he said there was this jetty down there. We were going to drive down and push it in the river, but as we got near the bottom we spotted this black four-by-four. It had its brake lights on. We thought at first it was a cop car, then realised it wasn't – it was this Audi, top-of-the-range job. Anyway, the driver's door was open – it was lit up inside, and this big fucking geezer was standing by the door. Dane was driving, spotted the car last minute 'cos we were larking about, and he braked too hard and we skidded. That's when the bloke looked round at us. I tell you the way he looked at us was scary.

123

He looked like he wanted to fucking kill us. And he was built like a brick shit house. Not the type you wanted to mess with at all, I tell you. So I told Dane to get us the fuck out of there. He slammed the car into reverse and we fucked off. That's when we drove to that car park where you found the car. We waited there for a good hour, ready to leg it, the first sign of the four-by-four, but it didn't come so we decided to fire it and fuck off. You've already mentioned the rest. We went along the towpath, just checking the four-by-four had gone, and then made our way to the main road and caught the bus. That's when we bumped into that man walking the dog.

Scarlett leaned in. "Jamie, just going back to the man with the four-by-four in River Lane – did you know him?"

He shook his head. "Never seen him before. And never want to meet him, thank you very much."

"Would you be able to describe him?"

"I've told you about him already."

"No, I mean do you think you'd be able to do an e-fit for us."

"You mean like a witness?"

Scarlett nodded.

"Fuck me, I don't know about being a witness. I ain't no fucking grass."

"We might be able to pull some strings regarding the burglary charge."

Jamie turned to look at his solicitor.

With arched eyebrows Trevor Campbell nodded.

Jamie returned his gaze to Scarlett. "You mean some kind of deal?"

"We can put in a good word for you, Jamie."

He flashed a cocky grin. "Drop the charges and I'm interested."

Scarlett smiled. There was some work to do yet but this latest piece of information would certainly kick-start the murder enquiry.

Thirty

"Latest update," said DCI Diane Harris, pointing the remote at the large interactive screen in the incident room. An image appeared. It was full body e-fit of a squat, heavy-built man, clean shaven, with a shaven head, dressed in dark, nondescript clothing, consisting of a mid-length leather jacket and jeans. She continued, "New suspect." She turned to face her seated team, "As you can see the facial features are not good, but this is a start. This man was seen on River Lane by both Jamie Hill and Dane Rolletts in the early hours of the morning before our body in the suitcase was found. He was standing beside a dark, believed black, Audi Q7. We haven't got a reg number for that vehicle but it was definitely an Audi Q7, described as being the latest model. Both of them were interviewed separately and gave us the same make and model – and these two toerags know their cars." She let the information settle in the thoughts of the team for a few seconds. "After they nicked the BMW from Hounslow they say they drove down River Lane with the intention of dumping the car in the river off the jetty, but they came across this car. It was stationary in the middle of the road and our suspect was standing beside the open driver's door and he turned round as they approached. Rolletts braked, skidded and reversed back up the lane, and then drove the car to where it was later found abandoned in the car park at Ham House. One of the interesting things Rolletts said is that he also saw the passenger door of this four-by-four open, and he got the impression that our suspect had been watching someone before they disturbed him. Now this could be completely innocent, but I think you know where I'm going with this. My thoughts are that whoever was the passenger in that vehicle was dumping the suitcase, and this guy" – she aimed the remote back at the e-fit – "was keeping a lookout." She lowered the remote. "This e-fit, together with the make and model of the Audi, will be circulated to all Metropolitan Police areas this afternoon for sightings and report. There will be a fresh action allocated to monitor and chase up any responses." Diane Harris triggered the remote again and three head-and-shoulders images of white females appeared. She glanced at them briefly and then returned her gaze to the room. "Okay, moving on. These are the three young women who were detained following the house fire in Camden Town last December. Because of the raids and arrests yesterday I decided to shortcut things and got DS Ashdown to phone Immigration and do the initial enquiry that way." She nodded at her detective sergeant on the front row. "Can I bring you in Gary – tell everyone what you learned."

DS Ashdown remained seated. Pushing his fingers through his hair he angled his body so that he could talk to most of the team. "As the gaffer says, I contacted Immigration at Dover yesterday morning and spoke with a supervisor in their intelligence unit and told him what I was after. It didn't take him long to find these girls' files. We've already heard that the officer who investigated the fire said that two of the girls were from Slovakia and one from Lithuania, but whereas the officer didn't get their full details, because they wouldn't fully cooperate, Immigration did." Gary Ashdown flicked his head toward the screen. "Going left to right we have Bozka Reznick, twenty-two years old, and Danika Kovac, twenty-one. These are Slovakian. In a nutshell, the girls told Immigration that they were tricked into believing that they had a job in the UK and willingly flew across here, only to be forced into prostitution once they had arrived. They say they were both raped by their abductors and repeatedly threatened. They were moved around several addresses for about eighteen months and had been in the house where the fire was for only a couple of weeks. They refused to name any of those involved in the trafficking, other than to say they were Albanian, and wouldn't divulge any of the addresses where they had worked for fear of reprisals against them and their families. Although their passports had been taken by their abductors they gave full details of where they were from and chose to be returned home. They were flown back to Slovakia within weeks following the fire and didn't come back for the inquest. Immigration has supplied me with their details and I have faxed Interpol with a view to them being traced and interviewed." He flashed a glance at DCI Harris and continued. "The last girl is Greta Aglinsky. She was nineteen when this photograph was taken. Greta wasn't as forthcoming as the other two. In fact the Immigration intel officer says she was petrified at what might happen to her family back in Lithuania. So other than give her personal details and confirm she was Lithuanian, she wouldn't tell them where she was from in Lithuania, and she wouldn't give any details of how she had been brought to this country. He told me that because they couldn't confirm anything and that because she hadn't got a passport they were obliged to release her after the customary three months. She was put up in a B&B in Dover but she disappeared within days. They have no idea where she currently is. She could be back out on the streets, and so with that in mind I've spoken with a couple of my ex-colleagues in Vice and sent them her details." The DS nodded his head at DCI Harris, indicating he had finished.

Diane Harris stepped towards the screen and slapped a hand over the photo of Greta Aglinsky. "There is an outside chance that Greta here could be our victim. Certainly in terms of her build and her age she fits the profile. So with that in mind we are cross-matching her DNA with that of our victim. I have asked for it to be prioritised, so we should know within the next two days if it is her or not."

Thirty-one

After morning briefing Scarlett grabbed a coffee and set to work on her report, detailing the outcome of the previous day's raids and arrests of Jamie Hill and Dane Rolletts, while her partner Tarn teamed up and went out with Ella Bloom on murder enquiries, chasing up possible suppliers of the suitcase the body had been found in.

Following Jamie's and Dane's confessions, and after getting the e-fit of the shaven-haired man on River Lane together with witness statements, she had handed over the pair to Southall CID to finish off the interrogation. Now she had to chase things up, so she put in a phone call to the DS leading the investigation. He proudly told her that Jamie and Dane had gone on to admit another ten burglaries and car thefts and had also given up the two other members of their team. They had been released on bail late last night and this morning detectives were currently out hunting down the other two thieves. Finishing the conversation Scarlett thanked him, but as she hung up she sighed. On the one hand, the information and result would make for good reading, but on the other she knew all she was doing was justifying the cost of resources used on the operation. She thought it was quite sad that everything boiled down to money these days.

Scarlett finished the report just before midday, and pushing back her chair took in the office. Only the office team were in: DS Brent Collins and DC Carolyn Young were at their desks, both of them on their computers. DI Taylor-Butler was sitting at Gary Ashdown's empty desk, on the phone. She knew that protocol determined that her report should first be seen by him, but following the debacle with the Lycra Rapist file she no longer trusted him with important paperwork. Deciding to bypass him, she headed off down the corridor and dropped it in the DCI's tray on her way out for lunch, during which she texted Alex to see if he had anything on the address they had tracked Rose's friend to. He didn't reply and she returned to work feeling slightly deflated.

The day went slowly. Scarlett ploughed through her backlog of paperwork and began work on the Lycra Rapist Crown Court file. She still hadn't heard back from Housing or Benefits and chased that up but the enquiry still hadn't been done. Biting her lips she asked if it could be prioritised. The woman she was speaking with said she'd put it to the top of her list, but detecting a lack of enthusiasm in the woman's voice, Scarlett ended the call with a heavy sigh.

Tarn and Ella returned late afternoon with no positive news. They had been unable to trace suppliers of the suitcase or even its country of manufacture. And so evening briefing was a quick affair, with nothing of note being offered up by anyone from the team. Afterwards, the majority decamped to the pub, but Scarlett wasn't in the mood to stay, and after a swift lager she bid everyone goodnight and left for home.

****

Unlocking the front door, she had just switched on her hallway light and deactivated the house alarm when her BlackBerry rang. Back-heeling the door shut she whipped out her phone and, recognising Alex's number, answered.

He said, "Sorry I couldn't get back to you earlier Scarlett, I had to go into the office and follow up on some enquiries."

"Oh, that's okay. No problem," she lied. "I just wondered if you'd heard anything."

"I have, actually. My contact from the council got back to me this afternoon. I couldn't speak with her but she left me a voicemail. Got some quite interesting info."

After a couple of seconds silence Scarlett prompted, "Come on then, don't keep me on tenterhooks. What have you learned?"

"I was going to tell you next time we meet."

"Don't you dare, Alex King."

He let out a short laugh. "I don't know, you're so impatient."

"Only because this is my sister. You don't know what it's like. I've been trying to find her for years, not knowing if she's alive or dead. This is the closest I've got."

"Okay, I'll give you the gist of what she's told me and then we'll sort something out." He paused. "It seems that guy we followed is part of a ragtag of squatters – street musicians and artists. Well I say ragtag, but they're actually very well organised. It would seem that they've occupied the flat we followed him to for the last couple of months. The owner died, and because he'd got no family the council had to clean it out. Apparently they left the window open after finishing one night and this group got in. Since then they've paid the bills and reconnected the utilities and the council are now having to go through the courts to get them evicted. Not surprising, it's not the first time this bunch have done this."

"Any names?"

Alex let out another short laugh, "A Mr John Smith is the name everything's billed to."

"Very original."

"Anyway, the council have done a doorstep visit and they've reported that at least a dozen people occupy the place. Now I guess this is not something you're going to be able to tackle legitimately with a posse of cops, so given the numbers living there you're going to have to come up with something pretty resourceful to get inside."

Scarlett lifted her eyes to the ceiling. "I've already given it some thought and I think I've come up with something to get us inside."

"Why don't I like the sound of the word 'us'. Is this going to end in pain?"

"Course not. Trust me, I'm a cop," she laughed, ending the call.

Thirty-two

The next morning Scarlett was out with Tarn, on enquiries, when the call came through that a body had been found in a dumpster on the Patmore Estate in Battersea. Uniform were already on scene and Communications were requesting that she attend. She set the postcode into the dashboard computer and Tarn began weaving his way through heavy traffic, occasionally leaving the main thoroughfare and using side streets as shortcuts, but in spite of some fast and erratic driving it still took them half an hour to get to their destination, a housing project comprising of a series of medium-rise flats and apartments only a stone's throw from the old Battersea power station.

Entering the estate, it wasn't hard to find the precise location of the discovery – directly in front of them the place was swarming with Uniform and a large number of the residents were milling around in disparate small groups.

Scarlett could see that a barrier of crime scene tape had been wrapped around a number of street lamps, sealing off-road access, and fencing in a good section of footpath and grassed area, either side of two blocks of flats. Several officers were doing their best to corral the nosy group of onlookers into the left-hand area of the cordon.

Tarn nosed their unmarked car toward the kerb and parked.

Scarlett got out. It was beginning to rain. She looked up, took in the heavy obsidian clouds dominating the sky and groaned. It looked like she was in for another soaking. She was fed up; it had done nothing else but rain for the best part of the week. She reached back inside the car and dragged her coat off the back seat, and as she slipped it on took in the theatre playing out before her, sympathising with the plight of the officers who were doing there level best to prevent contagion of the crime scene by a group of residents who were doing there level best to get the best view of whatever was happening on their estate.

Taking out their protective suits from the boot, Scarlett and Tarn headed toward the left-hand block of flats, where they spotted an active clump of uniformed officers. As they neared, a slim dark-haired female sergeant peeled away from the group and came to meet them. Scarlett recognised her: Abbie Wilson. She had been on the same group at Hammersmith when she had joined the police force nine years ago.

The sergeant greeted her, "Hi Scarlett. Long time, no see. I heard you'd gone into Homicide and Serious Crime."

"Hi Abbie, yeah, been there just over two years." She patted three fingers across her upper arm and said, "I see you've made sergeant. Congratulations."

Abbie smoothed a hand over the three stripes on her left sleeve and smiled proudly. "Yeah, eighteen months now. Took me four attempts, though. Time flies, eh? Doesn't seem two minutes since you and I were patrolling together."

Without warning a flashback of images cascaded from her subconscious. Seventh of July 2005. She and Abbie had been on patrol together when the first calls came in of a series of explosions on the London Underground and then later on a double-decker bus. She and Abbie had been whisked across to Tavistock Square to deal with the aftermath of the bus blast. Scarlett had nursed quite a number of seriously injured people that day following the suicide bombings. Occasionally, when she least expected it, like now, the imagery still visited her. She chased away the spectre, and tightening her mouth said, "Doesn't seem five minutes ago, hey Abbie? Some things you can't forget." Then, unpursing her lips, said, "Anyway, what have you got for us? Communications said something about a body in a dumpster."

Sergeant Wilson half turned and gestured with a backwards flick of her head. "Don't know about a full body, Scarlett. Body parts are what we've found at the moment. Certainly a couple of arms and most of a leg in a bin liner. I asked Communications to contact you because I know you're dealing with a dismembered body fished out of the Thames. Didn't know if it could be connected."

Scarlett met Abbie's gaze, "It won't be ours. Our body was minus her head and her hands."

"Oh, sorry about that. I wasn't aware."

"Never mind, Abbie. We'll take a look while we're here." Scarlett set off towards the mooching group of uniformed officers. Tarn and Abbie stepped in beside her.

She began unfolding her forensic suit as she walked. "Have you requested a senior investigating officer, Abbie?"

"No, not yet. I just put in a call and asked for your team to be informed. I've got forensics and CSI on their way."

"Okay, no problem. I'll see what we've got first, then ask for an SIO to join us."

Tarn said, "We're absolutely sure they're human body parts?"

Sergeant Wilson glanced sideways and nodded. "Absolutely. Seen them myself. One of my team came to the call. Climbed into the dumpster thinking it would be a false alarm. A mannequin or something. But then when he ripped open the bin liner he saw that the parts were real. The arms have been severed just below the shoulder and the leg has most of the thigh attached. Right shock for him, I can tell you. He threw up everywhere. I've sent him back to the station."

Scarlett asked, "How were the parts originally found? Who put the call in?"

"One of the residents," Abbie answered, dipping her head toward the low-rise redbrick block they were approaching. "This is Beattie House. A guy who lives on the top floor found them. Had a new TV delivered this morning and had brought the packaging down to dump it. He says the bin liner was right on the top of the rubbish when he opened the dumpster lid. It had a small tear in it and one of the hands was sticking out. Freaked him out, as you can imagine, and he rang us straight away." Sergeant Wilson stopped as she rejoined her group. She stared beyond them and said, "The dumpster is just around the side of the building. It's the one with the lid open. You can't miss it, there's a few officers guarding it. It's the refuse area for this block and the next. We've sealed the area off as well."

Scarlett began climbing into her protective suit. "Thanks Abbie, we'll take a look and see what we've got."

133

Thirty-three

Skender showered – his second shower of the day. The first had been eleven hours earlier, just after midnight, when he had arrived home after killing her.

Usually he had someone else to take care of the problems but he had decided to deal with this one himself, especially after the last fuck-up.

He had made the decision after the phone call late last night. He'd been in the house in Wandsworth when he'd taken it, and immediately rang Arjan and told him to pick him up. They had cruised the streets where he knew she was likely to be and it hadn't been long before they had spotted her. She was on her own, beneath the long railway arch, tapping her six-inch heels rapidly on the glistening cobbles in an effort to stave off the cold. They did a quick circuit to make sure no cops were about and then returned to the spot where she was standing.

Her look had been one of nervousness when he had pulled up beside her. He had witnessed it so many times in his girls. He liked to keep it that way. It gave him the edge. He had told her to get in and he had sensed the slight hesitation as she'd climbed into the back. "It's okay," he had said. "You not in trouble." In his rear-view mirror he had watched her give him an uneasy smile as she belted up.

"Where are we going?" she had asked.

"I have a little job for you. A friend of mine I want you to meet," he had replied and they had driven her back to the house in Wandsworth.

She had put up a little fight as they had dragged her down to the basement, but she wasn't much of a match for them and it hadn't taken too long for him to kill her once he'd got his hands around her throat. Then, before he had got Arjan to drop him back home at his flat, he had left instructions, with Henrikas, as to what he wanted happening to the girl. "I don't want her finding this time," he had commanded. "Do I make myself clear?" He had left Henrikas at the bottom of the basement steps nodding away anxiously.

When he had been dropped off, the first thing he did was to strip off his clothes and put them in the washing machine. Then he'd poured himself a large vodka, downed it in one and climbed into the shower. Wringing his hands in bleach he'd cleansed himself thoroughly, and then he'd gone into the bedroom and woken up Maria, ordering her to the lounge, where he lined up a small bag of coke on the glass-top coffee table and snorted it with her. The hour following he had screwed her until he'd collapsed.

****

Stepping out from his second shower, he dried his upper body and towelled his hair, then dropping the damp towel onto the bathroom floor he picked another off the heated rail, wrapped it around his waist and made his way into the open living lounge.

Maria was cooking, looking sexy in a tight black vest and lacy black thong. He could smell omelette.

He flopped onto the leather sofa, snatched up the remote and clicked on the 50-inch TV mounted on the wall. The news was on. A pretty, dark-haired newscaster stared back. He saw from the information running along the bottom of the screen that she was speaking live from Battersea. Behind her he could see it was a housing development of high-rise buildings and there appeared to be a lot of police activity in the background. He turned up the sound.

"A series of body parts, believed to be those of a woman, were found this morning in refuse bins in one of the flats behind me. Police and Forensics are currently on scene trying to determine the identity of the victim. As yet we have no information as to how the woman met her death. The police ask that anyone who saw anything suspicious around this complex, especially over the last twenty-four hours, contact them on the incident room number provided. All information will be treated in the strictest of confidence."

It took a few seconds for him to take in what the newscaster had said, but the information running across the bottom of the screen summarised what he thought she had just announced. For a split second his stomach emptied. He took a couple of deep breaths as he stared at the TV. The news had moved on to an update about the Russian plane crash at Karzan International Airport he'd been following; a cousin, on his father's side, had been among the dead. The last few days he'd hardly been off the phone to his family. Dealing with their sorrow had diverted him from his business affairs and last night had been his way of a sending a message that he was back on top of things.

But he hadn't expected this. Tightening his grip around the remote, as if he was squeezing the very life out of it, he could feel the anger within him beginning to rise.

Fucking half-wits. Someone is going to pay for this!

Thirty-four

By mid-afternoon every dumpster in the sealed-off refuse area next to Beattie House had been searched. In four of the bins, crime scene investigators had found and recovered seven black bin liners containing body parts. Each of these had been carefully opened and the gruesome contents logged and photographed.

In one bag they had discovered the torso. Its left shoulder had a branding mark in the shape of a crescent moon and star. It was an old scar. It created a huge stir among the team and Scarlett put in a call to DCI Diane Harris.

She arrived at the scene just as they were opening the last black sack. In it was the bloodied head of the woman.

For a brief moment Scarlett was dumbstruck – she thought she recognised the face from yesterday's briefing. She studied the features for a few more seconds before aiming a look at her boss.

Pointing, she said, "Does that look like who I think it is?"

Diane Harris's face took on a mystified look.

"Does that look like Greta Aglinsky?"

The DCI's look changed. Her eyes widened. "Do you know, Scarlett, I think it does."

****

It was early evening and the Homicide and Serious Crime Unit were assembled in the Major Incident Suite.

"This changes everything," announced DCI Harris, sweeping her gaze around the room.

Behind her, onscreen, were the various body parts found that morning in the refuse bins. They had been loosely assembled into a recognisable female torso.

The DCI gave a backwards flick of her head. "Fingerprints confirm this is Greta Aglinsky. And, when I say it changes everything, I don't just mean in terms of our investigation, but our whole future approach as to how we plan our moves and what we circulate." Deepening her troubled look, she continued, "A couple of things concern me with this find. Firstly, I think we were onto something with our enquiries into Greta Aglinsky. This tells me someone needed her out of the way. And permanently. It's my belief that Greta either knew the person, or people, involved in the murder of our, as yet, unknown victim in the suitcase, or had information which would identify them." She tapped the palm of her hand. "There are several things that make me say this. The first is the exact same branding mark on her shoulder as our headless victim. We have already heard that Greta was an illegal, brought in for the purpose of prostitution. And we have also heard that the gangs who bring them in brand them to identify them as their property. This suggests the likelihood that Greta and our headless victim were involved with the same gang. The other thing is the complete lack of any defence injuries on her body. She put up little or no resistance prior to being killed, suggesting that she was more than likely comfortable in their company and had no idea this was going to happen to her." Pausing for a moment she explored the room. Happy that she had everyone's attention, she continued, "The other thing the post mortem has revealed is that while her death was caused by strangulation, the pathologist has identified that, as in the case of our first victim, a knife with a serrated edge and a small angle-grinder was used to sever the limbs. Swabs have been taken from the severed areas to determine if there is any transference of DNA from our headless victim. That way we will definitely know if our victim's have been cut up by the same tools." Tightening her mouth she tapped her palm again. "I said there were a couple of thing which concerned me. Well, the second is that we have a leak!" She slowly checked the room. "I don't necessarily mean a deliberate leak, but it's fair to say that sensitive information from our enquiry has got out which has resulted in the death of Greta Aglinsky. For me, it's too much of a coincidence that one day after she crops up in our investigation she turns up murdered. And don't think for one minute I'm pointing the finger at any of you. We also shared this information with Immigration and Vice. So, more to protect ourselves, from now on every bit of information which needs to go out from this room will be scrutinised and logged." She aimed a direct look at DI Taylor-Butler. "Hayden, I want you to take responsibility for this."

The DI returned a quick nod and made a note in his journal.

Then she switched her gaze back to her team and added, "If you need to talk with anyone outside of this incident room about this case you run it past the DI first." She picked out a number of nods of approval and then continued, "Okay, now let's double-check on what we have in relation to this latest murder. At roughly ten-forty-five this morning, a thirty-two-year-old man was disposing his rubbish in a large refuse bin at the side of Beattie House, where he lives on the fifth floor, when he discovered a black bin liner containing two dismembered arms and a leg. A later search by us found a further six bin liners containing body parts which make up our victim, twenty-year-old Greta Aglinsky. We have also found another bin liner containing female clothing, which is bloodstained and which we believe is hers. Other than how she was killed, which I have already mentioned, that at the moment is all we have." While she spoke, crime scene photographs of Beattie House and the refuse area to the side of the flats appeared onscreen. Pausing again, she flashed a quick look behind her, took in the pictures and then returned her gaze to the squad. "Right actions in respect of Greta Aglinsky. It's imperative we find out where she was living, or where she has been staying during the last eleven months since she left the B&B in Dover. Who were her friends or associates she was in daily or regular contact with. We go back through her Immigration file. I also want to know where she was from and who her family are. They'll need to be informed. Go through Interpol when you do that." She took a deep breath. "The bloodstained clothing, which we believe is hers, is with Forensics. I'm hoping to get that fast-tracked. Also, we haven't found where either our two victims were killed." The imagery onscreen behind her disappeared. A couple of seconds later, photos of their headless victim and a 3D aerial shot of the river bank and woods at Ham appeared. "Right, now back to our first victim. We still haven't discovered who she is despite our media appeals. That is our main priority." For the first time since she began her conference a smile emerged. "On a more positive note, we may have a lead on the black four-by-four we circulated. A uniformed officer from Putney contacted the incident room yesterday. Apparently late afternoon, the day before our victim was found, she took a report of a hit-and-run involving a black Audi Q7, which ran into the back of a van. Witnesses have told her that after the accident, and before the Audi drove off, they saw the driver in a violent struggle with a young woman inside the car. The police woman is currently off duty but is back tomorrow morning. I've left a message for her to contact me the moment she comes on duty. I'm also hoping the incident has been captured on CCTV. Once I get the exact location I can ask for checks to be done with ANPR."

Breaking from her speech again she watched several members of the team exchanging knowing looks with one another. She knew they were having the same thoughts as her – this could be a breakthrough. ANPR automatically reads vehicle number plates and logs the movements of vehicles on almost every main road in Britain and the images are held in computers for two years. She clapped her hands and brought their gazes back to meet hers. "Okay that's it everyone for today. Tomorrow morning, collect your actions and let's get out there first thing. And one more thing: I don't need to remind everyone that these are very dangerous people we are dealing with. They've already killed twice, and brutally. Everyone needs to be diligent. Any suspicions you have you call in without hesitation."

Thirty-five

On the third floor of Beattie House Scarlett took a moment out from her house-to-house enquiries. Resting folded arms on the balcony she surveyed the housing project's communal area below. Beyond an expanse of threadbare grass, inside a fenced-in basketball court, she spied a dozen or so male teenagers playing raucously with a ball. She smiled to herself. *There's a lot of male testosterone flying around inside that court.* Although not as rough as them, she had empathy with their competitiveness. As a junior champion and a university runner she had always given it her all, and still pushed herself whenever she went out running, even though the majority of the time she was alone.

She brought back her gaze and pushed herself upright. Close by, at the periphery of her vision, she caught sight of Tarn, about to knock on another door. The next flat on, DCs George Martin and Ella Bloom were trying to get a foot in through a partially opened door. She and her team had been tasked with pressing doorbells and knocking on doors on the Patmore Estate, and so far it had not been an enjoyable experience. The ones who had answered their doors weren't exactly falling over themselves to talk. She remembered that she had encountered the same reaction two years earlier following a drive-by shooting outside Stockwell tube station. Four gang members from another estate nearby had killed a rival in front of the police and the car they had been driving crashed near here following a chase. One of the gang fled into the estate and a few residents had helped in randomly scattering the evidence. Although it was all eventually recovered, and the shooter arrested, feelings between the police and the residents were strained and led to high-visibility patrols for some time. It had taken high-level mediation between community leaders and the local district command team to get things back on an even keel.

Half turning, Scarlett was about to join her team when her BlackBerry beeped. She dug it out from her jacket pocket. It was a text from Alex.

"Can you ring me?"
"Busy, ring you in 1 hour"
Seconds later it beeped again.
"It's important."

She drew in a sharp breath through gritted teeth. Alex had something, just when she didn't need it. She swung her gaze towards Tarn and caught his attention. Holding up her phone and giving him a look indicating she needed to make a call, she set off towards the stairwell, dialling Alex's number as she walked.

It was answered after the first ring.

On a hurried note Alex said, "Sorry about this Scarlett, you know I wouldn't ring you at work unless I thought it was important."

"Is it Rose?"

"No." He paused. "It's about your mobile. Someone just activated it. I know where it is."

It took a few seconds for what Alex was telling her to sink in. "How do you know this?"

"Don't ask. It's another favour I called in. I got a call ten minutes ago and I knew you were at work but I thought it would be something you would want to know. It pinged up early this morning and it's still on. My contact's located it to a specific address in Wandsworth."

She trapped the phone between her ear and shoulder and took out her pen. "What's the address, Alex?"

He told her and she scribbled it down on the back of her hand. "Thanks Alex, I owe you."

"Let me know how you get on." He ended the call.

For a moment Scarlett stared at her BlackBerry, mulling over the information and thinking things through. Dilemma. It wasn't just her phone she was desperate to get back but her warrant card as well. Since it had been stolen she had monitored daily bulletins to see if it had been used to commit crime. So far it hadn't. Despite the murder enquiry she knew she needed to act on this. And quick.

Thirty-six

The location scribbled on the back of Scarlett's hand was a tree-lined street of Georgian grey-brick terraces. The street would have looked something in its heyday, now it was rundown.

From the front passenger seat of the unmarked car Scarlett checked the numbers of the houses they were passing. Tarn was driving and in the back were George Martin and Ella Bloom. Forty minutes earlier she had run a check on the address Alex had given her, and discovered it had a couple of intelligence tags, revealing that the premise was being frequented by illegal immigrants and was suspected of being run as a brothel. Following that she had decided to tell her colleagues about her phone call, knowing the only way she could get her warrant card and mobile back was with their help. As they had driven through heavy traffic together they had formulated a plan. Now, as they neared their target, they were ready to put it into action.

Scarlett patted Tarn's hand as they approached the number she was looking for. He slowed the car to a crawl and she saw that number forty-four was a two-storey mid-terrace with a side passage, barred by a tall metal gate. Its downstairs curtains were closed so she couldn't get a feel for the place – whether there was anyone in there or not – and for a moment it forced a quick rethink of the plans. But as they cruised past she locked onto the front door and saw that it was in bad state of repair. That made up her mind to go through with things.

She told Tarn to scout around the backstreets before they went in and they found a service alleyway that ran the length of the back of the terraces. Scarlett told Tarn to stop the car and turning to George and Ella pointed out the alleyway, directing them to make their way to the rear of the house. "Me and Tarn'll go to the front and we'll shout you when we're going in."

Acknowledging Scarlett's instructions with a quick nod the two detectives climbed out of the car and set off with a trot into the alley.

Two minutes later as she and Tarn returned to the tree-lined street, Scarlett's radio crackled into life. George and Ella were in position.

Tarn pulled up opposite number forty-four and killed the engine. There was still no sign of life in the premises.

Scarlett turned to her partner. "You don't need to do this if you don't want. This is my call. If you're uncomfortable, tell me now."

He met her gaze. "No, I'm good. The scrotes robbed you. They need to be taught a lesson. Let's do it."

Closing the car doors gently Scarlett and Tarn briskly soft-shoed across the road. Scarlett led the way, swinging her head back and forth, suspiciously eyeing the environment. Only a couple of women were around and they were at the top of the street with their backs to them. Closing in on number forty-four she could hear her heart beating double-time against her chest. She knew this wasn't what she was supposed to be doing, and although she had a well-rehearsed statement for the gaffer, she knew if it went belly up she'd be in for the bollocking of her life. She fought to push it from her mind as she neared the house, telling herself that it would be okay. She'd lock up two muggers, get back her phone and warrant card and everything would be hunky dory.

As they approached she gave the front door another once-over. It was old and well weathered. The black paint was flaky and peeling and it didn't look as though it would put up much resistance. She took another step nearer, feeling the tension cranking up inside of her.

Scarlett gently turned the handle and leaned against the door. It was locked. She knocked authoritatively and put her ear to the door. No answer. She pulled back her clenched hand further and hammered. It brought about activity. Inside she could hear the sudden outburst of fast footsteps. Not coming near – running away.

She yelled, "They're on their toes."

Tarn shouted, "Back!" and as Scarlett stepped aside he charged forwards, flinging himself, shoulder first, against the door. His thirteen stone of muscle splintered the old lock from its frame, smashing the door inwards and sending it crashing against the hallway wall. Tarn almost fell in with it. He caught himself, regained his balance, adjusted his footing and began running. Scarlett was on his shoulder, her eyes strafing everywhere for that unknown element that sometimes caught officers out. The adrenalin had kicked in. Suddenly, there was the noise of clattering furniture at the back of the house.

Dashing into a large square kitchen, Scarlett saw that the rear door was wide open, and through a big casement window she saw a tall, slim man running across the garden towards a high ivy-covered wall. In his wake he had scattered two wooden chairs across the kitchen floor in an attempt to slow them down.

Tarn was a good couple of yards ahead of her, already heading out into the garden as she hurdled over one of the upturned chairs.

She cried out, "Stop, police!" as loud as she could.

The fleeing suspect turned and she caught a quick glimpse of a dark curly-haired twenty-something man with an olive-skin complexion. He looked panic stricken. But her view of him was only momentary. He picked up his stride and reaching the rear wall leapt at it, grabbing at ivy, finding a foothold, and in just a couple of seconds he had reached the top and was dropping over the edge.

Tarn wasn't as surefooted, and rather than leaping he started scrambling and clawing his way up. Scarlett could hear him panting.

Scarlett screamed over her radio that their suspect was fleeing, hoping that George and Ella were in the right position behind the wall to collar him.

On the opposite side, in the alley, she heard Ella and George shout and picked up the sound of echoing footsteps involved in a chase.

Tarn was on top of the wall, about to drop over into the alleyway, when he flashed back a look. He called to her, "He's getting away! He's heading towards the main road. See if there are any mobiles in the area," before rolling over and disappearing.

Scarlett knew it was pointless her following. Her three colleagues were in a much better position to pursue. She ran back into the house, changing radio channels as she went and requesting backup for an escaped suspect. She gave out her location.

Within seconds she had a response. A patrol car was only five minutes away.

Heaving a grateful sigh she bolted through the house and out the other side onto the street, heading in the direction of the fleeing suspect. Scarlett trained her ears on the radio but it was frustratingly silent. Then, fifty yards along the road, it broke into life.

It was Ella gasping an anxious cry. "Suspect down! Repeat, suspect down! He's been hit by a car! Get us an ambulance!"

Thirty-seven

Sprinting into the main thoroughfare, the first thing Scarlett saw was a silver Corsa skewed at an angle across the central white lines on the road. Either side, in both carriageways, traffic had come to a halt and was beginning to build up. She slowed almost to a standstill.

By the nearside kerb Ella Bloom was crouching over their suspect. He was lying on the tarmac in the prone position, moaning. She saw that the front of his T-shirt was heavily bloodstained, and she could hear Ella telling him that an ambulance was on its way and not to move.

George was leaning in and speaking with the driver of the lead car on the opposite side of the road. Most probably a witness, she thought.

Tarn was standing beside the angled Corsa with a grey-haired lady, who had her face in her hands. She wore a stunned expression.

As she stepped nearer she could hear the elderly lady's high-pitched voice telling him, "I wasn't driving fast. I couldn't do anything about it. He just ran out in front of me."

Tarn placed a reassuring hand on her shoulder.

As Scarlett took in the scene she could see that her team had control of everything and in that same moment a strange sensation overcame her; she felt isolated and vulnerable. She tried to tell herself that it probably wasn't as bad as it looked, but as she set her eyes on their injured, groaning suspect she knew she was only kidding herself. This was a cock-up of monumental proportions! She wasn't just in for a carpeting; a worse fate awaited her once this was over.

In the distance, coming ever closer, the wail of sirens disturbed her thinking. Emergency vehicles were on the way.

****

Within ten minutes the area had become a circus. The street was full of cops and bystanders. Traffic was moving again, but slowly, as drivers rubber-necked their way past.

Scarlett was on the kerb, shoulder to shoulder with Tarn, watching a paramedic and two ambulance crew gently manoeuvring their injured suspect onto a spine board. He was still moaning.

She had sent George and Ella back to the house to secure it and to start the search for her phone and warrant card, her thinking being that if at least they had recovered the evidence it would go some way to justifying her actions and hopefully lesson the consequences coming her way.

A couple of minutes later, while watching the emergency team load the suspect into the ambulance, from out of the corner of her eye Scarlett caught sight of a marked car pulling up opposite. The driver's door sprang open and a slightly chubby uniformed officer hauled himself out. As he stretched up she spotted the two pips on his epaulettes. The duty inspector! And he didn't look a happy bunny. Worse still, she caught sight of DI Taylor-Butler emerging from the passenger side. He had a face like thunder.

Seeing them approach made her bristle. She nudged Tarn. "Make yourself scarce. Go and see how George and Ella are getting on." She caught his questioning glance and flicked her head. "Go on, bugger off. This is my mess."

Touching her arm and giving her a reassuring look he left her side, trotting off in the direction of the house they had broken into.

DI Taylor-Butler and the duty inspector were in step as they approached.

Stopping before her, ram-rod straight, DI Taylor-Butler dramatically drew his overcoat around him. "I suppose you've got a good explanation for this, DS Macey?"

She looked him up and down. She wondered why the DI never acknowledged her by her first name. Even the gaffer called her Scarlett. And why, whenever he pronounced her by her rank, did it always sound so condescending?

Prick! She took a deep breath, eyed both inspectors and said, "He did a runner. It wasn't our fault. We told him to stop, but he just ran out from the alleyway into the main road."

"And why were you chasing him?"

"I think he might be one of the guys who stole my warrant card and mobile."

"Let me just rewind a moment. You're saying *'you think he might be'* one of the villains who mugged you?"

Attracted by sudden movement beyond the two inspectors she switched her gaze. Looking over the shoulder of DI Taylor-Butler she could see that one of the emergency crew was closing the rear doors of the ambulance. A uniformed officer was climbing into the back to provide escort to the hospital.

She brought back her gaze. In answer to his question, Scarlett nodded.

The DI screwed up his face. "And how is he linked to our murder?"

She hesitated a second, before sheepishly saying, "He's not."

"Oh, he's not. So what on earth are you doing here?"

"I got a tip-off."

"A tip-off! Do you want to expand on that?"

"I got a phone call this morning to the effect that the guys who robbed me were at an address just around the corner from here, and that if I didn't act quick my phone and warrant card would be gone."

"So what you're telling me is that you've pulled your team away from the task you were given and come over here on a wild goose chase. A wild goose chase which has got a man seriously injured."

"He's a suspect! And it wasn't a wild goose chase. I've just told you that he's one of the guys who nicked my mobile and warrant card."

"Just a minute, DS Macey! I recall that when you originally told me about your mugging a few weeks back you said you couldn't identify them. Didn't you tell me they were wearing masks?"

"I did."

"So how on earth can you say he's a suspect?"

Thinking on her feet, she answered, "My informant told me that the guys responsible for robbing me were at the address and that he had seen them with my warrant card and phone." Then she embellished again. "He told me I needed to act sharp because it was going to disappear. So that's what I did." She paused. "I used my initiative."

DI Taylor-Butler glared at her. "What you did, DS Macey, is acted irrationally and without permission. Your poor judgment has caused serious injury to a man." A viperous sneer crept across his mouth. "You realise the IPCC is going to be all over this don't you?"

Scarlett felt her chest tighten. The involvement of the Independent Police Complaints Commission could mean suspension.

The DI said, "This informant. He is registered, I assume."

She answered softly, "No."

"So you've acted on information that has not come from a registered source?"

"He's someone I know. I trust him."

He shook his head. The sneer was changing to a wicked smile. "And I'm guessing the house where this suspect lived – you had a warrant to gain entry?"

Scarlett felt her stomach gripe. For a second she scrutinised the DI's face. That grin of his reminded her of a jackal. She was revving up inside. She knew he was belittling her in front of the duty inspector and yet she couldn't do a thing about it. He was highlighting every rule she'd broken. For a moment she stood there trying to think of something to say and then her radio broke into life. It was Tarn, asking directly for her.

Still meeting DI Taylor-Butler's eyes, she gave him a look which told him she needed to answer her radio. Then she depressed the receive button and responded, "DS Macey. Go ahead, Tarn."

"Serge, you need to get round here. We've found a body!"

Thirty-eight

Scarlett didn't even wait to get permission from DI Taylor-Butler for her to leave as she spun around and sprinted back to number forty-four.

Halfway down the street she spotted Tarn by the front doorway looking out for her.

Slowing her pace a few yards from the door she drew in a deep breath and gathered her composure. "You say you've found a body?"

Tarn beckoned behind him with his head, and stepping aside to let Scarlett pass he replied, "It's in the cellar. George and Ella are down there. It's a bit of a mess."

From her coat pocket she dragged out a pair of forensic latex gloves and pulled them on. Then, stepping into the doorway to the cellar she stood for a moment, facing a flight of stone steps, flanked either side by flaking lime-washed brick walls. A dull glow reflecting off the cellar's damp floor guided her eyes downwards. Already the temperature was cooler in this space and she caught the familiar tainted coppery smell of stale blood. She wondered what lay below.

As if reading her mind, Tarn, standing behind her, said, "I'll stay up here if you don't mind, I've already seen it, and I can tell you it's not a pretty sight."

Without glancing back she responded, "No problem. While you're up here, I want this place sealing off right now. And get hold of a pathologist and CSI." Placing a foot on the first step, she added, "Just a thought, as well. Have you checked over the rest of the house?"

"Not had the time yet. We'd just made a start when George found the body."

"Okay, get on with that then. We don't want to miss any more surprises." As Scarlett caught the sound of Tarn's turning footfalls she called back over her shoulder, "And while you're at it see if you can find my mobile and warrant card." Then, finishing off the sentence, by mumbling beneath her breath to herself, she ended, "They're what caused this shit of a mess in the first place."

Scarlett descended slowly and found herself in a long narrow room lit by a single bare bulb, dangling from a beam. The walls were a mix of brick and stone and like the stairway had been lime-washed. Here and there was evidence of damp in the form of mildew and black mould between the mortar. To her right, halfway along, was a bench constructed of brick with a stone slab. Upon it she could see a quantity of tools She stepped nearer and looked. A hammer, chisel, fretsaw and three long-bladed kitchen knives. Parts of the stone surface were stained. Scarlett thought it looked like blood. Her mind began racing.

As if from nowhere, Ella's head appeared through a gap at the far end of the room, making Scarlett jump. She clutched her chest. "Bloody hell, Ella!"

"Sorry, Serge. We're through here." Her head disappeared from Scarlett's field of vision.

Scarlett skirted past the bench, taking another look at its contents, before pulling her gaze back to where Ella had poked her head through. Before her was another doorway. She walked through into a much larger room, lit once again by a single bare bulb. This room, though, was not whitewashed, and so the play of light was not as good and most of the corners lay in shadow. Ella and George were in the centre of the room standing directly beneath the light, bathing their heads in a halo. By George's side was the corpse. Stepping forward, Scarlett targeted her gaze upon the body. It was naked and she could see it was male, though it wasn't whole. Both legs had been cut off, as had been the right arm. The dismembered limbs lay next to the severed joints. Beside the body was a bloodstained long-bladed kitchen knife and a small hand grinder plugged into an extension cable. She redirected her eyes to George and pointed to the knife and hand grinder.

George met her gaze. "Ella and I have already spotted them. Are you thinking what I'm thinking?"

Scarlett nodded. She was already on the same wavelength as the big man. She had known George a long time. He had been a detective when she joined and one who she had quickly learned she could rely upon to get a thorough job done. More importantly, he was someone whom she could trust. When she had first met him at the scene of a street robbery she had been impressed at how imposing he looked. He was not only tall at six foot seven, but back then, in 2002, he worked out. Over the years she had seen him pile the pounds on and his presence wasn't nearly as intimidating; nevertheless, she knew she would still rather have him in her corner if things ever turned sticky.

George was waiting for a response. Scarlett said, "Right, get this area sealed off as well. I want everybody and their grandmother here."

As she took a step back to the doorway she could hear Tarn yelling out for her. Increasing her pace, she made her way back to the steps.

Tarn was at the top of the stairs, looking down. On an anxious note he called, "Something's just happened with the suspect!"

Thirty-nine

Outside number forty-four Scarlett checked her watch. It had been forty minutes since she had called things in and everything was coming together. Scanning the street she saw that a sterile barrier, ten yards either side of the house, had been established, and four uniformed officers were on sentry duty keeping back a small number of curious residents who were eager to find out what was going on, plus a couple of journalists who had shown up, baying for answers. Behind her, four crime scene investigators were in the process of erecting a tent around the front door, to further protect the integrity of the scene. Tarn, George and Ella were inside with the crime scene manager.

Beyond the barrier, she caught a glimpse of DCI Diane Harris's car turning into the street. She lost sight of it as it pulled toward the kerb and disappeared out of view behind the bustle of onlookers. Her stomach emptied and she took a deep breath. She knew she would have some explaining to do to the DCI beyond the appraising her of their body find. A few minutes later, against the backdrop of diminishing daylight, Diane Harris appeared ghost-like in a white protective suit, marching towards her. Scarlett stepped off the footpath to meet her. She noted the seriousness etched on her face.

"Okay, tell me exactly what we've got. I've picked up some of it already from Hayden on the phone. And I also understand that we've got a suspect on the run, who's possibly the killer."

Scarlett could feel her neck getting warm. She guessed she was colouring up. "Has he told you how we came to find the body?"

"I've got his version of events."

Scarlett could see her mouth was set tight as she spoke. Not a good sign. She gulped. "Look, Boss, I take responsibility for my actions here, especially pulling off the house-to-house enquiries, but I got a phone call from a trusted source who told me that my stolen mobile was at this location and rightly or wrongly I decided to act."

"Well the gist of what you've said is the same, but his choice of words are somewhat different. Go on"

"Well, we got here at just after two. Tarn and I took the front and I sent George and Ella round the back. When I did the knock we heard a commotion inside the house and someone running away. We forced entry and saw this guy – the suspect – making a run for it across the garden. We chased after him but he got over the wall, and as you know he managed to get to the top of the street, where he ran out into the path of a car and was knocked down." Scarlett watched her DCI nod. She continued. "While dealing with the accident, the DI turned up with the duty inspector so I sent Tarn, George and Ella back here to see if they could recover my phone and warrant card. That's when they found the body."

Diane Harris nodded again. "In the cellar, I'm told?"

Scarlett answered with a nod.

"And I understand the body is that of a male and some of the limbs have been removed?"

"Yes. Both legs and his right arm. We think we disturbed our suspect just as he was cutting the body up."

"And we don't yet know who the victim is, or the suspect?"

Scarlett shook her head. "We never got the chance to speak to him. After the accident he was uncommunicative and there was blood all over the front of his T-shirt. We thought he was badly injured. I'm guessing, especially since finding the body, that the blood was actually from the victim and wasn't as a result of the accident, and obviously given that he's escaped, he wasn't as badly injured as we thought."

"It would appear so. Apparently within a couple of minutes of the ambulance leaving the scene he attacked the escorting PC and used his own gas on him. The paramedic in the back also got a face-full as well. The suspect was last seen disappearing into a nearby estate. We have enough resources out there searching for him including the helicopter, and CCTV are looking as well, but he appears to have well and truly gone to ground. I've given Hayden the job of co-ordinating everything." She paused and gave Scarlett an enquiring look. "Have your team started going through the house yet to see if we can get any IDs?"

"They're inside with the crime scene manager now. That's one of their priorities. And I've got the pathologist on his way to examine the body."

"Okay, well done. You seem to have everything in hand on this front." Then her voice took on a more severe note. "But this

155

doesn't let you off the hook. I'm going to do what I need to inside and then you and I are going to have a little chat."

****

Pulling her facemask down, Scarlett lifted her head and drew in a deep breath as she climbed the last step and emerged from the cellar. She had been cooped up in the confined space for the best part of an hour suffering the corrupt smell from the dismembered corpse and decided she needed not just some fresh air but a change of scenery. She had left DCI Diane Harris down there with the pathologist and the crime scene manager. Stepping into the hallway she was surprised to see DI Taylor-Butler in the front doorway. He was looking up the staircase, his face wearing a troubled look, and she noticed that he wasn't wearing a protective suit.

"Do you want something, Boss?"

He jumped, pulling back his gaze. His face flushed as if he had been caught out doing something he shouldn't. Then, just as quickly, his appearance shifted, taking on a more composed look.

"I'm looking for DCI Harris."

Scarlett thumbed over her shoulder. "She's down there with the pathologist and the CSI manager. Is there anything I can help you with?" Then, dipping her head towards him, she said, "You shouldn't be in here without your protective suit on."

His face tightened. "I do know about forensics, DS Macey. I've no intention of coming into the house. And no, I don't need your help, thank you. I think you've done enough damage for one day, don't you? It's the DCI I need to speak with regarding *your* escaped suspect."

She could feel her hackles rise. She took a deep breath, pulled up her face mask and turned her back on him. She muttered, "I'll tell DCI Harris you want to speak to her," and walked back towards the musty cellar.

****

Scarlett sat in the front seat of Diane Harris's car, fiddling with her recovered mobile. Her phone had been found during the first

156

cursory sweep of the house. They had visited both floors, double-checking every room to make certain there was no one else in the house before everything was sealed off for forensics, and Ella Bloom had found it, together with her warrant card, lying on a bedside cabinet in one of the second-floor bedrooms.

She finger-tapped the screen, checking the phone log. The battery was very low but it hadn't been used. With a feeling of relief she turned it off before it died and dropped it into her bag.

Next to her, the DCI was on her BlackBerry. She could make out that she was speaking with DI Taylor-Butler, requesting another update, and although she could only hear one side of the conversation it was enough for her to gather that their suspect was still at large. She listened in as the DCI brought him up to date with the state of things at number forty-four; forensics had already found further evidence of butchery down in the cellar, and there was significant splattering of blood across the tiles in the bathroom on the first floor. "There's a fair bit of work to do here, Hayden. Forensics are setting up lights so that they can work through the night and I've persuaded the pathologist to do the PM this evening as well, so I'm going to be tied up for the next few hours at least. Can you make sure everything's sorted back at the incident room and carry on co-ordinating the search for the prisoner?" The DCI finished by telling him to rally the team together for an eight-thirty p.m. briefing.

DCI Diane Harris ended her call and studied her BlackBerry screen for a moment. Then with a long exasperated sigh she pocketed it and shuffled sideways to face Scarlett.

"Bit of a fuck-up don't you think?"

"I'm sorry, Boss, I just didn't think…"

Diane Harris raised her hand, brokering Scarlett's silence. "That's just it Scarlett, sometimes you don't think." She held Scarlett's gaze. "Look, you're bright, enthusiastic, hard working, and as a supervisor I couldn't wish to have anyone better, but sometimes you're your own worst enemy. You know Hayden has a downer on you and yet you do everything you can to wind him up. You don't need me to tell you that he's pretty pissed off with you at the moment. He wants you off the team. He's blaming all of this on you. Without going into any great depth as to my conversation with him, words such as reckless, belligerent and maverick were used. In fact I'll be honest: he wants to pursue a neglect-of-duty discipline against you."

Scarlett bit down on her lip. "Jesus, Guv."

"Jesus is putting it mildly, Scarlett. I have to say, as regards your initial actions I'm pretty pissed off with you as well. Your saving grace in all this is the discovery of that man's body." She paused for a moment, her gaze drifting over Scarlett's shoulder, somewhere outside the car. A couple of seconds later she snapped it back and locked onto Scarlett's eyes. "Because I have faith in you, and because I'm also not too impressed with Hayden and his childish sniping myself at the moment, I've stuck up for you. But this is the last time. I've told him that you rang me this morning and told me the info you'd got about your phone and warrant card and that I'd given you permission to go to that house. I know he doesn't believe me, but he can't do anything about it." Pausing for a moment, she added, "And yes, there will be an IPCC investigation because of the accident, but the fact that your prisoner attacked an officer and escaped means he's not seriously injured. And also, given that he's wanted for murder it won't go anywhere, so you can rest easy on that front."

Scarlett could feel her eyes starting to water. "Thanks, Guv."

"Don't thank me. I did it because of all the hard work you've put in recently. I know what your qualities are and right now I need you as part of my squad. The way you can start repaying me is to just do your job. No more going off at a tangent. Yes?"

She wiped away a tear from one eye with a knuckle. "Yes. I'm sorry."

Breaking into a half-smile, DCI Harris said, "Apology accepted. Now get yourself together, Scarlett. We've got a murderer to catch."

Forty

The atmosphere in the Major Incident Suite was a mix of excitement and anticipation. The team were buzzing. The investigation had taken an unexpected twist, but they were ready for the challenge.

DCI Diane Harris poured herself a glass of water and while taking a sip looked at the pictures on the large screen behind her. Three crime scene photographs, taken from different angles, depicted the naked dismembered man laying across the bloodstained brick floor in the cellar of the house in Wandsworth. Beside them was a blown-up page from a passport presenting the head-and-shoulders photograph of a dark-haired, handsome young man and his identification details.

Diane set down her glass and faced her audience. "We believe we have identified our victim in the cellar as twenty-two-year-old Henrikas Astrosky. Mr Astrosky met quite a nasty death. He was stabbed three times in the chest, four times in the back and once in the neck. He also has numerous defence injuries to his hands and arms where he has put up some form of resistance. The pathologist says none of the wounds in themselves would have proved fatal. His death would have been as a result of significant blood loss." She paused for a moment before continuing, "Henrikas was Lithuanian. At the moment, identification has been by done by matching his face to the passport we found in one of the bedrooms. We don't know if those are his correct details, but the passport appears to be authentic. We've submitted his details to Interpol and they will be liaising with the Lithuanian authorities. We are also checking with Immigration to see if he came legitimately into this country, and if so when and where." The DCI picked up the remote and added two fresh pictures to the screen: the headless and handless female corpse in the suitcase, and the assembled female body parts found in the dumpsters on the Patmore Estate. "Professor Niall Lynch, the pathologist who attended the latest scene in Wandsworth, not only examined the body but also the knives and hand-grinder found there, and following his post mortem has concluded that the same instruments used to dismember Henrikas here were also used on our other two victims Greta Aglinsky, and our still as-yet-unknown female found in the Thames. Although the forensic work is still in the very early stages, CSI are pretty confident that the house in Wandsworth is the site where all our three victims met their deaths. There is significant blood staining, some of which is quite old, not only in the cellar but also in the bathroom on the first floor, where attempts have been made to clean it up. Though, thankfully, not too successfully. Plus, in one of the bedrooms they also found an identical suitcase to that which our headless body was found in. And I'm told the place is full of dabs, so hopefully we'll come up trumps with a fingerprint hit for our killer." She set down the remote, picked her glass back up and took another drink. "As regards the house, we have intelligence reports that the premise's were being used as a brothel. Scarlett and her team have spoken with a few of the neighbours, and although none of them were willing to go on record, they have confirmed that the house was being used for that purpose. We've learned that a number of regular females used the place and it had daily male visitors. This latest incident has certainly brought about developments, but it's also created a lot of work. Unfortunately, time's run away from us tonight to conduct any more enquiries, but tomorrow each of you will have a bundle of actions. Especially, we need to focus on our escaped suspect. He is at the centre of all this. So tomorrow we concentrate on identifying him." She finished her water. "Unless anyone has any questions then we'll call it a day."

****

It was after ten p.m. before Scarlett got home. She was drained and she could feel a headache coming on. From the fridge she took out a carton of cranberry juice and poured herself a glass, and finding two paracetamol in her bag she swilled them down. Standing in front of the fridge and eyeing the contents made her realise how hungry she was, but all that remained was one pack of opened ham, some cheese and some limp and shrivelled vegetables, reminding her that she hadn't shopped for over a week. Letting off a curse she binned everything and switched her attention to the freezer. All she found there was a frozen sliced loaf. She prised off a couple of slices and slotted them into the toaster.

While waiting for the frozen bread to toast she rang Alex on her BlackBerry. She'd not spoken with him since that morning and knew she owed him this call.

He answered almost immediately.

Scarlett said, "Sorry I haven't got back to you until now. You wouldn't believe the day I've had."

"Did you get your phone and warrant card then?"

"Certainly did, thank you."

Before she could continue, Alex asked on a high note, "And did you get your muggers as well?"

"Funny you should ask that." She gave him a re-run of her day, catching the noise of the toaster racking out the toast just as she ended her story. The smell of the cooked bread wafted across her nostrils, invigorating her tastebuds.

"Wow! So a result then?"

"Well, of sorts. Letting the suspect get away is a bit of a bummer and I got a bit of a bollocking for going to the house without permission."

"You're kidding me. You find a body, catch the killer and you get a bollocking! It's not your fault he's escaped."

"It's not really to do with that. Me and my DI don't hit it off. He went off on one because I went to the house without permission in the first place. And when he asked me the source of my information I wouldn't divulge your name, which pissed him off even more. He accused me of being reckless and failing to take orders. You know how it is with your army background."

He sighed, "Tell me about it."

"Anyway, the DI wanted to make something of it but my DCI's been great about it. She's gone out on a limb and backed me up, which has put the DI's nose out of joint. I'll have to watch my back for a while but it felt good getting one over on him."

"So I guess you're gonna have your work cut out over the next few days?"

"You're right about that."

"What do you want to do about Rose then? I don't know how long she's gonna be at the Notting Hill address. The council could get a court order next week."

Scarlett took a deep breath. After a quick think she said, "Look I'm scheduled for this weekend off. I'll ring you Friday night as soon as I finish work. If you're up for it we'll go to the flat then." Hearing Alex agree she bid him goodnight and ended the call.

Biting into dry toast the image of the woman she had seen down in the Underground subway sprang inside her head. She dearly wanted it to be Rose and she dearly wanted to see her after all this time.

But before that there was other work to do. A serial killer was still out there.

Forty-one

Pulling up her face mask Scarlett entered number forty-four with Tarn following. They had been given the task that morning of liaising with the crime scene manager, retrieving any exhibits of note and bringing back to the evening briefing the status of the forensic examination. Other members of Scarlett's team were doing house-to-house along the street, while DS Gary Ashdown's team had gone back to the Patmore Estate over in Battersea.

Scarlett stopped in the hallway and listened. She could hear shuffling noises and voices in the rooms above. She pulled her face mask away from her mouth and called out the crime scene manager's name. Within seconds there was a call back from the next floor. She peered up the stairway and saw Mason Gregory peering over the banister.

He called down, "And to what do we owe this pleasure?"

"Hi Mason, just come to see how you're getting on," Scarlett replied.

"We've done the cellar and ground floor and we've almost finished this floor. We should have the whole house done by today."

"Found anything of note?"

With a smile he said, "Some interesting apparatus in the bedrooms up here, which you're more than welcome to come and look at. It's made me realise I've led a very sheltered life."

"As if, Mason Gregory."

He let out a laugh.

"Any more surprises?"

"No more bodies, if that's what you mean. We've videoed and photographed the basement and done a thorough search. The evidence certainly confirms that more than one body has been cut up down there. We've swabbed the area and got samples, so DNA should give us an idea if more than three have been done down there."

"And what about up there? The bathroom's been used hasn't it?"

"There's certainly lots of blood spatter in the bath and on several rows of tiles above it, which looks to me as though there's been a bit of a fight up here. An effort has been made to clean it up, but whoever's done it has not made a very good job of it. The bathroom door's been forced as well. If you ask me, one of our victims has taken refuge in there before being attacked, and if I were to lay my reputation on the line I'd say it was the man you found in the cellar yesterday. The bloodstains between some of the tiles look to be quite fresh."

"Mind if we have a look round?"

"Be my guest."

Scarlett replaced her face mask and made her way to the cellar. Pausing on the top step she recalled yesterday's events. The coppery smell of blood had lessened. The strongest smell now assailing her nostrils was one of damp. She made her way to the bottom. Tarn was only a couple of steps behind. As before, a single light bulb lit the way. Staying away from the lime-washed walls she negotiated the thin corridor, carefully skirting past the stone and brick slab. As she passed she saw atop the slab a yellow plastic pyramid marker placed next to a dark stain and she noted that the tools she had seen on it yesterday were no longer there. They would be in a sealed exhibit bag in the back of one of the forensic vans.

At the end of the corridor Scarlett and Tarn stepped through the doorway into the main cellar chamber, where they halted and took in the surroundings. Four tripod lights had been strategically placed, one in each corner of the room, but currently they were not ablaze. Dotted around the floor were more yellow forensic markers and in the dim glow Scarlett made out more dark stains covering the brickwork. The image of the dismembered man flashed back inside her head, but the vision was weak and only fleeting. It disappeared in seconds.

Scarlett nudged Tarn. "Come on, I've seen what I need to see down here. Forensics have sorted it. Let's have a look upstairs."

The front reception room was gloomy; heavy maroon drapes were drawn across a large bay window. And it smelt fusty. Some of that smell was stale cigarette smoke. Two large sunken tan-leather settees and a wide armchair dominated the room. An eighties-style pattern carpet in garish colours, well worn and heavily stained, covered the floor. In one corner, next to a faux gas fire in a black Victorian surround was a large-screen TV on a heavy black glass and metal stand. Scarlett noticed a number of porn DVDs scattered in front of the TV, and hanging on the walls around the room she took in gilt-framed prints of Asian males and females in erotic poses. There were no forensic markers in this room but the furnishings and smooth surfaces were covered in fine metallic powder where they had been dusted for fingerprints.

Returning back to the hall, Scarlett and Tarn took the stairs up to the first floor. They met Mason Gregory on the landing.

"We're done here. Just got the floor above to do and that's it. Feel free to have a nosy. Except for the bathroom, where we've found the blood, all we've got is loads of semen stains and dabs."

Scarlett watched him take the stairs up to the second floor and then stepped into the nearest bedroom. What struck her first as she pushed open the door was the colour scheme – crimson-red walls with a black ceiling. She stopped in the doorway and ran her gaze around the room. A large mirror, fastened to the ceiling above a four-poster bed covered with red-and-black satin sheets. The top sheet was half off the bed, giving her a view of a heavily sex-stained bottom sheet. A shudder ran through her and she screwed up her face. On a velvet-padded wingchair next to the bed was a black leather full-head mask and a whip. Then she took in the leather restraints at each corner of the bed.

"Can have some fun here, hey?" said Tarn, leaning over her shoulder.

"Disgusting," exclaimed Scarlett. "Just look at those sheets."

"You can be so picky some times."

Scarlett elbowed her partner and backed out of the room, pulling closed the door.

"Let's have a look at the bathroom."

In sharp contrast to the bedroom this room was bright and airy. It was fully tiled in white, with a black border running around halfway up the walls, and contained a relatively new white bathroom suite. On some of the tiles above the bath there were fluorescent yellow stickers, and staining from the Luminol spray which had been used to find the blood. It appeared as if a lot had been uncovered, given the number of marks and streaks she could see.

She was about to close the door when a shout came from above. It was Mason Gregory.

"I think you two need to come up and see this!"

Scarlett exchanged a brief glance with Tarn and then the pair trotted up the stairs.

Mason Gregory stood in the doorway of the bedroom at the front of the house. It was the room where Ella Bloom had found Scarlett's phone and warrant card. In his hand he held out a burgundy-coloured booklet. He said, "We've just found this in a coat pocket in the wardrobe."

Forty-two

Talk in the major incident briefing room died down as DCI Diane Harris strolled to the front of the room. There was a bounce in her step and she looked remarkably refreshed given that she had been working over twelve hours. She wore a dark-blue knee-length skirt and matching jacket with a white cotton blouse. Her hair had been pulled back into a ponytail, though a few strands at the front had worked themselves loose, dangling over her ears. She made an attempt at brushing them back as she faced her team.

On screen behind her appeared the front cover of a Lithuanian passport, together with the passport's polycarbonated personal data page, which portrayed a tanned, curly-haired young man.

"Our escaped suspect," she announced, flicking her head backwards. "Twenty-three-year-old Andrius Machuta, and as you can see from his passport, like all our victims, he's from Lithuania. Finding this at the house has been our first bit of good luck in this enquiry and has moved things up significantly. We've already faxed this to Interpol, and although we have his passport we've now put out an all-ports warning, should he try and get another one and attempt to leave the country. We've also circulated his details and his photograph. Once we put out his photo across the media the pressure will be on him." Pausing and issuing a smile she continued, "Forensics finished with the house in Wandsworth today and I'm told there is an abundance of material to process, including blood and other trace evidence, as well as fibres and literary dozens of fingerprints, which is not surprising given what the house has been used for. Neighbours have confirmed it is a brothel. A number of complaints have apparently been made to the local council about it, and one neighbour has been keeping the car numbers of all visitors, so we have lots to be getting on with. Some of those actions will be prioritised. As to the owners of that house, however, I'm afraid we have drawn a blank. It was bought in cash eighteen months ago through a foreign company based in the Cayman Islands. That company has issued shares which are held in Dubai, so we've no means of finding out who is behind the company." Her mouth tightened. "The people behind this are no amateurs, and until we get hold of our suspect we are stuck with not being able to find out who is behind this. What I have no doubts about is that what we have uncovered here is a prostitution ring involving illegal immigrants and that the people behind it are ruthless." She let what she had said sink in. "The only other thing of any note is with regards to the black four-by-four. The policewoman at Putney who was dealing with a hit-and-run RTC involving a black Audi Q7 has e-mailed us with details of the incident." She glanced at some notes she had made. "The accident happened around four-fifty p.m. on the evening of the day before our first victim, the headless body in the suitcase, was found. Apparently the black four-by-four ran into the back of a builder's van in heavy traffic on the A316." She raised her eyes and checked a few faces and added slowly, "The location is less than a mile from the house in Wandsworth." She held their looks for a few seconds before continuing, "The van driver was already stopped in traffic so he jumped out to view the damage and speak with the driver. As he approached the Audi, he says the driver was having some sort of fight with a young girl. The driver was leaning over the back of his seat and had hold of the girl by her hair. He got the impression that she was trying to get away and he was punching her in the head." Diane Harris glanced up from her notes. She still held everyone's attention. She continued, "The van driver banged on the window and the Audi driver shouted back at him to 'fuck off'. He shouted back that he was going to call for the police and at that the Audi driver started the car and drove away. The van driver had to jump out of the way or he'd have been run over. Although he didn't get a good look at him he has given us a basic description of the Audi driver and he also got the registration number. He describes the driver as being white with a shaven head and overweight. The number checks out as belonging to a black Audi Q7, but the last registered keeper notified DVLA nine months ago that he had sold it. We've contacted that owner this afternoon and he's told us that he sold the car for cash to a shaven-headed overweight man who he believed was foreign. We pushed on the foreign bit but all he was able to say is that he believed the man to be Eastern European. We've arranged to get e-fits done tomorrow with both these witnesses." She broke off, eyeing the room, and folded her note. Then she said, "With regards the description of the girl, unfortunately the van driver hasn't been able to give us much at all. Just about as basic as before. All we have is that he got the impression that the girl was an older teenager, probably eighteen or nineteen, and that she was white, slim build, with longish brown hair. He thought she was wearing a silver-coloured vest-type top. That's it, I'm afraid." She finished off her briefing with a round-robin of her team. Detectives fed back on their assignments but there was nothing of significance. She gave a quick clap and said, "Okay, that's it for today. Tomorrow it's the actions I've already mentioned, plus I want someone to liaise with ANPR and feed in the reg number of the Audi, see if we can get a hit and, fingers crossed, the image will be good enough to pick the driver. And we finish off house-to-house in Battersea and Wandsworth." As the team rose from their seats Diane Harris pulled away the elastic from her ponytail and shook out her hair. Feeding the freed tresses through her fingers she eased back her neck. She could feel the tension between her shoulder blades. It had been another long day and she could feel the tiredness creeping up. She was ready for home.

Forty-three

Skender turned off the steaming shower, dragged his towel off the hook and smoothing a hand over his recently shaved scalp he swiped away clinging water droplets before vigorously towelling his upper body. Stepping out into the drying area he began slowly strolling towards the locker room. After a few yards, checking he was the only one in the changing room, he stopped at the full-length mirror and looked, flexing his pumped-up chest and arms. He always felt tight following a weights session and liked to check his pose before finally drying himself.

The muted sound of his ringtone coming from inside his locker interrupted him. He hoped it was the call he'd been waiting for. Quickly wrapping his towel around his waist and knotting it, he hurried to where he had dumped his sweaty gym clothes before jumping into the shower. Picking out his jogging bottoms, he removed his locker key from the pocket and unlocked the metal cabinet. His mobile was still ringing. He checked the listed caller before answering; it was who he had been expecting, though the name listed wasn't his real name.

He answered, "I hope you're going to give me good news?

He listened to the man on the other end. When he had finished he said steadily, "Good. You let me know the minute he's found. You make sure I get the first call before you go and get him. Understand?"

The man spoke some more. Then Skender answered, "Listen, I don't give a fuck. I need to get to him first. If he is caught he can do us a lot of damage, including you." He let his last sentence hit home and then followed up with, "You give me that call. That's what I pay you for – to sort out problems. So sort it out." Then on a menacing note he added, "You'd better not let me down."

He ended the call and stared at the mirror. His reflection had a hardened, granite look.

Forty-four

Alex leaned forward in the driving seat of his car and cleared the misted windscreen with the back of his gloved hand. He gazed out through the smudge he had made.

"How's the investigation going? I see on the news you've named a chief suspect."

Scarlett wiped her own side of the windscreen, clearing her view of Kensington Place, where they had parked up half an hour earlier. Keeping her eyes fixed on the road outside she replied, "We had to do that. We know nothing about this Andrius. He's well and truly gone to ground since his escape. We have no idea who his friends or associates are and to be honest we're also struggling to track down anyone connected with the house in Wandsworth. It's as if everyone has disappeared into a big black hole.

"What about the owner?"

"That's another problem. The place is registered to a company in the Cayman Islands. No way of tracking them down."

"Sounds like a real tangled web."

"The whole investigation is tangled. Three dead bodies! We still haven't managed to identify the first victim. We believe she's Lithuanian, only because the other two are and of course the suspect."

"It'll come good in the end. It always does. Just a bit of patience and a bit of luck."

Scarlett sighed. "Hope so."

"A bit like this job."

Scarlett pulled her eyes away from the road. "I'm hoping we can end this tonight." She held a sideways view of Alex. He had his gaze fixed beyond the windscreen. "We've chased around enough now. I've got my fingers crossed she's here."

The windscreen was starting to mist up again. He gave it another wipe. "That's if it is Rose we've been following."

"It is Rose, I'm telling you. I know it's been over ten years since I last saw her, but that look she gave me on the Underground. She recognised me and I recognised her."

"Well, we'll soon see won't we?" He reached for the door handle, "Are you good to go then? If we stay here much longer, someone is going to clock us and report us. Or worse still, one of that lot susses us." He motioned his head towards the block of maisonettes. "Then we will have blown it."

"That's the last thing I need."

"To be honest, Scarlett, we have to do this tonight. My council contact tells me they've got a court order for this place. The bailiffs'll be here either tomorrow or the day after to evict them."

Scarlett lifted her bag out from the footwell, delved into it and pulled out the A5 colour photograph she had secreted there before leaving work yesterday. She sprang her door, triggering the interior light.

Alex snapped into action and deftly turned it off.

Scarlett screwed up her face and mouthed, "Sorry."

He dipped his head at the photo. "Are you sure this is going to work?"

"It should give us a foot in the door." She pushed the passenger door wider and swung out her legs. "Come on, partner. If anyone asks, you're a detective."

He sprang his own door. "Do I get a badge?"

****

Scarlett and Alex made their way up the stone stairwell as quietly as possible to the fourth floor, where they stepped out onto the balcony.

"It's the third flat along," said Alex, nodding the way ahead. "Look: you can see the flag hanging out of the window."

Scarlett tiptoed ahead. Yards from the flat door, she saw clearly the black-and-white anarchist flag Alex had mentioned, hanging from the opened top light. She also picked up the sounds of a couple of guitars being strummed and several people singing, coming from inside the flat. She didn't recognise the song. It sounded like some folk ballad. With a brief look Scarlett checked Alex was okay. He returned a nod and she banged loudly on the flat door.

The music and singing stopped. For a good ten seconds there was silence, then a male voice shouted, "Who is it?"

It made Scarlett jump. Composing herself, she replied, "Police."

There was another long pause. Scarlett picked out the sounds of scuffling.

Alex broke into a smile. He whispered, "Probably getting rid of the gear!"

After a few more seconds the man shouted from behind the door, "What do you want, man?"

"To talk to you," Scarlett replied.

"What about?"

"A missing girl."

There was another pause and then a female voice piped up. "What missing girl? What's her name?"

Scarlett said, "Look, just open the door so I can talk. This is not a bust. We've got a fifteen-year-old girl who's been reported missing and someone has told us she could be here. I just want to check that out."

"There's no fifteen-year-old girl here," the woman's voice replied. "There's no one that young with us."

"Look, just open the door, will you? I need to do a quick check and then I'm gone. As I say, this is no bust and I'm not here to turn you out. I just want to check things out."

Scarlett could hear soft voices exchanging with one another behind the door. A couple more voices had joined the man and woman in the hall. She couldn't make out what was being said. Then she heard the sound of things being dragged and scraped back, and a chain and bolt being released before the door finally opened. A thin, straggly haired man in a green combat jacket appeared. He held on firmly to the door. Scarlett recognised him as the man she and Alex had followed over a week ago. She watched him scrutinising her. Seeing his face take on a puzzled look she shied away her head. She knew he was racking his brains trying to work out where it was he had seen her, so she quickly flashed her warrant card, pocketed it and blocking his view of her face she held up the A5 photograph she had brought from work. It was a photo of a blonde-haired teenage girl. Yesterday afternoon she had furtively removed it from a missing-from-home file Uniform were dealing with back at the station.

"This is who we're looking for. Her name's Rachel."

He studied the photo. "Never seen her. I'm telling you man, she's not here."

"Do you mind if me and my colleague just check? Just to satisfy ourselves, so we can tell our boss."

The sentry turned around to face a man and two women standing a couple of yards behind him in the hallway. Scarlett watched them all exchanging glances. He turned back to face her and on a raised note said, "We've no one with that name staying here. I'm telling you she's not here. Now, will you kindly go?"

Scarlett hardened her look. "Look, my friend, we can do this the easy or the hard way. The easy way is we come in do a quick check of the place, satisfy ourselves she's not here and leave. The hard way is I now get on my phone and call up a dozen of my colleagues and we give this place a turning over. I'm pretty sure we'll find some gear here and then we bust the whole lot of you for possession and you spend an uncomfortable night in the cells. Now, which is it to be?"

He loosened his grip of the door. "And that's all you're here for?"

Scarlett waved the photograph. "Honest. We just want to make sure she's not hiding out here and then, once we're satisfied, we're on our way. That's the last you'll see of us. Do you think if this was a bust only the two of us would show up?"

The man turned back again and flashed the others an acquiescent look and then stepped back, opening up the gap.

Scarlett stepped into the hallway with Alex tightly behind her. Her stomach fluttered nervously as she brushed past the doorman. As he closed the door she saw an old armchair and two long wooden buttresses leaning against the wall – the items she had heard being dragged away before the door was opened.

In the room at the end of the hallway a light was blazing. Following the man they passed a bare staircase leading to the rooms above. He led Scarlett and Alex into a large square room occupied by a ragtag-looking bunch comprising seven men and three women. She knew from what Alex had told her that the squatters were a bunch of musicians and street artists. Not the types to be confrontational, but nevertheless they outnumbered her and Alex four to one and she slipped a hand into her coat pocket, wrapping her fingers around her police-issue incapacitant spray.

The group were lounging around the room on sleeping bags and old mattresses. Rucksacks spewing out their contents were dotted around, giving the place an untidy look. It stunk of cannabis, though there was none in sight. A window was open at the far end; Scarlett remembered what Alex had said earlier and could guess where the spliffs had gone. Looking around the room, Scarlett checked the faces again, though she hadn't spotted Rose when she'd entered. The expression on the face of the man who had answered the door had changed.

Scarlett knew that look.

Racketing his head between her and Alex he arrowed a finger. On a raised note he said, "I know you two. You're the guys who chased me and Rose on the Underground."

At that moment, behind her, Scarlett picked up the sound of clomping feet on bare boards; someone was rushing down the stairs. She spun around just in time to catch a glimpse of a flaxen-haired girl in jeans and a parka making for the door. She shouted for her stop. The girl reached the handle, turned it rapidly, flung the door open and was out through the entrance even before Scarlett had made a step.

"Alex, she's getting away!" Scarlett yelled and set off after her. By the time she'd reached the outside walkway the girl was fleeing into the stairwell. She screamed "Stop!" but it drew no reaction as the girl disappeared down the stairs.

Fuck!

Haring after her, Scarlett dashed into the stairwell, saw the girl two flights below and leapt after her, taking the stairs two at a time. By the time the girl had reached the bottom Scarlett had made ground and was only one flight behind.

At the bottom of the stairs the girl flung out a hand and straight-armed the entrance door, half bursting, half falling out onto the footpath. Scarlett followed.

Spinning away left, the girl raced towards the main road. Scarlett was only yards behind now and screamed at the top of her voice, "Rose, for Christ's sake, stop!"

Her cry brought about a response.

Forty-five

Scarlett had a firm hold of Rose's parka sleeve as she led her toward Alex's car. He triggered the locks and Scarlett opened the back door. As she steered her into the rear Rose made a feeble attempt at shucking her off. Scarlett gripped Rose's sleeve tighter.

Rose stopped resisting, threw her an indignant look and said, "There's no need for this, I'm not going to run away." As she dropped into the seat she added, "Anyway what's with the tough-cop stuff, Scarl?"

Scarlett flashed a look of surprise. Another memory triggered. It had been a long time since she'd been called that. And Rose was the only person to call her Scarl since being unable to pronounce her full Christian name at the age of two. Scarlett looked at her for a few seconds, then answered, "Because I'm not letting you get away. It's taken me too long to find you."

"Why all this fucking pretence?"

Arching her eyebrows Scarlett met Rose's annoyed glare. "What do you mean pretence? And stop swearing, Rose."

She huffed. "This tough-cop attitude. You're not fooling anyone."

"What are you on about, Rose?"

"You! Telling my mates back there you're a cop. I heard you."

Scarlett let go of Rose's sleeve. "I am a cop."

Rose threw her a flabbergasted stare. "Since when?"

"Since Mum and Dad got killed, and you…." She wanted to say more but knew the timing wasn't right. She didn't want to antagonise her sister further.

Still wearing her astounded gape, Rose said, "Well fuck me! What happened to Mrs Top Barrister?"

For a moment Scarlett stared at Rose. She sensed a note of resentment in her voice. It got to her, but she took a grip on herself and answered, "Gave it up. After what happened to Mum and Dad I joined the Met." Proudly she added, "Been a cop nearly eleven years."

Rose let out a short laugh. "Well fancy that. My sis is Old Bill and me a dropout." She shook her head. "Well at least Dad'll have been pleased." Her face dropped. "This is what this is about isn't it? Mum and Dad's killing. You're arresting me aren't you?"

Scarlett held her gaze. "No, I'm not arresting you. I've been looking for you for years. Believe it or not, Rose, I just want to take you home."

"Bullshit."

"It's not bullshit, Rose." She paused and held up her hands. "Alright, some of it is about what happened to Mum and Dad, but you're not under arrest. I just want to know what happened. Okay?"

Rose turned her head away. She replied softly, "You're wasting your time then, aren't you?"

Scarlett wanted to say more. Rose had a lot of questions to answer, but again she knew this wasn't the time or the place. Alex's voice broke into her thoughts.

"Your place, then?"

Scarlett glanced across the car roof. Alex was opening his door. His timed intervention was perfect. She exchanged looks and nodded. Then, child-locking the back door, she slammed it shut and jumped into her own seat.

Alex started the car.

As he pulled away from the kerb Rose piped up, "If I'm not under arrest, then why are you locking me in?"

Scarlett half turned and in the confined space she caught a whiff of stale drink on her sister's breath. It smelt sour. Cider? She was also aware of an odour coming from her clothes. It was the unpleasant smell of cannabis mixed with dampness. Scarlett said, "I've already told you. I've been looking for you for the last eleven years and I'm not about to let you go again now I've found you. Not at least until you and I have had a good chat, anyway."

Beneath her breath she muttered back. "Bleeding liberty, that's what this is."

****

Half an hour later they pulled up outside Scarlett's house. As she opened the door Rose said, "Isn't this Aunt Hanna's house?"

Rising from her seat, Scarlett said over her shoulder, "Was Aunt Hanna's house. She died, Rose. Two years ago. Cancer." She opened the rear door to let her sister out.

Rose shuffled sideways and met Scarlett's gaze. "I'm sorry. I didn't know." Pausing, eyeing the Victorian frontage up and down she added, "I liked Aunt Hanna. We had some good fun with her when we were little. Remember?"

Scarlett did remember. She tightened her mouth and nodded.

"So this is yours? Did she leave it you?"

Scarlett still held Rose's gaze. "It's both our house. She left it to you as well."

Rose swung her legs out onto the footpath. "Neat," she said and set off up the path.

Scarlett unlocked the front door, and as Alex followed Rose into the hallway she deactivated the alarm and then tapped in the code to set the door chime. If Rose made an attempt to leave she'd know. As she shut the door she double-locked it.

Rose stuffed her hands into her parka pockets. "I'm not a prisoner, you said. So why all this? If I want to leave, I will."

Scarlett took a deep breath. Rose had her back to her. She pulled off her shoes, tossed them against the skirting and then snapped, "You just don't get it, do you Rose? I don't think you understand the state of your situation here. You are a major suspect in Mum and Dad's murder and you're acting as if nothing has happened."

Rose set off towards the lounge. She shrugged her shoulders, answering back, "Whatever," and went through into the front room.

Scarlett stiffened and balled her hands into fists. Alex tapped her on the shoulder, threw her a sideways glance which said "leave it", and slipped past her issuing a weak smile. "I'll make us a drink while you two get reacquainted."

Scarlett sensed the wit in his comment and let out her own smile. Then, slipping off her coat and hanging it up, she walked into the lounge.

Rose was lolling on one half of the sofa. She still had her hands jammed into her coat pockets.

Scarlett said, "You can relax, Rose. Take off your coat and make yourself comfortable." She nodded towards her sister's feet. "Would you mind taking off your shoes?"

Rose looked at her defiantly. "I thought you said half of this house was mine. If I don't want to take off my shoes I don't have to."

Scarlett threw back her sister an angry glare. Grinding her teeth together she said slowly, "Rose, you are trying my patience. Will you please take off your shoes?"

Alex appeared in the door way, leaning against the jamb. "Listen, you two, you've not seen one another for eleven years. Why don't the pair of you just rewind and start again?"

Both sisters fixed their eyes on Alex. As he turned back to the kitchen they locked eyes with one another. Slowly Rose bent down, untied the laces of her battered trainers, and making a loud huffing sound, toe-heeled them off.

She wasn't wearing any socks and Scarlett saw that her feet were covered in grime. A feeling of sorrow and remorse overcame her.

Forty-six

In her kitchen Scarlett tidied away the still-warm plates from the dishwasher. Then she dragged out the cutlery. Above her she caught the sound of the bath emptying. She stopped what she was doing and strained her ears. Within a minute she heard the bathroom door opening.

Rose called down, "Can I borrow something to sleep in?"

Scarlett responded, "Sure, help yourself. Front bedroom, second from bottom drawer, in the unit next to the wardrobe."

Hearing her bedroom door open she allowed herself a cautious smile. It felt as if Rose was finally settling into the situation, though she knew from experience she dare not take anything for granted. It was too early. The past four hours had been a struggle and a strain. Scarlett had been so conscious of every aspect of what she had said. She had pried and probed Rose, but only about her lifestyle and what she had been doing these last few years. She had so much wanted to question her about the killing of their parents but deviated away from that line of enquiry. Alex had eased things. At times he'd taken control of the conversation, joking about how hard it had been to follow her and the guy she had been with on the Underground, despite his army surveillance training. Especially how easy she'd given them the slip. Rose had laughed and explained that Gareth, the man she had been with, was a good friend she'd met in a squat eighteen months ago, and then she'd given them the run-down on how she had managed to survive on the streets. Scarlett had been mesmerised by some of her sister's tales, thinking that some of them overshadowed her own frightening experiences as a cop on the streets of London. She was also astonished as to how close they had been in proximity to one another over the years, expressing her surprise that she had not noticed or bumped into her sooner. She reiterated that she had been searching for her for the last eleven years, but when Rose shied away her eyes, she pushed it no further, and moved on to the story of how she came by owning their aunt's house. Avoiding mentioning their parent's death she told Rose that she had moved in with her after university while she searched for a job. Within weeks of doing so she had learned that Aunt Hanna was battling leukaemia and that the first few years of living with her had been spent going backwards and forwards to hospital while she underwent treatment. "Initially Aunt Hanna fought the cancer. She had blood and bone marrow replacement and at one stage it went into remission. We had a fun couple of years together. You know what Aunt Hanna was like." She saw Rose nodding and continued. "Life and soul of the party. Most of the time she was like a teenager. Remember how it used to wind Mum up? How she used to tell us to ignore her?"

Again Rose nodded, a smile lighting up her face.

"Well, she never changed. She carried on even when she got ill again." Scarlett could feel a lump emerging in her throat. She gulped it away. "The leukaemia came back three years ago. She had more treatment but it didn't work this time. She died two years ago."

As she finished her story she saw Rose's eyes start to water. She lifted her voice. "Aunt Hanna never once got down. She was funny right to the end. Many a night we laughed together until we cried." Scarlett felt her own eyes filling up as she finished.

That was when Alex had come to the rescue again with his offer of ordering pizza for them all.

And with the telephoning of the pizza shop had come the first sign of a change in Rose's demeanour; she had finally taken off her parka and slunk back into the sofa.

Hearing Rose's soft footfalls coming down the stairs brought Scarlett's thoughts back to the moment. She continued to put away the cutlery. As she returned the plastic holder to the dishwasher Rose appeared in the doorway. Scarlett glanced her way and saw she was wearing one of her long T-shirts.

Canting her head and running a fan of fingers down through her fair tresses Rose said, "God, this feels so good. It's years since my hair felt like this."

Scarlett couldn't believe the transformation in her sister. She still looked pale and gaunt, but now there was a sheen to her skin and she couldn't help but notice for the first time that her striking features reminded her of Mum. *Like her ghost looking back.* And, like herself, Rose had inherited their mother's long shapely legs.

"Gosh, Rose, you look so different. You look good." Then she said, "I'm just going to stick the kettle on, do you fancy a warm drink?"

"Do you have any herbal tea?"

"I've got some green tea."

"That'll do. Do you need any help?"

Scarlett nodded towards the lounge. "No, I'm fine. Everything's sorted. You just make yourself at home."

With that Rose spun around and walked away.

A large grin lit up Scarlett's face as she made the hot drinks. For the first time that evening she felt good. She was still wearing the smile as she strolled into her lounge and rested the steaming cups on the coffee table.

Rose had her legs tucked beneath her on the sofa. "Alex not around?"

"He's gone home to Twickenham. Left while you were in the bath. He thought we might want some time together."

Rose steered away her eyes and settled them on the hot drinks. "He's nice. Your boyfriend?"

Scarlett tightened her mouth. "Just a friend."

"Well he's a nice friend. Does he work with you?"

"No, he's a consultant. Something to do with his old job. He used to be in the army."

"How come he was with you tonight then? I thought I heard you tell the others at the flat you were cops."

"A little bit of deceit, I'm afraid."

"Well it worked. That was very clever what you did back there."

Scarlett threw her a questioning look.

"You know for years when we find a new squat we spend the first couple of days doing drills and rehearsing what to do if the cops come or the bailiff or landlord. You threw everyone off guard with your 'missing girl' story."

Scarlett grinned. "That's my job."

"That was sneaky."

"I'll take that as a compliment."

"It wasn't meant to be."

"I know."

There was silence between them for a few seconds, then Rose took on a more serious face. "So if Alex isn't a cop, it really wasn't official what you did tonight."

Scarlett shook her head. "Like I said, I've been looking for you for years. It was Alex who spotted you a couple of weeks ago in the Underground."

Rose picked up her mug and grasped it in both hands. She blew inside it. "So no other cops know I'm here?"

"Nope. Just me."

"So if I wanted I could just walk out of here?"

Scarlett's chest tightened. She took a deep breath. "You could," she said slowly, "but I'd rather you didn't. It's taken me so long to find you. I'd love you to stick around for a while." *At least long enough for me to interrogate you about Mum and Dad's killing*, she wanted to add, but bit her lip.

Rose sipped her drink and still not looking up replied, "Do you mind if we don't talk? Not anymore tonight. Not being rude, but I'm stuffed from that pizza and I'm knackered. I haven't been able to switch off like this in a long time. You don't know what it's been like. I'm constantly on alert. Someone always trying it on or kicking the door in and threatening me."

"Sure, no problem." Scarlett suddenly felt guilty. "What about some TV? *Big Brother*'ll be on."

Rose lifted her eyes and threw her an inquisitive look. "What's *Big Brother*?"

Scarlett couldn't stop herself letting out a loud laugh. "What's *Big Brother*!" She reached for the TV remote. "Believe me, Rose, you have not lived!" She aimed the remote at the TV. "You don't know what you've been missing."

****

Scarlett awoke with a start. She had fallen asleep in the chair. The television was still on, but the sound was muted. Across from her Rose was still on the sofa, also asleep. For a few seconds she watched and listened. Rose was breathing heavily, her lips quivering as she exhaled. The noise coming from the sides of her mouth wasn't quite a snore and it triggered another memory. When they had shared a room together back home it used to keep her awake many a night. But now it made her heave a sigh of relief. As she watched her stirring she couldn't help but wonder what was going on in that haunted labyrinth of a mind. She hoped tomorrow her sister would have a change of heart and open up about what happened to their parents.

Forty-seven

Rose awoke in a panic, covered with sweat. The dream had visited her again. Jolting upright she could feel her heart pounding against her chest and her breath was trembling. It took her the best part of ten seconds to steady her breathing, taking in long gulps of air. In a moment she would be back in control again. It was always like this.

Then, in the gloom of her surroundings, she remembered where she was – in the spare bedroom of Aunt Hanna's house. Her sister was next door in Aunt Hanna's old bedroom.

She dropped her head back onto the pillow and lay in the dark. Listening. All she could hear was the sound of her own breath – panting. An image stuck inside her head, reminding her why she had woken up in this state. It was the blurred ghost of her father again. He was looking up at her, his face fixed in shock, holding his stomach. She could see the dark blood seeping between his fingers. Close by, two shadowy figures were coming towards her. He was screaming at her to run. It was his last dying words.

Forty-eight

Scarlett awoke with a woolly head. She'd had a restless night. At one stage, in the early hours, she thought she'd heard Rose scream out, but when she pulled herself fully awake and heard nothing else she guessed it had been a dream. Following that it had taken her some time to drop off. Laying in the dark she had been preoccupied with the thought that Rose might do a runner, and although she hadn't heard the door chime activate she needed to make sure and so she had gotten up and sneaked a listen at Rose's door. When she'd heard her heavy breathing she'd returned to her room and left her door open a fraction – just in case. After much tossing and turning she had eventually dropped off.

For a split second, as her eyes roamed around her bedroom, a feeling of dread overcame her. Was Rose still in the house? She wasn't sure how deeply she had slept since she had dropped off. Whipping back the duvet she swung out her legs but then halted as she caught the sound of voices below. Holding her breath and concentrating her hearing she gradually realised it was coming from the TV. She heaved a satisfying sigh and reached for her dressing gown. She needed a coffee.

****

Downstairs, stopping by the open lounge door, Scarlett poked her head through and found her sister curled up on the sofa watching *Jeremy Kyle*.

"I see you're hooked on reality shows already."

Rose turned her head. "This is unbelievable. There's a woman here who's only nineteen, she's just got out of prison for assaulting a neighbour, and she's come back home to her parents, and now she's stealing from them and regularly getting drunk and abusing them. People in our squat behave better than her and they've had far more troubled lives."

Scarlett wanted to say that she had witnessed similar behaviour from Rose leading up to her disappearance, but bit her lip. "I'm putting the kettle on, do you want a drink?"

Rose turned back to the TV. "Can I have a green tea, Scarl?"

In the kitchen Scarlett made them both a warm drink and some toast and made her way back to the lounge. She put the drinks and toast on the coffee table and picking up her mug of coffee retreated to the armchair. Tucking her feet beneath her she said, "Do you fancy doing anything today? Doing some shopping?"

Without looking her way Rose replied, "I thought I was a prisoner."

"Rose!" Scarlett's initial response was high pitched. Then she caught herself. "We discussed this last night. I did this for your own sake and I explained to you why else. It's time to be honest, Rose." She took a deep breath. "You're still wanted in connection with the death of Mum and Dad...."

Rose jerked up from her slouching position, "Does that mean you're handing me in?"

Scarlett held her sister's wild stare. "If you'd let me finish Rose, I was going to say I don't think you did it. I know you were doing some crazy things back then, but I don't for one minute believe you would hurt Mum and Dad like that. If I thought otherwise, you and I would not be having this conversation."

Rose eased back against the cushions. "I didn't kill them, Scarl. I had nothing to do with their deaths. Honest."

"I believe you, Rose."

"So what are you going to do with me?"

"For now, nothing. I obviously want to know your side of the story. And when you feel ready I'll be here to listen. But today I have a day off and I want to chill, and what better way to do it than go up west and do some shopping and take in some lunch. Maybe even go to the theatre. What do you say?"

"Sounds good, but it's going to have to be on you Scarl, 'cos I've got no money."

Scarlett smiled, "Oh but you have, Rose. You've got quite a bit of money." She watched her sister's face take on a look of surprise.

"I've got money?"

"Couple of hundred grand! At least! From Mum and Dad's insurance and sale of the house. Aunt Hanna and me put your money in a trust for when we found you." She paused. "And although the house is in my name, half of it is yours."

The astonished look on Rose's face morphed again to one of shock. "Fuck me!"

"Rose!"

"Sorry, Scarl, but this has come as a right bolt out of the blue for me. Last night I thought I was being locked up and this morning you're telling me I'm free as a bird and rich."

"It's certainly put paid to you going back to your squat."

Rose screwed up her face. "Why's that?"

"Well, you're going to have to own up and tell them you're now a capitalist."

Rose started to laugh, picked up a cushion and threw it at Scarlett.

Forty-nine

After breakfast Scarlett opened up her wardrobe to Rose and let her choose some things. She selected some skinny jeans, a T-shirt and a jumper. She was a few pounds lighter than Scarlett but they fitted her well enough. Then Scarlett plucked and shaped Rose's eyebrows and helped her put on some make-up. She only applied it lightly. Rose had already confided she didn't want to look as "dolled-up" as her sister, letting off a nervous laugh. "No offence, Scarl, I love the red hair, but your make-up is far too wild for me." However, when Scarlett pushed her in front of the hall mirror her face lit up.

"It's years since I've done this. I've spent most of the last few years covering up and hiding myself away from everyone."

"Not anymore, Rose, if I have anything to do with it. Now you look like the Rose I remember."

Rose stared back through the mirror at Scarlett, her bottom lip trembling.

For a couple of seconds there was an uneasy silence before Scarlett broke it by saying, "Right – time to hit the shops. You need a wardrobe of your own."

****

They took the train to Waterloo and then jumped on the tube, getting off at Oxford Circus, where they spent over two hours traipsing in and out of department stores. The first thing they chose together was a winter coat for Rose. With some reluctance Rose binned her old parka following some hard persuasion from Scarlett.

As she bundled it up and pushed it into a bin she said, "I've had that coat for five years. It was a bargain from a charity shop."

Seeing her sister's sorrowful look made Scarlett a little uneasy. She wondered if she was forcing things. She touched Rose's arm and engaged her hazel eyes. Exact mirrors of her own. "We don't have to do this if you don't want."

Rose seemed to think about the question for a short time, but then a smile broke out. "No, I'm enjoying this. For years I've envied those who could afford it and wondered what it would be like. It's nearly as mind-blowing as some good skunk...." She stopped herself as Scarlett's face changed. She gave a mischievous grin. "Only personal use and I don't do it all the time, Officer. Can I accept a street caution for that confession?"

Scarlett burst out laughing. "Come on, let's go and get us some food."

They chose a small Italian restaurant and ate a pasta dish each; Scarlett had wine and Rose drank an Italian beer.

Wiping her mouth with her sleeve after she drained her glass, Rose said, "That tasted wonderful. I can't remember when I last had beer. We can only usually afford cheap cider and then it's passed around."

It was another throw-away comment from her sister, but it hit home. Scarlett couldn't imagine what the last few years had been like for Rose.

Scarlett settled the bill and they did a few more hours' shopping together. This time Scarlett shopped for herself. She added a pair of expensive jeans to her wardrobe. Trying them on in front of Rose she told her about how she had been mugged for her bag and how her last pair of Armanis had been torn chasing her attackers. Then she told her about how she had tracked down the two robbers a few days ago, thanks to Alex, discovering that one of the attackers had been murdered by the other, who was now on the run.

Paying for them and strolling away from the store Rose said, "You lead a pretty exciting life, Scarl. But I can see you need someone like me around to look after you."

Scarlett gave her a sideways look.

Rose was wearing her mischievous grin again. "If you'd had me with you, you wouldn't have got mugged in the first place. It seems I need to teach you some proper street skills."

Scarlett couldn't help but giggle. "Come on, let's make a day of it. What do you say we go to the theatre? Let's see what we can get cheap tickets for."

At the bucket shop several offers were made but they both honed in on *The Bodyguard* at the Adelphi Theatre. Catching each other's gaze they recalled how they had watched the original film together numerous times with their mother.

That evening, for two hours, they sang along together to the hits of Whitney Houston. As it finished, they both had tears in their eyes.

****

After the theatre they headed home, walking the last of their journey from Richmond station arm in arm. In the hallway they kicked off their shoes and dumped their shopping. While Rose went through into the lounge Scarlett slipped into the kitchen to get them both a drink. She got herself a glass of wine, and in the fridge she found a couple of bottles of Alex's Budweiser beers which had been there a while, picked one out and poured it into a tall glass. She guessed Alex wouldn't mind.

Entering the lounge Scarlett saw that Rose had made herself comfortable on the sofa again and she handed her the beer and settled into the armchair.

Scarlett sipped her wine, watching her sister devour the first half of the beer. As she saw her pulling it away from her lips she asked, "Had a good day?"

Rose looked over her glass. "Really good, thanks. A few memories came back today. Especially watching *The Bodyguard*." On that note she dragged her eyes back.

Scarlett saw them cloud over as Rose returned to her beer. "Me too. It's a long time since I've done something like this."

Swallowing, Rose replied, "What about tomorrow?"

"Can't. Back to work I'm afraid."

"That murder you told me about? The guys who mugged you?"

Scarlett nodded and took a drink of her wine.

"Are you on some murder squad or something then Scarl?"

"It's called the Homicide and Serious Crime Unit. I'm based at Sutton Police Station. Been there a couple of years. We deal with all kinds of stuff. Rapes, murders, that kind of thing."

"Like Dad, eh?"

"Things have changed since Dad was in CID, but yeah, a bit like that."

"He'd have been proud of you, Scarl."

"I'd like to think so."

"I know so. You were always his favourite."

191

Scarlett pulled her glass away and engaged her sister's gaze. "He loved us both, Rose."

"You were the blue-eyed one though. All I gave him was grief."

Scarlett didn't immediately reply. She held her sister's gaze for a good few seconds. "That's in the past now, Rose. You have to move on."

Rose pulled her eyes away and downed the remainder of her beer. "It's alright you saying that. You're not to blame for their deaths."

An awkward silence followed. Scarlett placed her unfinished wine down on the coffee table and still leaning forward said, "Do you want to tell me about that night?"

Clasping her empty glass Rose straightened herself. "There isn't that much to tell." She looked Scarlett in the eyes. "I'm being genuine when I say that. That night is just a complete muddle. I've spent so many years trying to hide away from it that it's all mixed up now. It's eleven years ago, as you know, and a lot of water's gone under the bridge since then. The first few years after it happened I got myself in a bit of a mess. Started drinking really heavy. Anything I could get my hands on. Some days I was just completely out of it. Then one day Gareth and a couple of the squatters found me. I was sleeping rough in an old warehouse and in a real state, as you can probably imagine. If they hadn't have found me when they did I don't think I'd be here now. I've got a lot to thank them for."

Scarlett pondered on what Rose had just said. Picking her wine back up she settled back in the chair. "There must be some memories, though?"

"There is, but like I say it's all so mixed up now."

"Well, what do you say I get us another drink and you lead me through it?"

****

Scarlett got them both another drink and settling back into her chair she said, "Rose, try not to think of this as my job. Tonight this is one sister to another. Just tell me what you remember. Go through things slowly." While she was being honest in what she was saying, she knew she still had to draw on her interview training

192

if she wanted to get the best evidence from Rose to help her catch their parents' killer.

Rose replied, "Where do you want me to start?"

Scarlett shrugged her shoulders." The night it happened. Whatever you remember about it. If you remember, I wasn't around, I was at uni, so I've no idea what went on. The first thing I learned anything was when the police woke me in the early hours and told me Mum and Dad were dead. Everything I've learned since has been from the detectives who worked on the case. And, of course, what was in the papers at the time. That wasn't much. The only bits I've managed to put together are that Mum and Dad were out having a meal on their wedding anniversary and that supposedly the police contacted Dad and told him you'd been found drunk in the street and taken to casualty. He and Mum came to pick you up and the next thing a couple on their way home from a night out found Dad's car crashed into a tree. Mum had been killed by the crash and he'd been stabbed. And of course you had disappeared. That's it in a nutshell." She paused. "Is that right?"

Rose wore a shamed look. "Some of that's right, but it's like I said it's so mixed up in my head."

"Just tell me how you remember it. No matter how small. I promise, Rose, I won't judge you. I just want to know what happened. Especially now I know you didn't kill them."

"You believe me, then."

"Of course I do! Not once did I think you'd killed them. No matter what the police kept telling me. Don't get me wrong, I believed what they said about the drunken bit. Mum would tell me, from time to time, that they were having a few problems with you. But that was different. Teenage drunkenness and murder are two different things."

"Honestly, I didn't kill them, Scarl."

"The first time you told me that I looked into your eyes and I knew you were telling me the truth."

Rose's eyes glassed over and then she started to sob.

Scarlett set down her glass and joined her sister on the sofa, wrapping her arms around her shaking body.

Through tear-filled eyes Rose met Scarlett's concerned look. "But I think it was my fault they got killed."

Fifty

With a finger, Scarlett delicately wiped away the tears from her sister's eyes. She said, "It's time to unburden yourself, Rose. Time to let it out."

Rose drew in a deep breath. "It's as you say, Scarlett, I was giving Mum and Dad a hard time. I know now how selfish and childish it was, but every day they'd be on about how well you were doing and how you were going to be this great barrister one day and I was so jealous of you. I just wanted them to acknowledge something good about me for a change."

Scarlett felt hurt and saddened. Sighing, she replied, "I don't think Mum and Dad meant it like that. I know they loved you just as much as me. I guess it was because I was at uni. Don't forget you were only sixteen at the time. You weren't ready for any of that, so probably that's why they went on so."

"I know that now, Scarl. I've had a lot of time to run everything through in my head and work it out, but it's like you just said, I was only sixteen. A child really. A spoilt child. And I just rebelled by getting drunk and giving them grief."

"And did things happen on that night like I've been told?"

"The bit about them coming to get me from casualty's right. But it wasn't because I was drunk."

Scarlett threw her a questioning look.

Her face took on a hurt look. "Honest, Scarl! Sure, that night I did go out for a drink, but I didn't get drunk. My drink was spiked – I think by this couple I met"

Scarlett raised her eyebrows.

"Straight up, Scarl. It's the truth. I only had a couple of drinks and then something weird happened to me."

"Okay, I believe you. Just take me through it. Slowly."

Rose took in a deep breath and exhaled slowly. "Well, that night I'd sneaked out as soon as Mum and Dad went out. I'd arranged to meet up with some schoolmates in the park. One of the lads had bought half a bottle of vodka and we passed it around. I only had a couple of sips and then it was empty. That's when someone said, 'Let's go into town.' I thought about Mum and Dad, about them being out for their wedding anniversary, and I just thought there'd be no harm in it. That I could have a couple of drinks and I'd be back in the house well before they got home."

"So you went into town?"

Rose nodded. "I wasn't really dressed for it like the others, so I stuck at the back. When we went into the pub we all went into a corner and two of the older lads bought the drinks. I had a couple of halves of lager, but then I needed the toilet. When I came out they'd all gone. I thought they might have been waiting for me outside, but when I went out they were nowhere to be seen. I couldn't believe it. I just set off running, to see if I could catch up with them, but as I got to the corner of the road I bumped into this couple – literally – and I ended up on my arse. The man helped me up and asked me if I was okay and what I was running from. I told them what had happened and that I was looking for my mates. The girl said they were just about to go in the bar I'd come out of and she said, 'Seeing as your mates have gone why don't you join us and get yourself cleaned up and we'll get you a drink?' I told them I'd got no money, and the man just said, 'Our treat.' So typical me at the time just thought free drinks and so I said yes. We went back into the bar and the man bought me a pint of lager while I chatted with the girl. They seemed nice, the pair of them, and we got drinking and talking but I never got to finish my drink. Within twenty minutes I came over all weird. I started feeling all wobbly on my feet and I started slurring my speech. I couldn't even think properly. The next thing I remember was the police around me and I was at the hospital."

Scarlett scrutinised the puzzled look on her sister's face and said, "So how did you end up at the hospital?"

"The police took me there."

"So how did that come about? Can you remember?"

She shrugged. "Not really. It's all a blur. And it's such a long time ago now."

Scarlett acknowledged with a nod. "Just tell me what you remember."

"Well, as I say, I just remember suddenly coming over all weird. Everything just began spinning and I felt sick. I can remember the girl saying she would help me to the toilet. The next thing I'm outside. The girl and the guy are holding me up and trying to get me in the back of this car. I started freaking out. I think I started

196

fighting with the girl. I'm not sure. Anyway the next thing the police were there and I was in the hospital. But even that's a blur. And then Mum and Dad turned up."

"They'd come to pick you up?" Scarlett interjected.

Rose nodded. "I tried to tell them what had happened, but they just wouldn't listen to me. They just kept saying I'd spoilt their evening and that I was a selfish, spoilt brat. Even Mum was going off on one. It was awful, Scarl." Her eyes took on a pleading look. "On the way back home I was trying to make them listen to me. Trying to tell them I wasn't lying and that's when this car came from nowhere. Rammed into us from behind and we skidded off the road and smashed into a tree."

"Rammed you?"

Rose nodded.

"Definitely rammed you? Not an accident? It didn't swerve or skid before it hit?"

"No. I'd come round by then. It just hit us from behind. One minute we were all shouting at one another and the next minute there's was this loud bang and we're skidding off the road and into a tree. It happened so quick!"

Scarlett straightened herself against the cushions of the sofa. Sitting rigidly, she said, "What happened after that?"

Rose's mouth tightened. Slowly she shrugged. "I'm not really too sure. Again everything is just a blur because of the accident. I just remember coming to in the back. I must have been thrown off the seat when we crashed. I can remember thinking my head hurt and I put my hand up to it. I saw I was bleeding. I started to panic and I shouted for Mum. When I looked to the front all I saw was this tree trunk through the smashed windscreen. Then I saw Mum." Rose's face paled. "She wasn't moving. Her face was all bloody." She paused a moment and then said, "I knew she was dead." She paused again, drifted her gaze up towards the ceiling and after a few seconds returned her eyes. "I can remember thinking, 'Where's Dad?' He wasn't in his seat and his door was open. My door was stuck and I had to kick it open. It was dark. There were no lights anywhere. We were on this country road." She paused again and continued, "When I say no lights – there was a car by the edge of the road. It had its headlights on. The doors were open. And that's when I saw Dad." Her face took on a scared look. "He was on the ground holding his stomach. I could see blood all over his hands. There were two men standing over him. He looked at me and just shouted at me to run. And that's what I did. I ran into the woods and just kept running."

Scarlett leaned forward and placed a hand on Rose's shoulder. "Did you see who the men were?"

Rose shook her head vigorously. "No! They were dressed in dark clothing. Everything was happening so quick. I can remember thinking that both of them were quite stocky – a lot bigger than Dad. And I can remember that one was taller than the other. Quite a bit taller. But that's all. It was so dark. As I say, there were no street lights. We were on a country lane."

"Anything else you remember, Rose?"

"Yes! Remember what I said about the car at the edge of the road?"

Scarlett acknowledged with a quick nod.

"I told you the doors were open."

Again Scarlett nodded sharply.

"Well the light was on inside the car and there was someone sitting in the back. I can remember at the time thinking that it was the guy from the bar. The one with the girl I'd bumped into."

"You're sure about that?"

"At the time yes. That was the first thing that came to mind when I saw him."

"Okay Rose, you've done ever so well. I want you to concentrate now on the man you saw. Had you seen him before that night?"

Rose shook her head. "Nope. Never seen him before."

"And you're confident that was it the same guy? The one with the girl? The one who you think spiked your drink?"

She nodded frantically. "That was the first thing that entered my head as soon as I saw him."

"Okay, hold that thought. Did he tell you his name?"

Rose shook her head again. "If he told me I can't remember. I do remember he had some kind of foreign accent. Italian? French? I don't know I'm not good with accents. Anyway he was foreign. The girl was also foreign. She looked to be slightly older than him and he said it was his sister."

"When you say older, do you know roughly how old?"

"I would say in their twenties. So now they'll be in their thirties, won't they?"

Scarlett nodded and said, "Did you recall if she told you her name?"

Rose's mouth pinched. "No." She stared into Scarlett's eyes. "You think I'm stupid don't you?"

Scarlett offered a reassuring smile. "No I don't, Rose. You were sixteen. Like you say, you'd just been dumped by your mates and these good Samaritans turn up offering to buy you a drink. Who wouldn't say yes?"

"You're just saying that to make me feel good."

"No I'm not, Rose. It could have happened to anyone. It has happened to a lot of people. Trust me, you're not the first and you won't be the last."

Fifty-one

Scarlett was in the office early catching up on her paperwork. It had piled up during her two days off. She had left Rose in bed. Before leaving for work she had looked in on her and saw that she was fast asleep, snoring away gently. Scarlett had thought she looked so peaceful, especially given last night's revelations. After all this time she now had a completed version of events about what had happened to their parents eleven years ago, though frustratingly it had not provided her with the evidence as to who was responsible for killing them. Nevertheless, finding and speaking with Rose had certainly untangled some of the Gordian knot of their murders. She had far more than the detectives who had originally investigated their killings – four suspects. She would give it a couple of days and then coax Rose into giving better descriptions of the three men and the woman she had seen that night. One thing she'd already determined was that she wasn't going to tell anyone that she'd tracked down Rose. She knew from last night's questioning that, mentally, Rose was not ready to be interviewed. Especially as a suspect, which she still officially was. No, she would handle this herself. She, more than anyone, knew how important it was to maintain trust with a witness. The fact that this was her sister increased that importance.

"Who was that I saw you with yesterday?"

"DI Taylor-Butler's voice made her jump. He had appeared by her side without her noticing. Her stomach emptied and a sudden coldness flooded over her. Without looking up from her paperwork she replied, "Yesterday? Who was I with?"

"Yes. I saw you going into Dorothy Perkins with a fair-haired woman. I've not seen her with you before."

Scarlett daren't look up at him. She kept his looming figure in the corner of her eye. She could feel herself flushing. She swallowed hard and thought fast. Controlling her voice she answered, "Oh her! It was a friend from my uni days. She was in London for the weekend so we caught up."

"Oh yes? She looked a lot younger than you."

She pretended to cough while thinking up a response. Half covering her mouth she said, "She's only a couple of years younger. She was starting her course as I was finishing. We shared a flat together for a while."

He started to drift away from her side. "Pretty, anyway. You'll have to introduce me to her if I see you two again."

Scarlett rolled up her eyes and watched the back of him striding away. *You've no fucking chance of that happening.* Then she caught herself. What was Taylor-Butler doing in Oxford Street on a Sunday? She knew he had issues with her. Had he taken to stalking her? She checked him as he left the room. As the door clattered shut she took a deep breath. Was she getting paranoid? One thing was for certain, she knew she had to get Rose out of the house. In the eyes of the law she was harbouring a criminal and she didn't need any more complications in her life right now. She lifted her mobile out from her bag and dialled Alex's number.

*****

Following morning briefing Scarlett returned to her paperwork. CPS had notified her that the Lycra Rapist had entered a "not guilty" plea, and his trial had been set for seven weeks' time and she had to get a full file together. Across from her Tarn was working through the forensic schedule, matching it with the exhibits they had seized. She had temporarily dragged him away from the murder enquiry.

Briefing had not thrown up anything earth shattering to move the investigation forward. There were still no firm sightings of Andrius Machuta and the Audi Q7 hadn't been found. The e-fits, from two witnesses who had seen the driver of the Audi, had come back and were on display. There were similarities in the features of both, but neither of the images had anything which would make the men stand out. The e-fits had been circulated and later that day DCI Diane Harris was holding another press conference.

The ringing of the desk phone disturbed her and she glanced up, catching Tarn's gaze. She gave him the nod to answer it and returned to her task. But she didn't have her head down long. The excited note in his voice brought her interest back. Tarn eyes were grabbing her attention and she watched him scribbling notes as he exchanged conversation with whoever was on the phone. She could tell from his patter that it was someone else in the job. Two minutes later Tarn was hanging up. He flourished another quick note on some scrap paper and then flashed an excited look.

"We might have found Andrius."

Scarlett straightened. "Where?"

"Brixton. That was communications. They've just taken a call from someone who said they think they've seen the man we're after on Brixton Station Road. They say he's gone into an old abandoned railway station there. I've asked them to pull up the location for us and send it."

Scarlett put down her pen and scooted back her chair. "Come on, let's tell the boss."

Ten minutes later she, Tarn, DCI Harris, DI Taylor-Butler and the office-bound detective sergeant were in the HOLMES office sat in front of a computer screen. One of the female operators was typing the location into Google. As she typed she said, "There's only limited CCTV covering that section. It's the railway arches that run down towards Brixton Market and the leisure centre. Some of the arches are lock-ups and shops and I've just done a check and the location Communications have given comes up as an old station which used to be on the Liverpool line. It was abandoned shortly after the war." As she finished talking several colour images appeared on screen. She flicked to one and tapped it open. Displayed was a metal railway bridge spanning the road and beside it a bricked-up archway with a painted blue door set into the wall.

Pointing to the screen the operator said, "This picture is a couple of years old. The blue door is securing the entrance to the old Coborn Road station. Communications have said that the person who phoned it in said they saw our suspect going in through this door. You can see on this picture its metal but he must have somehow managed to force it."

DCI Harris dipped her head towards the screen. "Get me a print of that." Then she turned to DI Taylor-Butler. "Hayden, get everyone back for a briefing and get on to SO 19. I want a firearms team as backup and I want a secure cordon putting around that station. Andrius is going nowhere until we can get an arrest team down there."

Fifty-two

Skender and Arjan parked their BMW close to a back-street garage in a residential area a few streets away from Brixton Station Road. There were only a couple of people around and no one gave them a second look as they each put on a baseball cap, pulling down the peak to hide away their eyes.

Skender hunched up the collar of his leather coat and set off at a trot, calling back over his shoulder, "We've only got half an hour max before this place is swarming with cops. Come on!"

Arjan picked up his pace, chasing after Skender awkwardly because of his bulk.

By the time they had arrived at the blue metal entrance to the old railway station Arjan was gasping for breath and sweating profusely.

Skender pressed a finger to his lips, signalling for Arjan to hold his breath. Then, taking a quick look around, slipped his fingers into the gap between the metal door and the wooden jamb. He tried to ease it open but it resisted and he had to give it a good tug, causing it to issue a long creaking noise. He paused for a second, listening. Hearing nothing he squeezed into the space he had made and found himself emerging into rubble-strewn waste ground. In front of him was the ballast remains where tracking had once been and that stretched to a raised platform on which was a dilapidated concrete waiting room. Where windows and doors had once been were now gaping holes. He set off at a sprint, crunching over the ballast and in a couple of seconds he had reached the old platform and hoisted himself up. He could hear Arjan wheezing behind him. Within a few more seconds he was entering the waiting room. He saw Andrius curled up in the far corner and stepped towards him.

The Lithuanian had been asleep but his eyes soon snapped open when Skender's feet scraped over broken glass.

Skender saw the shocked look register in Andrius's face and couldn't help but produce a mocking grin.

Andrius pushed himself up into a sitting position, forcing his back against the concrete. "Skender!"

"Correct," he replied menacingly, closing in on him. For a moment he stared down, shaking his head. Then, reaching down, he grabbed his jaw and squeezed.

Andrius cried out.

Skender locked his eyes upon the Lithuanian. "Andrius, you've let me down."

Through a pinched mouth he spluttered, "I'm sorry, Skender. I'll make it up to you."

"I know you will."

Behind, Skender heard Arjan arrive. He was way out of breath. He watched Andrius's eyes dart from himself to Arjan and back. Skender saw the Lithuanian's eyes widen as he swung them back to Arjan. He guessed that he had spotted what Arjan was carrying.

Andrius returned his gaze to Skender. His face was a mask of horror. "I promise I won't say anything," he machine-gunned out.

"I know you won't." Without warning he slammed a fist into Andrius face and his head rocketed backwards against the concrete.

There was a dull crack and Andrius sank to the floor.

Skender reached behind and Arjan offered up the green plastic container he was carrying. Skender unscrewed the lid and tipped it an angle, sloshing the liquid over Andrius's head and shoulders.

The strong whiff of petrol soon filled the room.

Andrius spat out some of the petrol that had fallen into his mouth and in between chokes he screamed, "No! Please Skender! I won't say anything! Honest!"

Handing back the container to Arjan, a sneer crept across Skender's face. Stepping backwards he reached inside his coat and pulled out a zippo lighter.

Arjan's eyes went wide with terror. "No!"

Skender flicked the lighter and instantly Andrius burst into flames.

204

Fifty-three

"How the fuck did this happen?" DCI Diane Harris demanded angrily. She was looking down at the smouldering remains of Andrius Machuta. The fire brigade had put out his burning body ten minutes earlier, after receiving a 999 call from a passer-by on Brixton Station Road who had heard the screams. She turned away and exchanged glances with DI Taylor-Butler, Scarlett and Tarn. "This is no fucking coincidence," she continued. "This is the second time someone of significance, connected to our investigation, has been murdered. This time it has to have been leaked by one of our own. Us and SO 19 are the only people who knew Andrius was here." She set her sights on DI Taylor-Butler. "Hayden, I want a thorough investigation carried out. I want to know who the fucking mole is." Then she stormed out of the smoke-reeking waiting room into the fresh cold air and stopped in the middle of the old platform. The DI, Scarlett and Tarn joined her.

Diane Harris surveyed the area slowly and then returned her gaze to the three members of her team. "I know there's limited CCTV around this location, but someone must have seen something. The fire brigade said an accelerant was used on him. Most probably petrol. Whoever did this had to transport and then carry it here. Check out the streets nearby. See if anyone saw someone carrying a can or something similar. And check service stations within a two-mile radius. And get Forensics down here. I want this whole place going over with a fine-tooth comb." She thrust her hands in her pockets and began walking towards the platform ramp. She called back over her shoulder, "Someone is going to pay for this!"

****

It was gone nine p.m. before Tarn dropped Scarlett off at home. It had been a long day with very little to show for it. Both teams were stretched to their limits, given that they now had four crime scenes, and DCI Harris had told them at evening briefing that she had put in a request for more resources. And although she had not aired it everyone knew that an internal investigation had begun, delving into the possibility that among them was a corrupt cop. The atmosphere in the incident room could have been cut by a knife, and no one had spoken as they filed out from briefing – the team had adopted a siege mentality. As she opened her front door she knew that the next few days were going to be difficult. She just prayed that the person who had betrayed them was not someone from her team. Now though, she still had things to do. She had to check in with Alex and catch up with her sister.

Scarlett took a quick swig of juice from the fridge, grabbed a banana from the fruit bowl and ate it while she changed into her biking leathers. Then, uncovering Bonnie from beneath the plastic sheeting she wheeled her Triumph onto the road and set off to Alex's. Given the time of night, traffic was comparatively light and there were a few moments when she could open up the bike; the whole time, though, she checked her rear to see if anyone was following. She still had the jitters following the comments made by Taylor-Butler that morning.

She made Alex's place in twenty-five minutes, parked her bike next to his car at the rear of the block of maisonettes and took the back stairs to the third floor. Alex answered the door almost straight away bearing a welcoming smile.

Scarlett kissed him on the cheek. "Has she been okay?" she asked, stepping into the hallway.

"Absolutely fine," Alex replied, closing and locking the door behind her. "We nipped into the city to get her a few more things; I also got her a phone." He dropped his voice. "Did you know she's never owned a mobile? I've spent this afternoon programming everything in and showing her how to use it." He paused and added, "And she wanted to go to the squat."

Scarlett's eyes widened.

"Don't worry. She just wanted to catch up with them. Especially Gareth, and tell him she was okay and what was happening. They weren't there though. The council have taken back possession of the house. I've promised her I'll find out where they've gone. I've said we'll go looking for them."

Scarlett presented an anxious face.

Still speaking softly Alex said, "You've got to stop worrying, Scarlett. If she wanted to do a runner she would have done it by now. She had plenty of time this afternoon. She just wants to catch up with the people who she's lived with for past eleven years. They're the ones who've looked after her, remember."

Scarlett relaxed. "I guess you're right."

He touched her arm. "You've got to trust her."

Scarlett nodded. "I know." She unzipped her leathers, took off her boots and piled them in the hallway. "Thanks for everything you've done today. What do I owe you?" She walked towards the lounge.

"She spent just over a hundred on new things and ninety-nine quid for the phone. I didn't get her a dear one. Just one with basic functions. I paid cash and I got a pay-as-you-go. I've registered it in a false name. I also got a couple of spare SIMs. I've shown her how to swap them. No one can trace it to her."

"Thanks Alex. Much appreciated." Scarlett entered the open-plan lounge. She always felt enthused to do something with her own house whenever she stepped into his place. In keeping with the 1930s building his interior was art deco inspired, with dark drapes covering floor-to-ceiling balcony doors and furnishings of chrome and Perspex with retro accessories. It was truly stylish. The only thing out of place was the wall-mounted large-screen TV playing a music channel. Nevertheless, it blended in well enough.

Rose was sprawled the length of the three-seater hide sofa. She looked like she'd made herself at home. She met her with a smile and flashed her mobile. "Hey Scarl, got myself a phone."

"Yeah, Alex just told me." She tapped her sister's ankles, indicating for her to draw them up and then joined her on the sofa.

Rose said, "I wanted to ring you but Alex said you'd be busy. I've not been able to use it yet. Only a couple of the guys at the squat had phones but I don't know their numbers."

Alex slipped past into the open-plan kitchen. He took out a couple of glasses from a cupboard and set them down on the central island. "Drinks?"

"I'll have a glass of wine," replied Scarlett. "Just a small one. I'm on the bike."

Rose said, "I'll have a beer if you've got one." Then, setting aside her phone, she asked Scarlett, "Had a good day? You've been a long time. Did you catch your mugger-cum-murderer?"

As Alex brought across the drinks and handed them round, Scarlett told them about the latest incident at the abandoned station.

When she'd finished, Rose shuddered. "Good God, Scarl, you deal with some right stuff. I don't think I could stomach that. It's like something from a horror film."

Alex said, "I wouldn't say it's a fitting end, but it'll certainly save the cost of one trial."

Scarlett couldn't help but smile, "Do you know, sometimes you've got the black humour of a cop. I keep telling you, you should join. You'd make a good cop."

"No chance. I've had enough of rules and regulations to last me a lifetime. I'm happy doing what I'm doing, with the odd bit of private detective moonlighting and being a sheriff's deputy when you need me." He took a long drink of his beer. "Have you caught who's responsible?"

Scarlett shook her head. "We think it's all linked. You know, with those other two women we found murdered – the Lithuanian street worker and the headless woman in the suitcase we found in the Thames."

Rose pushed herself up. "Headless woman in a suitcase?"

Scarlett gave Rose a potted version of recent events, for fear of alarming her. She didn't tell her that one of the team may be a bent cop, whose leaks had probably caused two of the victims to be killed.

Rose hung onto every word. When she'd finished she said, "Wow Scarl. What a case. I know that kind of stuff went on but not this close to home."

Rose's comments made Scarlett sit up. She hadn't thought of it like that. This was just her everyday work. She had never viewed it in proximity to where she lived before. It made her realise why some people get nervous when incidents happen around them. She took a drink of wine, glanced at her watch and then nodded to the TV. The sound had been muted. "It's going to be on the ten o'clock news. Can we watch it? I'd like to see it if you don't mind. The gaffer did a press conference this afternoon and I'd like to see what she said."

Alex picked up the remote and switched channels. The news had just started; the anchor was announcing the headlines. After twenty seconds it flashed across to the local London studio and another broadcaster aired the Brixton Station Road murder as the main event.

For the next twenty minutes three pair of eyes were glued to the TV. Scarlett agitatedly sat through world events of a bird flu outbreak in China, escalation of fighting in Syria and more of the courtroom saga involving Nigella Lawson's personal assistants. The national news finished with a weather forecaster warning of gale-force winds and heavy rain sweeping across Britain during the next forty-eight hours. Then it switched to the London local news. The opening shot was of the blue metal entrance door to the old abandoned Coborn Road railway station. A line of blue-and-white crime scene tape was fluttering in front of it and standing sentry was a highly visible police officer. Then it panned across to a dark-haired female reporter who was standing beside DCI Diane Harris. The reporter gave a brief introduction: "Here I am on Brixton Station Road. Earlier today, behind that blue door, police discovered the badly burned body of a man in the old station waiting room. With me I have Detective Chief Inspector Harris, who is leading the hunt for the killers." Then the microphone was thrust towards Diane Harris. Without a hint of nerves the DCI delivered a clipped response, outlining that a passer-by had been alerted by the cries of the burning man, had found him on fire, and had called the police and fire brigade. She then elaborated on how horrific the murder was and how important it was they catch the culprits as soon as possible. Then she added, "At this moment in time, we are exploring a link to the discovery of a body we found in the cellar of a house in Wandsworth. We are currently trying to trace a number of people who visited and used these premises, whom we believe are of Eastern European origins. There may be also links to another murder we are investigating of a young woman and we have an e-fit of a man we want to trace who may have evidence crucial to that investigation." The picture changed and one of the digital e-fits of the driver of the Audi Q7 appeared on screen.

Suddenly Rose stiffened.

Scarlett sensed it and she flashed a sideways glance. Rose was transfixed to the TV. Her hand was covering her mouth.

Scarlett said, "Rose what is it?"

"Him!" she exclaimed, pointing to the screen.

"What about *Him*?"

"Remember what I said, about that car that had pulled up and how two men were standing over Dad and he told me to run? Remember I said they were big and that one was taller than the other?"

Scarlett nodded.

"Well that picture they've just shown on the telly looks like the smaller of the two. I know it was eleven year ago, but I'm telling you Scarl, he looks dead like one of those I saw. Especially with the shaven head."

Fifty-four

"Are you absolutely certain Rose?" Scarlett had drawn her legs up onto the sofa and shuffled around to face her sister.

"I'm not a hundred per cent sure but he reminds me of one of those men I saw standing over Dad when he was bleeding." Her face took on a thoughtful look. "It's triggered something else as well! I remember now that the taller one also had a shaven head. That one, whose face was on the TV, was the one who chased after me, but he was a bit fat and a lot slower than me so I was able to get away."

"And is this the first time you've seen him since that night Mum and Dad were killed?"

Rose nodded vigorously. "Once Dad told me to run and I'd got away that was it! I was terrified! I didn't know what to do. I just wandered around and hid. I was shit-scared. I didn't know if the police would believe me or if they'd think I had something to do with it, especially as one of them was someone I'd been drinking with. I didn't know what to do and that's when I started drinking." She paused. "I've told you the rest about the drinking and dossing down. That's when I met some other homeless people and just fell into their way of life. Most of the time I was out of it with booze. For the first year or so my life was a blur. I just moved around a lot, sleeping rough, until those friends from the squat found me. After that I spent the rest of the time moving from one squat to another and keeping my head down. I have to say that ever since that happened, and I saw those two, I've given every shaven-headed guy a second look, but I've not seen either of the two men since that night. Well, until I've just seen his mug on telly. And I'm telling you, I'm sure he looks like one of those I saw standing over Dad."

"God Rose, this is so weird. The bloke we're looking for in relation to our murders could be the same person involved in Mum and Dad's killing. How much of a coincidence is that?"

Rose's face lit up. She pulled out her legs from beneath her and pushed herself up on the sofa. "One thing you said a couple of minutes ago just clicked."

"What's that?"

"These murders you're working on. The two men who mugged you and the woman in the same house? Did I hear you say something about the woman being Lithuanian?"

"Yes. But to be honest we know very little about any of them. We don't yet know if the women who were killed were illegals. We're inclined to think they were. The one whose body parts we found in Battersea we believe was killed and cut up in the house in Wandsworth." Scarlett dipped her head and pointed towards the TV. "The same house where Andrius, who's also Lithuanian, and who we found burned to death in Brixton this morning, was staying. It's also the same house where we found another Lithuanian man killed, who was one of the men who mugged me." She engaged her sister's eyes. "I hope I've explained that okay. It's all a little complicated. Why do you ask?"

"I don't know if this is a coincidence but a young Lithuanian girl has been staying at the squat with us. We found her hiding in an old garage a couple of weeks ago and brought her back." She diverted her gaze and shook her head as if something was disturbing her thoughts. Then she returned her eyes and said, "She was in a bit of a state. She speaks pretty good English and she told us that she and a friend of hers had been tricked into coming to England and that when they'd got here some men had kept them prisoner in a house." She paused and her mouth tightened. "She told us she been raped by one of them." She paused again. "And they'd hurt her. They branded her on the back, near her shoulder, with a soldering iron, like they do cows."

All the time Rose was talking Scarlett could feel herself becoming more and more rigid. When she finished she said, "Does the branding look like a crescent moon and a star?"

Rose's forehead creased and she nodded. "Certainly a crescent moon, now you mention it. Don't know about the star. There's another mark but it just looks like a bit of a blob to me. It was a real mess, to be honest, when she was found. It had gone septic. By rights she should have gone to hospital, but she was too scared to go, so one of the girls treated her and she's a lot better now. But it's left a nasty scar." Rose threw Scarlett a questioning look. "Do you know her or something? Is she wanted?"

Scarlett shook her head. "Did she explain how she got be in the garages where your friends found her?"

"She said she'd managed to escape. The men who'd kept her prisoner were taking her and her friend to another house. They told her she was going to work for them." She paused then added, "She thinks as a prostitute. Well that's what she said. She was certainly dressed as if she was."

"Did she say how she'd managed to get away?"

"She said they put her and her friend in this big black car, but there was only the driver with them. Not long after they'd set off it got stuck in traffic, and her friend attacked the driver and she'd managed to get out and run."

"What happened to her friend?"

Rose shrugged her shoulders. "She doesn't know. She just ran until she found that empty garage. She'd been there two days before we found her. She daren't move." She paused a moment and added, "Very much like what happened to me." She paused again, only momentarily, before continuing, "She was terrified of what the men would do to her if they caught her. She thinks something bad happened to her friend. She said the men who held them were really evil."

For a minute Scarlett was thoughtful. She ran through everything Rose had just said, desperately trying to piece things together. A new twist had been added to what she was working on and yet things were becoming clearer. After thirty seconds she asked, "Did this girl tell you her name?"

"She's called Grazyna. She did tell me her second name but I can't remember it. And she did tell us the place she came from in Lithuania, but I can't remember that either. I'd never heard of it."

"No problem, Rose. What about her friend she was with? Did she tell you her name?"

Rose took on a studious look. She appeared to be thinking over the question. After several seconds she shook her head. "She did but I'm sorry, Scarl, I can't remember it. It's a name I've never heard before. I think it began with a K, but I'm not sure."

Scarlett leaned forward, fixing her sister's look. "Something you said just now about the car they were put in. Did you say Grazyna told you they got into a big black car?"

Rose nodded. "Yes."

"Did she say what type of car it was?"

Rose seemed to think about the question again. After a few seconds she answered. "No, I don't think so. I'm sure she just said they were put into this big black car. Why, is it relevant?"

"Could be. We have a sighting of an Audi Q7, which is a big black four-by-four, on a lane close to where the suitcase with the headless woman was found. The driver of that car was the shaven-headed man whose e-fit you've just seen. We've not yet been able to identify who the woman is we've found."

Quick as a flash Rose said, "And you think it could be Grazyna's friend?"

"It would certainly fit." Scarlett clasped her hands together. "One thing I've not mentioned. The headless woman in the suitcase had a recent scar on her shoulder. She'd been branded as well, with a crescent moon and a star, which also fits with what happened to your friend Grazyna." Scarlett unclasped her fingers and pushed herself back. "Just one more question, Rose. Did Grazyna mention the names of any of the men who'd held her and her friend prisoner?"

"She told us the driver's name who she'd managed to escape from." Rose nodded toward the TV. "She told us that his name is Arjan. She said he was Albanian. She told us so we could keep a look out for him."

Scarlett spun sharply and met Alex's look.

He was sat on the edge of his seat. He had hardly touched his beer.

Scarlett said, "We have to find where Rose's friends have gone; this Grazyna is crucial to our investigation."

Fifty-five

DCI Diane Harris stood at the front of the incident room, a serious look etched on her face.

Behind her on the interactive screen was the latest body find – Andrius Machuta's charred remains. There were also various photos of the old abandoned station where the brutal killing had taken place.

She began the morning briefing.

"While I'm not yet pointing the finger, the sad fact is that someone, and I believe it's someone in this room, has leaked information which has caused the deaths of at least two people crucial to our enquiry." She let her opening words hit home a few seconds before progressing. "In the case of Greta Aglinsky, it could have been Immigration and Border Control, but not in this latest killing. Only this team knew where Andrius Machuta was located. And, although SO 19 were told, the common denominator in both these murders is within this squad." She paused and scanned the room looking for a reaction on the faces of her team. While no one looked guilty there were a lot of sheepish faces. Continuing, she said, "I will get to the bottom of this, make no mistake, and once I find out who is responsible that person will not only be off the team but they will be under arrest. I have already spoken with the commander and an internal investigation is already underway." She paused again, taking a deep breath. "While I know it puts everyone under the spotlight I'm afraid there's nothing I can about that and I can't halt this investigation. All I can say is that if you are innocent you have nothing to fear." Pausing again she let the thread of what she had just said peter away. After a few seconds she said, "Right, now to the work of the day." She brushed the sides of her slacks as if removing something before moving on. "We have a killer or killers out there who have now murdered four people. We still haven't found out the identity of our headless woman in the suitcase but it is natural to think she like the other victims is Lithuanian, especially given the identical branding to that of Greta Aglinsky. And it is also reasonable to believe the two women are street workers, given the premises in Wandsworth, which we believe we will link Greta to once forensics come back. As to the two men, Henrikas and Andrius, we do not yet know what part they play in all this. Diane Harris took on a more thoughtful look. "The only suspect lead we have at present is our shaven-headed friend" – the head-and-shoulders digital e-fit appeared on screen – "who was sighted on River Lane by our car thieves, standing next to a black Audi Q7 in the early hours prior to the body in the suitcase being found at the bottom of that lane, and also is identical to the driver of a black Q7 involved in a minor RTC two days before that, only a mile from the house in Wandsworth, and who was seen fighting with a young female in the back of the car. As you all know this e-fit was aired on London news last night and although a number of calls came in with names, none of those are definite. Following up those names is a priority today. If anyone is in the least bit suspicious about who they are talking with you immediately call for backup." Directing a finger at the e-fit on screen she continued, "This man is extremely dangerous. I don't want any heroics." She lowered her hand. "We also still haven't found the Audi Q7. Our viewing team are still going through CCTV and I have an ANPR enquiry out. Also today an enquiry will be allocated to check on what CCTV there is around the Brixton Station Road area to see if we can pick up anyone acting suspicious." She pushed her hand in her jacket pocket. "That's it, everyone. Back here tonight for eight o'clock briefing."

****

Scarlett and Tarn together with a Uniform team had been tasked with carrying out house-to-house enquiries in and around the residential streets leading away from Brixton Station Road. They had also been given responsibility for liaising with the Forensics team who were working in the abandoned station where Andrius Machuta's body had been discovered.

Trudging the streets with Tarn, Scarlett was having difficulty focussing. She had a heavy heart and was experiencing a great deal of guilt and shame. She felt as if she was not only betraying the squad by not disclosing what she found out from Rose last night, but also that she was betraying DCI Harris, who she respected immensely. She had a name for their suspect and she couldn't mention it. She wanted to, but she had difficulty with how she could introduce it without mentioning where it had come from. Rose after all was still a suspect in their parents' murder. And although she now could give a good account of herself it would still mean arrest and a couple of days in a cell while it was cleared up. She knew Rose wasn't ready for that and it would complicate the relationship they had just resurrected again after all these years. It was a dilemma she knew she had to deal with, and soon, if she wanted to retain her credibility and her place on the team. She had her fingers crossed that Alex and Rose would come up trumps today with finding where the people had gone from the squat. That way she would have access to Grazyna and that should go some way to clearing up the problem of revealing the e-fit suspect by name.

****

Scarlett was shattered, physically and mentally, by the time she got to Alex's place. Rose greeted her at the door in buoyant mood, skipping away back to the lounge, calling back over her shoulder, "Drink, Scarl?" as Scarlett closed the door behind her.

"I could murder one," she replied, prising off her boots and unzipping her leather motorbike jacket.

Entering the lounge, she saw that the ten o'clock news had just started and flopped onto the sofa. Alex was busy in the kitchen, preparing something on the work surface. Rose was pouring a glass of wine.

Alex looked her way. "I'm just making us a sandwich – cheese and tomato – want one?"

Scarlett was handed the wine. She raised her glass. "That sounds delish."

She took a sip of the chilled white wine, removed the glass from her lips and eyeing it said, "That hit the spot."

"How's your day gone, Scarl?" asked Rose, plonking herself beside her.

Rose's sudden movement bounced the cushion up and Scarlett had to quickly place a hand over the top of her glass to stop the wine slopping over the rim. "More to the point, how's you two's day gone? Did you find your mates?"

Rose shook her head, "We went to a couple of the places where they normally hang out but there was no one there." She glanced over her shoulder to where Alex was plating up the sandwiches. "We're going to try some other places tomorrow aren't we?"

Alex nodded, taking a bite of a sandwich. Then, balancing three plates, he joined them, handing them each a plate.

He settled in the chair looking at Scarlett. "We'll find them, don't worry. And we'll find your witness."

Fifty-six

Everyone was on their best behaviour. Two detectives from Professional Standards, or the "Rubber-Heel Squad", as they were more commonly known, were sat in morning briefing. Very little in the way of results came from it. Lots of work was ongoing but no fresh leads were being delivered. Scarlett kept her head down, doodling on her pad, feeling as if a great weight was bearing down her. From her lowered head she eyed the two Professional Standards detectives with wariness. The last thing she wanted was to be interviewed by them right now. She prayed that Alex and Rose would find her sister's friends today.

Scarlett made her way to the office following break-up of briefing and picked up her things from her desk ready to begin her day. Tapping the edges of a bunch of house-to-house forms into line she caught the sound of Professional Standards talking with DI Taylor-Butler in the corridor outside and she attempted to jolly Tarn along for them to leave.

"I've just got a couple of phone calls to make, Scarlett," he replied, picking up the phone.

Hearing the doors opening behind her she stuffed the pink forms into her bag and answered back, "Okay, I'll just be with the HOLMES team next door. Just come and collect me when you're done." With that she hurried off, slipping past the two Professional Standards investigators coming though the doors, without giving them a glance.

****

During mid-afternoon Scarlett and Tarn got a breakthrough, of sorts. Two streets along from Brixton Station Road a mechanic who worked in a small garage remembered seeing two strangers pull up in a silver car near to the premises shortly after eleven p.m. on the day Andrius was murdered. After parking up, he described seeing the men get out of their car, put on baseball caps and then walk off down the road in the direction of Brixton Station Road. He told them he hadn't been able to see their faces, but was able to say that one was taller than the other and that the smaller of the two was overweight. He described them as both wearing mid-

219

length black leather jackets and that the silver car they came in was a BMW. Unfortunately the man didn't see them come back to their car because he was working in the back of the garage.

They got a statement from him and phoned it in.

Scarlett had just returned her BlackBerry to her bag when her personal mobile rang. She pulled it out, viewed the caller and saw that it was Alex.

"Got to get this, Tarn," she said urgently and turned away, swiping the screen to answer as she took a few steps out of earshot from her partner. "Hello," she answered, deliberately not calling Alex by name.

"We've found them!" he said.

Scarlett cupped a hand around her phone. "Where?" she hissed quietly.

"Rose and I are with Gareth now. We found him at his old stomping ground at Charing Cross. Rose is speaking with him now. She's trying to persuade him to go for a coffee."

"Listen, Alex, hold onto him. Don't let him get away. I'm coming across there right away." She ended the call and dropped her phone back into her bag. She glanced up to see Tarn looking in her direction. She walked towards him. "Tarn, I've got to go, something's cropped up."

He gave her a puzzled look.

"Can't say too much at the moment. I've got to meet with someone urgently. Can you cover for me for a couple of hours?"

His bottom lip tightened. "You're not doing a Lone Ranger on me again are you?"

She threw him a grin. "No way, Tonto."

The edge of his mouth curled up and he shook his head at her.

Scarlett said, "Promise I'll fill you in soon. You couldn't drop me off at the Underground could you?"

"Sure thing, *Kemosabe*," he winked.

Fifty-seven

Scarlett caught the train from Brixton, jumped off at Stockwell and then took the Northern Line into Charing Cross. Emerging from the station she texted Alex to say she had arrived and got a text back to say they were in a coffee shop on the Strand. Putting in a brisk walk she found the place five minutes from the station. Alex, Rose and her friend Gareth were sitting at a table by the window. She joined them, offering out her hand to Gareth as she sat.

He took it and gave her a weak handshake saying, "I can't believe I'm collaborating with the cops, man."

Gazing across the table she took in Gareth's dishevelled appearance. His shoulder-length light brown hair was lank and greasy. The combat jacket, which she had seen him wearing on the last couple of occasions, was stained and the cuffs were frayed. Though she had to admit one thing as she looked him up and down – he was a good-looking man. Thinking about her sister she couldn't help but wonder what his background story was and how he had ended up living rough.

Rose flicked his upper arm with her fingers. "We've already talked about this, Gareth. You're not collaborating with the cops. You're helping us catch our parents' killers and the people who hurt Grazyna. And anyway, Scarlett is my sis. She's a good cop."

He looked Rose in the eye and shrugged. "You've changed."

Rose's face took on a hurt look. "That's not fair, Gareth. I haven't changed. I've just seen things differently over the last couple of days. I've kept it bottled up all these years and now I know it's time to sort things out. Catching who killed Mum and Dad has always been my aim. Catching up with my Scarl has brought it to the fore."

He held up his hands. "Your call, Rose."

Scarlett locked onto Gareth's blue grey eyes and said softly, "I'm guessing Rose has explained everything to you?"

He nodded. "I've known about her parents' – your parents' – murders a long time. She's filled me in with what's happened recently and also the thing with Grazyna."

"So you know how important it is we speak with Grazyna then?"

His face gave up a look of reluctance. "She came to us for help. Everyone from the squat has issues, man, especially with the law. I'm not too sure about this."

Rose reached across and took his hand. They exchanged gazes. She said, "Look, Gareth, you still trust me don't you?"

He seemed to think about the question for a few seconds before responding. "Yeah, I guess so."

"Good. Well you don't think I'd be going to all this trouble to cause you any problems? Especially after everything you've done for me. Grazyna is just like I used to be – lost, grappling with her problems and a long way from home. Can't you see we're trying to help her? My Sis is trying to help her."

Scarlett interjected, "Gareth, I know you have issues with cops. I can't imagine for one minute what your life has been like over the years. Just speaking with Rose over the last few days has certainly opened my eyes, but I'm definitely not here to add to your burden. Grazyna and her friend were tricked into coming to this country, held prisoner and seriously hurt, and we now believe her friend was murdered. Grazyna can help us put these men away for a very long time. It is imperative we talk to her."

Gareth stroked his chin, exchanging looks between Scarlett and Rose.

Rose's face displayed a pleading look.

For the best part of thirty seconds there was silence around the table and then Gareth answered, "Okay, man. But no pressure on her. If she doesn't want to talk you walk away and let her be."

Scarlett crossed her chest. "Promise. Just let me talk to her for five minutes."

"And you have to promise to leave us out of it, 'cos we don't want to get involved. And you won't tell anyone where we are once I show you."

Scarlett gave him a reassuring nod. "I promise about that as well. It's only Grazyna I need to talk with."

"Okay, man, we need to catch the train, we've got a place at Charlton. I'll just make a call and tell them we're coming."

Fifty-eight

Gareth's new squat was in a Victorian house, among a row of derelict villas on the Woolwich Road. The overgrown, weed-infested frontage was boarded up and Gareth took them around the back, across a muddied and rutted string of adjoining gardens to where one of the houses had a weathered door instead of boarding.

Gareth motioned towards it, "We found that door in one of the gardens and put it on a couple of days ago and we've already informed the council we've taken possession of the house and asked for a council tax bill." He opened the cracked, peeling door. "We do everything legit, man. This way it makes it harder for them to evict us. Once we were left alone for almost three years, you know."

They stepped over the threshold onto bare boards.

Scarlett recognised a number of faces from the maisonette squat. They were sat in an array of chairs set out in a semicircle in front of a glowing wood fire burning in an open grate. The room was partly filled with wood smoke but it was warm. Four people got up and Rose went to them and gave each one of them a hug. One asked how she was and two of them told her she looked well.

Scarlett searched among the faces even though she didn't know what Grazyna looked like. She turned to Gareth, "Grazyna?"

Gareth turned his attention to one of the women who had hugged Rose. Scarlett thought she looked to be in her early thirties. She was small and slim with long dark hair in a thick French plait, and she wore a baggy purple woollen jumper which had long sleeves covering her hands.

Gareth gave her an exploring look and she flashed her eyes upwards to the ceiling.

"She's up in the back room with Phillipa and Andrew."

"Is it alright to go up and speak with her?" enquired Scarlett.

"I'd like Phillipa and Andrew to stay with her while you talk. Just as witnesses," Gareth responded.

"Sure, no problem." Scarlett gave Alex and Rose a look which told them she was going up alone and she walked to where she guessed the stairs would be. She was right. A bare, narrow, rickety wooden staircase ran up the middle of the house. Either side the walls were covered in peeling flowered wallpaper. She had to steady herself on the walls as she climbed because the handrail was missing. As she clomped up the stairs she experienced a drop in temperature and by the time she had reached the top her breath was leaving her mouth as fine wisps of fog.

On the small landing she called out to Grazyna, and a man's voice to her right answered, "In here."

The door to the bedroom was ajar. Scarlett pushed it. This room was carpeted. The pattern reminded her of the eighties. In parts it was threadbare and a number of sleeping bags were dotted around the floor.

Though Scarlett had never seen what Grazyna looked like she instantly spotted which of the three she was. Grazyna's face had a recognisable Eastern European look, with high cheekbones and piercing blue eyes. She was wearing a duffel coat which looked too big for her and a pair of jeans and boots. Scarlett smiled as she stepped towards her. "You must be Grazyna?" she said, holding out her hand.

Grazyna looked uncomfortable but took her hand.

Scarlett could feel her shaking as she grasped her cold hand. She tapped the back of it. "I'm Scarlett. I'm a detective with the Metropolitan Police. I'm guessing you've been told why I'm here?"

Grazyna nodded.

"My sister Rose, downstairs, who until a couple of few days ago was staying with you in Notting Hill, has told me all about what happened to you. I'm here to help you."

For a few seconds she eyed Scarlett up and down then blurted, "I'm scared. The men you want hurt me and my friend. They said they would do the same with my sister back home. She is only fifteen. I'm terrified for her."

"I promise you nothing will happen to your sister. Once you tell me who she is and where you are from I will get the police there to protect her and your family."

"You can do that?"

Scarlett nodded, "I can do that, Grazyna. I will do that just as soon as you give me some details."

"And you will protect me against these bad men?"

"I can promise you that as well. We will give you a place to stay and look after you while they go to court. If they've done to you what I've been told, they will be locked up and put in jail for many years."

"And my friend Kofryna. I think she is in danger. She didn't manage to escape like me. I don't know what happened to her. I don't know where she is. I think they will have beaten her. Maybe even rape her like they did me."

Scarlett let go of her hand and took a step back. Giving her a serious look she said, "I'm sorry to be the one giving you this sad news, but we think the men who held you prisoner killed your friend."

Grazyna's hand shot to her mouth. She paled. "Oh God!"

"That's why I'm here, Grazyna. I want to put away the men who killed your friend, but I don't know who they are or where they live, but you do. With your help we can put these people in prison for a long time."

"And you can promise that these men will not hurt me?"

"Yes I can promise that."

"And you can protect my sister and my family back home?"

"They will not come to any harm. As soon as you tell me where they live I can sort that out."

Grazyna shifted her gaze between the two people she was with and then returned it to Scarlett. "I trust you. I will tell you."

For the next quarter of an hour Grazyna outlined how she and Kofryna had met up with Andrius and Henrikas back in Lithuania and how they had told them they would have work if they came to the UK. She told Scarlett of the horror heaped upon her and Kofryna following their introduction to Skender, the Albanian, who told her he had bought them and that they had to work for him. She then told her of the rapes, and the brutality of the branding carried out by Arjan and his friend. Finally she finished with her escape and meeting up with Gareth and his crew.

Scarlett let off a low whistle. "That is a horrible story, Grazyna. How you must have suffered. As I say, now you've told me all that I need to do something about it. But, I can't do it on my own. I work in a team and I have to inform my boss of everything so I can support you and keep you from harm."

Grazyna offered an unsure look.

"I can see this is pretty frightening for you, but you have to trust me on this. I made a promise to you and the only way I can keep it is by informing my boss."

"And he can be trusted?"

"It's a she. Her name's Diane. Yes, she definitely can be trusted. She's a good person." Pausing for a moment, she fished out her BlackBerry from her pocket, and tapping the phone called up DCI Harris's mobile. As she hit the call button, she looked Grazyna in the eyes and said, "You need to know that Andrius and Henrikas are also dead. We think this Skender and Arjan, who you've mentioned, killed them."

Fifty-nine

On the phone Scarlett arranged to meet her DCI in the same coffee shop on the Strand where they had been earlier. She told Diane Harris very little, other than she had found a couple of crucial witnesses in the case and asked her to come alone.

Then she contacted her partner Tarn and told him the same.

After that, Scarlett, Rose, Alex and Grazyna left the squat and made their way back to the train, where they travelled back to Charing Cross station, and then headed up the Strand.

Once they were settled around a table in the coffee shop and had ordered drinks, Alex said his goodbyes, informing Scarlett that he thought it would be best if he wasn't around when her boss arrived, that it would only complicate things further. Then he left.

Tarn arrived within minutes of Alex leaving and pulled himself up a seat.

Scarlett introduced him to Rose and Grazyna and gave him a quick resume of everything that had gone on over the last few days and informed him that the DCI was also going to join them.

His face bore an incredulous look once she had finished. He said, "Bloody hell, Scarlett. No wonder you've been so secretive. Does the boss know all this?"

Shaking her head and pursing her lips she responded, "No. I'm going to tell her I tracked Rose down last night, otherwise I'm in for the high jump, but I'm going to tell her the truth about finding Grazyna this morning, and I want you to pretend you were with me when we found Grazyna. Now you know everything, I want you to just go along with me when I tell the boss."

Tarn shook his head. "You're certainly not giving me much option in this are you?"

"What do they tell you at training school? Always obey an order from a supervisor, even if you don't like what you're being asked to do?"

"I don't think covering up a lie is included."

Scarlett laughed. "Oh, Tarn Scarr! I happen to know you've told a few porkies in your time. Just think of your loyalties here. Anyway I'm going to make you a hero." She reached across the table, tapped his sleeve and gave him a wink. "Now let me get you a coffee. You look like you need one."

****

Diane Harris arrived ten minutes later wrapped up against the elements. The wind and the rain had picked up since Scarlett and the group had entered the coffee shop and she remembered the weather warning on the news the night before.

Pulling away a spare chair from another table and issuing a greeting smile Diane Harris unwound her scarf from around her neck, unbuttoned her coat and squeezed herself in between Tarn and Rose.

She looked at Scarlett first. "This is all very mysterious. I know I said we have a leak in the office but I wouldn't have thought this was necessary."

"I think it might be when I tell you what I've got," Scarlett replied.

As the DCI shook off her coat Scarlett poured out her story. While she talked the DCI repeatedly switched her gaze between Rose and Grazyna.

They both shied away their eyes, diverting them to their cups of coffee.

Upon Scarlett finishing, DCI Harris clasped her hands together and clamped her eyes upon her. "You say you tracked your sister down yesterday?"

Scarlett nodded.

"So why couldn't you tell me this, this morning, in my office, once briefing was done, if you didn't want it leaking out?"

Scarlett could feel her neck flushing.

Rose snapped up her head and interjected, "Because I told her not to. I told her if she told you I would disappear again and this time no one would find me."

Scarlett met her sister's eyes. Inside she was thanking her. She returned her gaze to her DCI. "Rose is still circulated as wanted in connection with our parents' murders. If I'd have brought her in, even though I knew she'd not done it, she would still have to go through the process of being arrested and interviewed and so on. It would just have slowed everything down, and she was the one person who could support Grazyna and fill in all the blanks as to who the two Albanians are. And be able to persuade her that

228

she could trust us." When she finished she pushed herself back and heaved a sigh. *Most of that was true*, she told herself.

The DCI was silent for a while. Her face took on a thoughtful look. She unclasped her hands and laid them palm flat on the table. "Right, plan of action. We need to protect Rose and Grazyna until these Albanian's are under lock and key. Scarlett, you're right when you say they're crucial witnesses, and you've rightly pointed out that while we have a leak in our department we can't afford for these two to be compromised. This Skender guy and Arjan have already murdered four people to our knowledge. What I'm going to do is go back to the office with Tarn and make some phone calls. You go nowhere near it. You go home with Rose and Grazyna, pack up some things for a few days and wait for me there. I'll phone you and then come by and pick you up."

Scarlett asked, "Where are we going?"

"You, Rose and Grazyna are going to a safe house until this is all ended."

Sixty

The safe house was a three-bedroom detached house in a quiet street in Ham, backing onto woodland. DCI Diane Harris helped Scarlett in with her bags, checked over every room with her, ensured her personal radio was working, and that she had a spare battery and confirmed there was enough charge in her BlackBerry. Then she handed over a set of keys.

She said to Scarlett, "Right, you three are to remain here, and you only leave on my say so. You do not answer the door to anyone but me, is that clear?"

Tight-lipped, Scarlett nodded, roaming her eyes around the room. The furnishings were basic, but it was comfortable, and eyeing a TV in the corner, she thought they at least had that to see them through the boredom.

"I am the only person who knows you three are here. I've used this house before, and I've managed to pull a few strings with the Yard to get it. You'll be okay here." She opened the front door and an icy blast came in. She shot a glance over her shoulder. "The weather's picking up out there, they've forecast ninety-miles-an-hour winds over the next twenty-four hours. Once I've gone lock everything up and keep yourselves tucked up. I'm going back to the office to pull together the operation to get Skender and Arjan off the streets, once and for all. I'll try and keep you in the loop, but I'm going to be pretty busy over the next day or two so just hang in there until you hear from me."

Scarlett gave her a nod, holding onto the door, which bucked in the wind as the DCI walked to her car. She watched her leaning into the gusts thinking that she didn't envy her having to go back into work on a night like this. She was in a much better place right now, she told herself. As the DCI pulled off the drive Scarlett shut the door, locked it, put the two security bolts in place and then returned to the open-plan kitchen-cum-lounge.

When she entered Rose was rifling through the carrier bags on the work surface. Earlier while packing she had had the foresight to empty the fridge and freezer. Watching her sister picking out the salad stuff she was glad she had – she was famished.

Between them they put together a salad, microwaved a jacket potato each and oven-cooked three chicken fillets.

Rose brought to the table a bottle of wine she had smuggled into a bag. She poured herself and Grazyna a glass but Scarlett resisted. Although she would have loved to have had a glass with her meal she knew she had to keep a clear head and remain focussed until this was all over. Scarlett made herself a coffee instead.

After the meal they all cleared the table and while Rose and Grazyna hand-washed the dirty pots she made a phone call to Alex. Although she didn't tell him where she was she explained that they were in a safe house and would be staying there until the Albanians were arrested. Before ending the call, Alex asked her to ring him tomorrow morning and to take care, and as she finished speaking she found herself staring into space and musing. It had been a long time since Alex had said anything affectionate to her – since they'd split up seven months ago, in fact. She wondered if he was telling her something. Before she could dwell on it further her phone rang again. It was Tarn. She took it. He told he was just checking in and said that the DCI had just called it a day. He said, "We're all in at half six tomorrow morning. We're doing a number of raids. The boss has informed everybody about the two witnesses you found, but she hasn't mentioned Rose and Grazyna by name. And she's also named Skender and Arjan as our suspects." He paused and continued, "Hey and guess what?"

"What?" she asked.

"We've actually got a hit on the Skender guy! His full name is Skender Dosti, he's forty-two and he is Albanian. Came here fifteen years ago. He was arrested in Soho seven years ago for assaulting a woman but for some reason the case never went to court. We've got a couple of addresses for him, from back then, so we're hitting them tomorrow morning first thing. I'll let you know once he's under arrest."

Scarlett thanked him and asked him if the boss had questioned him about her story about Rose.

"Never raised it, Scarlett. She thinks it is as it is. She's none the wiser."

"Good. Thanks for backing me up. Again!"

"No problem, Scarlett, that's what partners are for." Then he said, "Speak tomorrow. Sleep tight," and ended the call.

She had just put down her phone when it rang again. She picked it up – DS Gary Ashdown. She took the call.

"Hi Gaz, what's up?"

"Nothing. The DCI just asked me to check in with you – see if everything is okay. See if the witnesses are comfortable."

Scarlett flashed a look at Rose and Grazyna. They were just putting away the pots and cutlery. "They are, thank you. Everything is fine."

"Good, glad you're all okay. Oh and by the way, good job finding them. Commendation coming your way when this is done. I'm envious."

"It's a team effort at the end of the day, Gaz. I've just got lucky."

"Well you ought to have seen Taylor-Butler's face when the DCI told us all at briefing. You've really put his nose out of joint."

"Oh God, that's me tip-toeing around the office on broken glass for a while."

"And we've also got a hit on one of the suspects."

"Yes, Tarn's just rung me and told me."

"Oh, Okay. Anyway, just to say, don't worry, everything is going smoothly this end. You can relax and someone will contact you tomorrow."

"Thanks Gaz, much appreciated."

"Goodnight Scarlett."

Scarlett disconnected the line, and thinking how thoughtful some members of the squad were, put down her phone. If only Taylor-Butler could be the same, she said to herself. It would make her job so much easier.

Still in contemplative mood she glanced up and saw that Rose and Grazyna had finished the pots and were pouring themselves another drink. She said, "I'm going to get myself some fresh air and check everything's okay outside before I settle down."

Rose raised her glass of wine. "Okay, Scarl, I'm going to put on the TV."

With that Scarlett unlocked the kitchen door and stepped out onto the wooden decking that spanned the width of the house. The sharpness of the cold instantly hit her, although she was surprised not to feel the gushing winds from the raging storm – the position of the house had to be shielding her. For that she was grateful; standing out here, in a strange kind of   way, was refreshing. In the few hours they had been there the heating had kicked in, and although it had chased away the fusty smell she had noticed when they had first arrived, it had now made the place unbearably hot and stuffy.

Pulling closed the back door Scarlett took in a lungful of fresh air and stared out over the garden. At first the darkness of the night was impenetrable, but as her sight adapted she began to pick out bits of her surroundings. She could make out that the garden was mainly lawn. It stretched before her for approximately fifty feet and then it met a bank of trees that was the beginning of woodland. She could see and hear that the line of trees were taking the brunt of the fierce wind – the skeletal treetops whipping to and fro, their boughs creaking and groaning against the wind. She shivered and listened.

She had been standing like that for a good few minutes when another noise grabbed her attention. It was coming from the road at the front. It sounded like the noise of tyres hissing on wet tarmac. She remembered the DCI telling her that she wouldn't be visiting her until tomorrow, and that she would ring her first. Scarlett had an uncomfortable feeling about that noise. She hurried back into the house and at a smart clip took the stairs to the front bedroom overlooking the street. Not turning on the light, she went to the window and eased back one side of the closed curtains and peered through the gap. Her eyes were drawn to the brake lights of a silver car stopped ten yards away on the opposite side of the road. The rain battering the bedroom window was creating a red halo effect around the brake lights. She caught her breath and stared. For the best part of two minutes nothing happened, then the brake lights went off, the interior light came on and both front doors opened. As the two men in dark clothing stepped out onto the rain-sodden tarmac her heart missed a beat. Both of them had shaven heads and while one was tall and looked well made the other was overweight – Skender and Arjan.

Scarlett let go of the curtains and raced back downstairs.

Sixty-one

"They're here!" she cried, tearing into the lounge.

Rose and Grazyna were on the sofa. Their heads whipped around.

"Skender and Arjan! They've found us. Quick! We've got to go."

Rose and Grazyna didn't need a second warning. Both their faces displaying panic, they shot off the sofa and bolted for the kitchen door.

Scarlett knew she would have just enough time to activate the alarm button on her radio. She snatched it from the coffee table and hit the red "status zero" button, which would instantly register in the Communication Room, overriding all radio chatter and sending out a GPS signal as to their location. But she knew that any help could be at least fifteen minutes away. That was too long to hang around.

Seconds after Rose had flung open the back door Grazyna and Scarlett were through, following her down the garden at a sprint.

Scarlett yelled out, "Into the woods – quick!" Behind her she could hear banging, and guessed that Skender and Arjan were kicking in the front door. Although it had two bolts and a lock she knew it would only hold them back for a few seconds, and the noise of the glass top panel shattering confirmed as much.

At the bottom of the garden there was only a thin privet hedge. Scarlett threw herself sideways at it and fell through.

Rose and Grazyna followed her and they all crumpled together in a heap. The force of their bodies coming together knocked the radio from Scarlett's grasp and she didn't see where it went. Half scrambling, half picking herself up, Scarlett set off at a sprint, reaching out to Rose, grabbing her by her sleeve. "Run!" she squealed.

The three of them were soon matching one another's pace. Scarlett led, pushing out her arms to fend away the whipping branches. The trees and the bushes were preventing her from running her best, and a feeling of dread and panic enveloped her. She knew she needed to focus. Dropping her pace just a fraction she looked back over her shoulder. She couldn't see a thing but she could hear the sound of bushes rustling not far behind.

"We need to separate," she called back. "If they catch up they've got us all. You two go left, I'll go right and make as much noise as I can to distract them. Help is on its way." With that she pushed her sister's arm, steering her away. She could just make out the fear in Rose's eyes as she seized hold of Grazyna's wrist and spun away.

Jogging, Scarlett watched them both weave between several bushes, and as soon as they disappeared from view she sucked in a lungful of air and put in a fresh burst, kicking out as she ran, trying to make enough noise to draw Skender and Arjan towards her, but it was slowing her down. She was having difficulty keeping her footing on the uneven woodland floor and on a couple of occasions nearly went headlong into the ground. And all the while, in between her panting breath, she was straining to hear.

Suddenly Scarlett heard the sharp snap of twigs and the beating back of branches. It was a lot closer than she had expected and her thoughts turned to panic. She shot a quick look back and caught her right ankle among some brambles, jarring her leg and sending her sprawling. She flung out her arms instinctively, hitting the ground hard, stars detonating behind her eyes like fireworks.

For a couple seconds she lay there. Then she took in a short breath and began to heave herself up. She had just got onto her haunches when a heavy blow thumped into her right hip, rocketing her sideways. A pain with the intensity of an electric current jolted through her and for an instant she saw stars again. When her eyes cleared and she regained her breathing she looked up to see the tall stocky figure of Skender standing before her. She could hear that his breathing was as ragged as hers.

"You dead! I fucking kill you!"

He bent down and seized her jaw, pulling her face towards his. He had a maniacal stare and his eyes bored right through her. Then he began to squeeze.

The pain was like nothing Scarlett had ever felt. She could hear squealing, and although she knew it was her own voice it felt like an out-of-body experience. As the thought entered her head that this was it, today she was going to die, another thought came to her. She delved into her jogging top and pulled out her police-issue pepper spray, plunging down on the trigger as she swung up

235

her arm. She heard the hiss but couldn't see what part of Skender's body she was hitting. When he released his grip and began screaming, she knew she'd hit his face. She didn't stop spraying until the can had stopped hissing and then she kicked out and up. Her knee jolted as she connected and his muscular frame buckled and collapsed beside her. Feet from her he was rolling around, clawing frantically at his face and squealing like a pig. She rolled to one side, dumping the empty canister, and as she pushed herself up she grabbed at a broken limb of a tree. Grabbing it with both hands, with all of her might, she swung it above her and sent it crashing down on Skender's head. She felt a crack and Skender stopped squealing, slumping forward, hitting the ground face first. As he lay unconscious she pulled back her foot and delivered an almighty kick between his legs.

Dropping the tree limb, Scarlett clawed for air. She had just filled her lungs when a crunching noise broke from behind. Instinct told her it was danger but before she had time to turn, a huge weight smacked into her side, lifting her off her feet, launching her sideways against a tree. Her ribs took the impact and air exploded from her mouth as a strident cry. As she collapsed into a pile of damp leaves she thought she could hear someone calling her name, followed by the sound of scuffles and shouts. She tried to lift her head and for a moment thought she saw two blurred silhouettes dancing, but before she could make sense of anything her heavy eyes finally closed.

Sixty-two

Scarlett thought she recognised a voice and she could feel someone tugging at her arms. As she came to the first thing she felt was a sharp wind stinging her cheeks. Her head felt weird and it was as if every part of her was filled with lead. She sprang open her eyes. A blurred vision of Alex was on his knees holding her in a half-seated position. As her sight came back into focus she saw he was dressed in army fatigues. Then she remembered where she was and what had happened. When she glanced sideways, Arjan was nearby, also in a crumpled heap. She swung her gaze back to Alex. She started to talk and felt something wet and sticky clog her throat. It choked her for a second and she began spluttering. Spitting out the residue in her mouth she tasted copper on her tongue and realised what it was – blood! It caused her to start.

Alex grabbed a hold of her. "Steady Scarlett," he called out.

She spat again and wiped her mouth with the back of her hand. Finally, looking at Arjan's prostrate form she was able to say, "What happened?"

"You don't remember?"

"I can remember Skender. But then I was hit from behind. That's it."

"That's where I came in."

Scarlett shot Alex a puzzled look. "You came in?"

"I couldn't leave my favourite girl to fend for herself, now could I?"

Her expression changed to one of bewilderment.

Alex eased back on his haunches and started to heave Scarlett up. "I've been watching out for you, Rose and Grazyna, since the coffee shop. I saw that boss of yours bring you to the house. I guessed it was a safe house, but when she left no one to guard you I thought I'd better hang around." As he helped her to her feet he added, "And it was a good job I did. You'd be a gonner now if I hadn't stayed."

Scarlett held Alex's gaze. She could feel herself welling up inside. "I don't know what to say."

"You don't need to say anything."

"Yes I do," she answered and wrapped her arms around his neck. "Thank you."

237

After a few seconds he prised them off, and wearing an embarrassed look, he said, "Hey, I can't have you going all soft on me. You've got your professional appearance to keep up."

In the distance the sounds of wailing police sirens approached them. Alex let her go and fixing her eyes said, "That's the cavalry arriving. Listen, I think it would be best if I did a disappearing act. I could end up having to answer a lot of questions if they find me here and I'd prefer not to. Let's just let them think you managed this all on your own, shall we?"As he set off jogging he glanced back, "I saw what you did to Skender there, at the end. The next time I make you mad I'll remember to keep a wide berth."

He didn't hang around to watch Scarlett break into a grin.

Sixty-three

Scarlett winced as she pulled herself up in the hospital bed. DCI Diane Harris placed a pillow at the back of her head.

"No permanent damage then?"

"Bruised ribs and a twisted ankle! A few cuts and bruises! A hip which doesn't feel as though it belongs to me at the moment, but no, no permanent damage," Scarlett replied, slowly rotating her neck and rubbing the right-hand side of it. "I'm sore as hell."

The DCI patted her shoulder. "Not as sore as Skender and Arjan. You really gave them a good working over. Skender has fifteen stitches in his head and a concussion, so they're keeping him in overnight for observation." Then she broke into a smile. "And his balls are the size of balloons." Relaxing her smile she continued, "Arjan has a couple of broken teeth, a busted nose and a lovely shiner. I've put armed guards on the pair. Neither of them are going anywhere." She paused, and with a shake of her head added, "You must have one hell of a temper when you're mad. I know one thing for sure, DI Taylor-Butler is going to be extremely careful around you from now on." She fixed Scarlett's eyes for a second and then they both started to laugh.

It made Scarlett's ribs hurt. She grabbed her sides. "Don't make me laugh, boss." Then, changing her face she asked, "How're Rose and Grazyna?"

"They're fine. Both of them. Thanks to your swift actions. The helicopter found them with the thermal imaging camera. They'd managed to get a good mile through the woods. They've both been taken to a victim and witness suite. We're getting them checked over by an FME. Once the doctor gives them a clean bill of health we're going to start video interviewing them." The DCI leaned in and dropped her voice. "While you were tucked away in the safe house the squad uncovered a number of things. Firstly we've found where both Skender and Arjan were living. We busted those addresses an hour ago and I've just been told that in Skender's house they've found a laptop identifying a number of addresses owned by him that we think are brothels. We're currently putting together an operation to hit those tomorrow. We're going in with Immigration and Border, because we're certain illegals will be there. We've also got CCTV evidence from a petrol station just a mile away from the abandoned railway station where Andrius Machuta was found. I've seen the footage, and it's timed and dated just half an hour before his murder. It clearly identifies Skender and Arjan pulling into the petrol station in a silver BMW, and Arjan getting out and filling a can with petrol. As to the BMW – that's across the road from the safe house and being recovered as we speak. Add to that the evidence from your sister and Grazyna and those two are going away for a very long time."

"How did they find the safe house?"

"We're working on that. We think we've identified the source."

"Someone from the squad?"

The DCI pushed herself up. "I can't say too much at the moment, Scarlett. Professional Standards have put a team on it. I should know something in the next few hours if all goes well." She began buttoning her coat. "And now, young lady, I'm going to say my goodbyes. I can't stand around chatting to you all night, there's work to be done. I've arranged for you to have a lift once you get released from here and they're going to take you to join up with your sister and Grazyna. Once you give your statement it's off home and I'll see you sometime tomorrow." She picked up her bag and pushed back the cubicle curtain, "And don't rush in. Everything is being taken care of. You've done your bit for this investigation."

Sixty-four

Scarlett awoke at ten-thirty a.m., having had six hours' sleep. Much of it had been restless.

Scarlett had been released from hospital in the early hours, having insisted on signing herself out, much to the consternation of the doctor. Then she had caught up with Rose and Grazyna at the Victim and Witness Suite, where they had finished giving their video statements. The three had then been dropped off at home by their police driver at four a.m.

Scarlett had given up her bed to Grazyna. She made up the sofa with a spare duvet, and then the three of them had exchanged their goodnights and gone to their beds. However, for Scarlett sleep had been a long time coming; the evening's activity had repeatedly tumbled around inside her head and she'd had difficulty relaxing. Added to that had been the pain. Every little movement had brought a groan, and it had taken her a long time before she had finally dropped off to sleep. When she had awoken, the pain started afresh and it had taken her the best part of three-quarters of an hour to shower, dress and put on her make-up.

She left Rose and Grazyna tucked up, quietly made herself some toast and coffee, swallowed down with a couple of painkillers the hospital had prescribed, and then set off to the police station. Initially she had thought about going in on Bonnie, but she was so sore and stiff she couldn't put on her biking leathers and so called a taxi.

****

She entered an office buzzing with activity. Most desks were occupied. People were on phones and at their computers. A couple acknowledged her with a wave and then continued what they were doing.

Slowly pulling out her chair, Scarlett eased off her coat and draped it around the chair back and then tentatively sat down. Opposite, Tarn leaned forward resting his arms on his desk. "How's the hero of the hour?"

"Once the pain's gone I'll be fine."

Lowering his voice and leaning further forward he said, "They've arrested Gaz!"

"Gaz! As in Gary Ashdown?" she replied with a surprised look.

Tarn nodded. "He's the leak!"

She looked across the room to where the detective sergeant normally sat. His place was empty. "How do you know?"

"It's come from the HOLMES team. Apparently Professional Standards have been monitoring certain individuals' phones. His among them. They've arrested him this morning at his home and rumour has it they've found a bagful of cash hidden in the rafters at his garage. It appears he knew Skender from his Vice Squad days. Looks like he's been on the take for years."

"Bloody hell!" Scarlett hissed. "I knew Gaz was a bit dodgy but I'd have never taken him for a bent cop."

Tarn pushed himself back. "I know. It just shows you doesn't it? You don't know who you can trust."

"He rung me last night."

"Gary did?"

Scarlett nodded. "Yes, while I was at the safe house. That explains how Skender and Arjan found us so quickly. He must have had someone track the call." She shook her head. "The bastard! He almost got us killed."

"Well, he'll be getting what comes to him," Tarn responded, pushing back his chair. "I'll get us a coffee shall I?"

"That sounds like a good idea."

Scarlett watched her partner making his way to where the coffee and tea-making facilities were in the squad room and then diverted her gaze to her in-tray. On the top was an A4 buff envelope with her name boldly written on it. Curious, she picked it off and tore open the seal. Inside was a bunch of papers. She slid them out and saw they were the DNA results from the house in Wandsworth. There were at least half a dozen hits of people who had visited the house. Even though their enquiry was just about sorted she was interested in seeing who had frequented the place when it was being run as a brothel – especially if any of them were known to her, or more importantly were celebrities of note. It was always handy to have some dirt on someone, even if she couldn't do anything with the information. She began to go through the sheets. She had not heard of the first three people but the fourth name caught her eye. She held the sheet before her and examined it carefully, double-checking the details, making sure it was who she thought it was. Then, easing herself up she stepped gingerly to the photocopier, made three copies, and returned to her desk where she folded the copies, together with the original, and secreted them inside her bag. Dropping her bag into the bottom drawer of her desk she lifted her gaze and scanned the room. No one was looking her way. She couldn't help but release a mischievous smile.

Sixty-five

That day DCI Diane Harris commenced evening briefing at four p.m. It was planned so that the whole team could clock off early to celebrate. She updated the team as to the present status of the investigation, informing them that from Grazyna's video interview she had identified both Skender and Arjan as her captors – Skender as the one who raped her and Arjan as the one who had branded her. She had also explained Andrius's and Henrikas's parts in her abduction. Following her naming of Kofryna as the friend she had come to the UK with, a request had been sent to Interpol for family DNA to be taken by Lithuanian authorities. The DCI sadly announced that it was strongly believed that Kofryna was the headless victim they had found crammed into the suitcase and dumped into the Thames. Then Diane Harris explained that the witnesses who had originally given digital e-fits of the shaven-headed man with the Audi Q7 had all identified that person as Arjan. And they had found the Audi. Arjan had apparently taken it to a crooked scrap dealer near Manor Park, requesting it to be crushed, but instead the owner had hidden it away with the intention of selling it on. It was currently in the Forensics drying room, and they had already found bloodstains in the boot and on the back seat, and it had not been hard getting a statement from the scrap merchant naming Arjan as the person bringing to him. It was another nail in the Albanian's coffin.

Raids had been carried out at three addresses owned by Skender, and they had found twenty-two young women illegally held in those houses, all from Eastern European countries and all working as prostitutes. Their keepers, all Albanian, had also been detained. Finally she introduced the evidence given by Rose. She had positively identified Skender and Arjan as the two men she had seen eleven years ago standing over her father after he had been stabbed following his car being rammed off the road. Before breaking up she told everyone that so far Skender and Arjan had exercised their rights and refused to say anything, but that she was pretty confident that once all the forensics came together they would both be charged with various counts of murder.

Her announcement brought about a round of applause.

She brought briefing to a close on a sour note. "In the last hour I've had it confirmed by Professional Standards that DS Gary Ashdown is the one who has been leaking information. I'm sure in the next few days everyone will get to hear just how deeply he has been involved in things, especially the damage he has done. But for now I'm simply here to announce that he is currently suspended and that in due time a file will be submitted to CPS." Pushing together her hands prayer-like, she added, "On a final note, I'd like to thank everyone for their hard work during what has been a difficult couple of weeks. I couldn't wish to have a better team."

With that, briefing broke up and the squad headed down to the pub.

****

Scarlett wasn't really in the mood to drink. She was stiff as a board and every little movement hurt like hell. She took a seat by a table and watched people milling around and chatting elatedly, noting especially that some of her teammates were getting louder with every drink they downed. She smiled to herself. They would leave this pub later tonight in a state of good-humoured drunkenness. On any other occasion she would have been one of them.

While nursing her drink she decided to phone Rose. Upon connecting she told her where she was and that she was coming home in the next hour. She asked her sister, "Do you fancy doing anything?"

Rose replied that she fancied going for a meal. She had spoken with Grazyna, who had revealed to her that she had never eaten in a restaurant before.

That got to Scarlett. "Tell her to get herself ready. We're going out to celebrate. We'll go to my favourite Italian." With that she ended the call, finished her half of lager and stiffly hobbled to the toilet.

When she came out DI Taylor-Butler was in the passageway, halfway through a pint of bitter. She heaved a crestfallen sigh when she saw him but carried on stiffly walking. She was about to pass when he put out a hand, stretching it across to the opposite wall, forming a barrier.

Scarlett threw him an icy stare. "I'm in no mood for your games tonight. I'm sore and I'm ready for home."

He dropped his arm, "Quite the cocky little madam now, are we? The DCI's blue-eyed babe again."

Scarlett felt herself stiffen. She slowly brought up her bag, unfastened it, picked out one of the photocopied sheets of paper, and cracked it open dramatically in front of his face, causing him to step back. "As I've said, I'm in no mood for this, but you've asked for it." She waved the A4 sheet. "I have here a DNA result of someone identified as being in the brothel in Wandsworth. That's you!" She thrust it directly in front of his eyes and held it there.

After a couple of seconds of silence the DI snatched it from her grasp and looked at the document. For a minute his look was one of anger, then his face changed. "This doesn't prove anything, DS Macey. If you recall I saw you at the house during the investigation. You asked me what I was doing there, remember?"

Scarlett nodded. Slowly the corners of her mouth curled up. "I thought you'd say that. But if you remember I stopped you in the hallway, near the front door. This DNA result is from substances found in the S&M bedroom. Now I'm sure, under normal circumstances, were this to be discovered, it would be a little embarrassing for a while – the fact that a DI likes a bit of correction as sexual gratification now and then – but eventually that would die down. However, given the fact that this DI belongs to a murder squad involved in the investigation of a double murder at this brothel, where bodies were chopped up, and in which vulnerable people were trafficked and raped, then I can't see you staying on in this squad. Can you? Especially if the newspapers were to find out about it." Scarlett prodded him in the chest. "You can keep that copy as a reminder. If you ever give me any more hassle I promise you the original gets leaked." With that she brushed past him, catching her sore hip, but she held back a grimace until she had stepped out into the fresh air.

Sixty-six

Scarlett had a good long soak in the bath. By the time she was dried the stiffness and aches had eased and she felt totally chilled. Dressing in jeans and a tight-fitting jumper she made her way downstairs to the kitchen, where she took two more of the painkillers the hospital had prescribed her. She knew she shouldn't drink after taking them, but she thought what the hell. She felt especially buoyant following her triumphant clash with DI Taylor-Butler. Now she was in the mood to celebrate.

As she stepped into the lounge she saw Rose and Grazyna already had their coats on. Grazyna's hair was plaited and she had put on a little make-up. It had totally transformed her appearance. And Rose had made an effort to hot-brush her hair into loose curls.

Rose handed Scarlett her coat. "Come on slow-coach, I've booked us a table at the Italian you said. I know the invalid can't manage anything more exciting tonight."

Taking her coat, Scarlett gave her a hurt look. "I can't believe you've just said that to someone who's just saved your life."

Rose quipped back, "That's what I pay my taxes for!"

Scarlett held her sister's twinkling hazel eyes. Then she shook her head, targeting her with a look of amazement. "What taxes?"

They both burst out laughing and made for the front door.

The previous day's storm had passed, leaving behind surprisingly warmer and much calmer weather given that it was early December, and the three had a slow stroll into the centre of Richmond.

The Italian Rose had booked was a restaurant Scarlett had been in on a number occasions over the years. She had been here on a fair few dates with Alex. *There was Alex again, entering her head.* She'd thought of nothing else since he'd rescued her last night. What was the term he'd used – "my favourite girl"! She knew she would have to sit down and have a proper talk with him. She wondered if she should suggest giving the relationship another go.

"I fancy a calzone," said Rose as they entered the restaurant.

It broke Scarlett's thoughts. She nodded. "That sounds good. I could eat a horse."

For the next half an hour they drank Peroni beer and chatted. Grazyna did the most talking, excitedly telling Scarlett that DCI Harris had said she could stay in the country until the court case was over, and that her boss had contacted Immigration and the local authorities, who had provided her with a temporary visa and a place to stay. She had also made her a promise to support her should she wish to stay permanently.

Scarlett was pleased for her and told her so. As she finished her beer, she aimed a look at her sister, who appeared to be deep in thought. She set down her empty glass. "Something on your mind, Rose?"

Rose offered a meek smile. "There is, actually. It's something that's been on my mind since I met up with Gareth. I've been waiting for the right opportunity to raise it."

Scarlett reached across and took her sister's hand. "I think I can guess. You're restless aren't you?"

"Does it show?"

"It's all been a bit sudden what's happened."

"Not just that. But this is not my life. This is your life, Scarl."

"So what do you want to do? Go back to Gareth and the others?"

Rose pursed her lips and nodded.

"And that's what your heart's set on?"

Rose nodded again. "Don't get me wrong, Scarl, I appreciate everything you've done for me, and I'm so glad we've caught up after all these years, but I couldn't live this life – your life. It would drive me up the wall. Even though at times life was hard on the streets, it was fun. And I love the freedom."

"But what about the house – the money?"

"Scarl, I'm not a materialistic person. The years on the streets have made me appreciate everything I get. You can look after the house and if ever I need a bolt hole I know where to find one. As to the money, I'm not giving that up, it will come in handy. I'll be able to live the life I'm used to but from time to time sneak in a few luxuries when I feel like them. I'll have the best of both worlds."

"Is that what you're set on?"

"Definitely! I hope you're not upset."

Scarlett squeezed Rose's hand. "Not at all. Anyway, I know where to find you now. You've got a mobile so I can always ring you and you can sneak away, meet up for coffee, and be a capitalist for a day."

Rose pulled away her hand and laughingly thumped Scarlett's arm, just as the waiter appeared with their orders.